THE
TATTOOED
WOLF

to Maleah --
Happy howling!

(signed)

THE TATTOOED WOLF

K. BANNERMAN

HIC DRAGONES

First published in Canada in 2005 by Double Dragon Publishing

This edition first published in Great Britain in 2014 by Hic Dragones
PO Box 377
Manchester M8 2DE
www.hic-dragones.co.uk

Copyright © Kim Bannerman

Cover design by Rob Shedwick

The moral right of Kim Bannerman to be identified as the author of
this work has been asserted in accordance with the Copyright, Design
and Patents Act, 1988.

A CIP catalogue reference for this book is available from the British
Library.

ISBN 978-0-9576790-4-7

Designed and typeset by Hic Dragones
Printed and bound by CPI Group (UK) Ltd, Croydon CR40 4YY

To Shawn, who always seems to know the perfect thing to say

PART I

"Adversity makes men and prosperity makes monsters."
Victor Marie Hugo

1

DAN SULLIVAN WAS NOT the sort of man you'd remember. He was broad shouldered and handsome with thick black hair and sharp eyes the colour of malachite, but for all his striking characteristics, something in his features denied description. His face was sheltered, closed, anonymous. This was Morris Caufield's first thought when the door opened and Sandra ushered Mr Sullivan into the office.

His second thought, as he stood to greet him, was that Dan Sullivan seemed much too young to be hiring a divorce attorney.

Caufield held one hand towards the wooden chair opposite his desk. "Please, Mr Sullivan, have a seat."

Mister. This guy was less than thirty, half of Caufield's age, and the word left his mouth sounding awkward and strained. Whenever someone so young hired his services—and it seemed to be happening more and more, much to his dismay—he couldn't help but feel a smattering of judgmental disdain. 'They all think it's easy,' he thought. 'But once the honeymoon's finished and reality sets in, they're all running for the door.'

He forced himself to stop; it was unprofessional to think like that, and he knew it. He tried to muster a more friendly demeanour with a warm and welcoming smile. But as each man sat down, Caufield realized that Sullivan's eyes had narrowed;

he'd noticed Caufield's cold tone. Something in those brilliant green eyes seemed unnaturally intense, even while the rest of his expression remained placid and benign. A thought pierced Caufield as sharply as a shard of glass. 'He cultivates his blandness,' he realized. 'This is a guy who *wants* to be forgotten.'

Sandra returned to the office with a tray holding two mugs of coffee. In her youth she'd been pretty and optimistic, but now she was nearing retirement and what had once been pert was now soft and squishy. When he'd hired her, almost twelve years ago, she'd been full of ambition, but now, with her slow, swaying gait and tired eyes, she reminded Caufield of a water buffalo. As she set the tray on the desk, Sandra asked, "Anything else, Mr Caufield?"

"No thanks, Sandy my dear," he replied and threw her a little wink. Once she might've winked back, but these days Sandra scowled and the creases of her cheeks deepened. She closed the door after herself and returned to her filing.

Sullivan reclined in the stiff chair as best he could and rested his elbows on the armrests, folding his hands together, waiting.

Caufield coughed to clear his throat. "So, Mr Sullivan," he began, checking his appointment log for a given name. "Dan. May I call you Dan?"

"Sure."

The voice was low and measured, with a hint of caution. Not too loud, not too soft. One hundred per cent Goldilocks.

"It's not normally my style to make an appointment on such short notice, but we had a few cancellations this morning."

Caufield shuffled through his papers, head down, searching for his pen.

"Well, you came with good references," Sullivan replied. "I would've waited, but I admit, I'll be happy to get this business finished with as soon as possible."

So this guy hadn't just plucked a random lawyer from the phone book. Good. Caufield tented his fingers, casting Sullivan a cocky grin to demonstrate that they were going to be allies, comrades through the battlefield of the legal system, and that he'd chosen his counsel wisely. More than a lawyer and client, they were going to be buddies. "Now, I just want to start off by saying that divorce is never an easy hurdle. It's a big change and a lot of ugliness gets stirred up, but I'm here to make the transition go smoothly. If you choose to take me on as your attorney—"

"I don't want you as my attorney," said Sullivan. The corner of his mouth curled up in a wry smile. "You see, I've done research into your background and I was most intrigued, Mr Caufield. Morris. May I call you Morris?"

Morris, interrupted in his opening speech, took a moment to find his voice. "What?"

"Here's the thing, Morris," Sullivan began, his eyes gleaming. "I want you to be my wife's attorney."

With a grunt, Caufield leaned back in his leather chair and folded his hands across his crisp cotton shirt and generous tummy. He cocked one eyebrow and grinned, intrigued. Most husbands who sat in that cold wooden chair were either fretting over losing their life's possessions or guilt-ridden about a discovered affair, but Sullivan, calm and quiet and calculating, exhibited neither emotion. He wasn't stupid, of that Caufield was certain, and he didn't let his motives slip out unintentionally.

"You must understand, Dan," he said with a chuckle, "that you can't hire a lawyer on your wife's behalf. Conflict of interest. Simple as that."

"I'm aware of that, but—" Here he paused, lowering his chin and fixing Caufield with that penetrating stare. "I need a man with a great deal of... how should I put it? Discretion."

"Your wife has certain knowledge that you would rather remain confidential, is that it?" Caufield tried to match Sullivan's focused stare but found himself faltering. Finally, he dropped his gaze to the desk between them. "So what is it? Money laundering? Something sexual? Maybe a fondness for heroin or little boys?"

"Nothing so sordid as that," Sullivan replied. The comments hadn't shaken him, much to Caufield's disappointment.

"Look, buddy," Caufield said as he raised one hand. "Whatever your wife tells her attorney is her own business, and if it helps her case, her lawyer will use it. Even if that lawyer is me."

"I know," Sullivan replied. His smile returned, but it was neither warm nor welcoming. Upon reflection, Caufield realized it was the controlling, calculating smile of a predator. Sullivan leaned in and, in a quiet voice, added, "But *your* secrets are well hidden, Morris. I hoped you could keep mine equally well."

Caufield felt his skin blanch. He coughed into his fist. "I don't know what—"

"Of course you do," Sullivan replied. Their eyes locked for a space of a minute, assessing each other openly. Caufield realized that further bluffing was a waste of time and effort. This strange, nondescript man sat without a twitch of impatience, without a hint of doubt.

Caufield lowered his voice and looked quickly to the intercom to ensure that Sandra wasn't listening. She did, sometimes, the cranky old hag. But the light on the little beige box was dark; Sandra was busy with her paperwork. "Listen, you goddamn bastard, I paid this month's fee."

"I'm not the one blackmailing you, Morris. But if you promise to help me, I'll tell you who's behind your little 'problem'. As simple as that."

"How do you know—" Caufield held up his hand and ran his palm over his balding crown. Beads of sweat had appeared on his brow. His heart sank as he said, "Helen hired you. She knows, and you're some damn private investigator?"

"Not at all." Sullivan rocked back in his chair and it squeaked under his weight. "I'm a limner for Warley Conservation Studio." When Caufield's face pulled down in a confused scowl, Sullivan leaned forward again and said, "I fix old manuscripts and paintings. I'm what you might call a restoration artist. I'm just very good at research, Morris, and I tend to notice things that other people miss." He smiled again, and this time the expression was more convivial. Those fiery green eyes seemed friendlier than before. "I never thought about private investigation; that would be an interesting career choice, wouldn't it? Hmm... I might look into that."

Caufield shook his head. "You have nothing to do with Helen?"

"If Helen's your wife, then no. I've never met her."

Caufield's heart soared with relief. "You'll help me with this mess I'm in, tell nobody, not even Helen, if I help you divorce your wife. That's what you're proposing?"

"Please."

Rage flashed across Caufield's face. He balled his hands into fists, felt his blood pressure rising as his cheeks turned crimson. "Goddammit, who the fuck do you think you are? Holding me hostage with my own blackmail? I ought to—"

"Ought to what?" Sullivan interrupted sharply. "You can't go the police, or you would've done that already."

Caufield huffed.

"Look, Morris, I'm not holding you hostage," he began, glancing at the full length windows along the northern wall of the office. They offered a spectacular view of Vancouver's skyline: the silver towers of the downtown core, the iconic lines of the Lions Gate bridge, the dark conifers of Stanley Park. From this vantage, the whole city was framed by the blue Coastal mountains and the iron grey streak of English Bay, a glittering metropolis encircled by forest and sea. The first drops of a gentle November rain pattered across the glass, and Sullivan closed his eyes as if to listen to the sound. Then, in the same quiet voice as before, he said, "I don't want your money, Morris. You'll be paid in full for your services. I need a divorce, and I need a sympathetic lawyer to represent her, but you're free to refuse my offer. I'll just take my business elsewhere." He glanced again at Caufield. "But you're a man in a bad position, Morris, just like I used to be. I want to help."

Caufield was flustered and grabbed a handkerchief from his pocket to mop his forehead. "If it's anything illegal—"

"It isn't. I'm simply requesting that you ignore one of her claims."

"That's it?"

"One claim. Use all the rest to her advantage, but ignore one story she'll tell you."

Caufield pulled his pen from his breast pocket and fiddled with it between his meaty fingers. "This accusation of hers… it must be something ugly, hey? Because you said you're a… a lim… a limi… a restoration artist, right? I mean, how many rules can an artsy-fartsy guy like you break?" He gave a strained chuckle, more like a nervous whistle in the back of his throat than a show of mirth.

Sullivan tapped his fist against the wooden arm of the chair, smirking at some secret joke. "Well, it's certainly not as bad as a fondness for heroin or little boys."

"Then why this? Why sneak around looking for someone to represent her, and then throw me over a barrel with my own problems?" He now tried very hard to leach the bitterness from his words. "I don't like being threatened, Dan. I don't like it at all."

"I haven't threatened you," came the cool reply, and the malachite eyes regained the coldness that chilled Caufield's clammy skin. "I need help, and so do you. A business proposal, Morris… that's what this is."

Caufield clenched his teeth. "A business proposal?"

"Yes."

"This story," he started, pulling a yellow legal pad close and clicking his pen, "is it true?"

"I wouldn't ask you to ignore it if it was a lie, would I?"

Caufield doodled circles to ensure the pen worked. He chewed the inside of his cheek, thinking, and realized he didn't have much choice. If Sullivan walked out that door, his offer refused, Caufield would forever wonder what would've happened, what might have been. Wasn't he desperate to have his life back? To know who knew his secrets? He took a deep breath that reached to the bottoms of his lungs. "Alright, Sullivan. I'll do it. I'm desperate enough to get these vultures off my payroll." Caufield took another deep breath to steady his rising temper. "I'll ask you the first thing I ask any client, Dan: why do you want a divorce?"

Expecting an answer, he was surprised when Sullivan stood, unbuttoned his jeans, and pulled down one side to expose his right buttocks. A wicked scar ran along the upper length of his muscular thigh and disappeared under his cotton boxers to emerge again above the waistband. It was puckered and scarlet, poorly stitched, and less than six months old. Caufield immediately recognized the knotted line of violent red as a bullet tract.

"She shot me, Morris," Sullivan said. "She tried to kill me. Twice."

Caufield studied the crimson wound. It was worse than any of his old army scars, even the pitted white one where a drunken corporal's dagger had sliced open his palm.

"Goddammit, buddy!" He shook his head slowly in awe. "Turn her over to the authorities!"

But Sullivan yanked his pants up again and said, "I can't do that."

"Because of what she knows?"

"Exactly."

"What's she going to tell me?" he asked, leaning forward. "What can she know that would keep you from throwing her crazy ass in jail?"

Sullivan gave a broad grin as he took his seat again. "Well, Morris," he said as he rested his elbows on the edge of the desk. "She's telling everyone that I'm a werewolf."

A PAUSE FILLED THE stagnant office. The furnace clicked on, filling the room with a whoosh of warm air, and Caufield glanced towards the windows, back to this client, out the windows again. Sullivan patiently folded his hands in his lap and waited for Caufield to reply. When the seconds stretched into minutes, Sullivan shifted his attention to the framed artwork on the wall behind the desk, well aware that it might be take a while for Caufield to process the information.

Caufield, thinking hard, finally said, "Did I hear you right?"

"I'm a werewolf," said Sullivan with a nod.

At this, Caufield gave a disbelieving laugh, thin and high like a punch had pushed the air from his lungs.

"You've got to be joking."

Sullivan shook his head, then nodded towards one of the paintings. "That one's an Emily Carr, isn't it? Nice."

Another pause. Caufield narrowed his eyes and stared at Sullivan, who now admired the artwork on the wall with great interest, self-assured and unwavering, as he waited for a response.

"Do you think I'm an idiot? I'm a busy man. I don't have time for this kind of crap."

"Don't take her as a client, then," Sullivan replied, shrugging. He brought his attention back to Caufield. "Really, I don't care if you believe me or not, Morris. I only want someone who appears to believe my wife. I can't have her running from lawyer to lawyer, stirring up problems, when all I want is a quiet divorce."

"You bring her to me and she starts screaming about fangs and the full moon and bull hooey like that, and I'm just supposed to nod and agree with her? We'll just set down her hallucinations as one more reason for the separation, the papers get lost in the legal system, and the whole mess is finished?"

"That's my hope."

"Well, you're right, buddy. I don't believe you. You're as crazy as her."

"Good."

"And I think you should have her locked away, if that's the kind of marriage you two had. Tried to kill you twice," he spat in disbelief. "Why didn't you hit her for a divorce after the first attempt?"

"I wasn't in any position to seek legal counsel," said Sullivan with a grin.

18

Caufield drummed his fingers on the edge of his desk and chewed his lower lip in thought. "You're a lunatic."

"If it makes you feel better to think that, fine."

"And what about your own lawyer? I mean, your attorney's going to find out—"

"My attorney is sympathetic to my lifestyle." Sullivan crossed his arms and glanced again out the window again. "There aren't many werewolves around, Morris, but we tend to look after each other. He already knows what I am because we've run through the woods before, a couple of times."

"Run through the woods?"

"Gone hunting. Changed skins. Left the world of men. Call it what whatever you want."

"You *are* a fucking lunatic."

Sullivan shrugged.

"Why not hire two werewolves for lawyers?"

"Like I said, there aren't many of us around. Payton's the only one—"

"Payton Grey? Of Rossland, Grey and Ricci?"

Sullivan grinned. "You know him?"

Caufield fiddled with his pen, wrote the name on the yellow pad and mused over the letters. "Of course I know him," he muttered. They had crossed paths a couple of times: Payton was a small, wiry man with a fierce competitive streak, whether in the courtroom or the racquetball court. Caufield thought how Payton was going to laugh—laugh like a sonofabitch—when they met up at next week's poker game and he told him this client, this madman with a scarred ass cheek and a maddening knowledge of Caufield's hidden secret, was pulling

Payton into his delusions. Caufield ground his teeth, thinking, then asked, "You've already hired Payton?"

"I have," said Sullivan. "Met with him yesterday."

"And he knows you think he's—"

"It's going to take us a week to get through this meeting if you keep asking me to verify everything I say," Sullivan replied bluntly. "Yes, Payton knows I think he thinks he's a werewolf, because he knows that I know he's a werewolf because I'm a werewolf too. Does that clarify everything?"

Caufield stared hard, waiting for the laughter to come, waiting for the joke to be revealed. Sullivan remained cordial but distant, arms crossed. There was no punch line; he was serious as all get out, and Caufield shook his head and sighed. If nothing came out of it, at least he'd have a damn funny story to tell Helen over dinner. "Alright then, Dan. Both you and your lawyer are... are—"

"Werewolves."

"Sweet Jesus—" Caufield muttered as he slouched back in his seat and crossed his hands over his belly, smirking "You've got my attention, Dan; I'll humour you. Tell me, from the very beginning, how you got into this whole bloody mess."

2

BEGINNING? WHERE DO I begin? Where does anyone's story start? I mean, our lives are compilations of experiences and memories, and there were many, many reasons why I found myself ensnared in my marriage, most of which had been imprinted on my personality long before I met my wife. I was stupid and young—that's good for a start. I was lonely too, far more than you can probably understand, Morris. I suppose I should start there, with the loneliness, with where it came from. If you can understand that, then you'll understand why I fell under her spell when anyone else would've run the other way.

When your parents know you're going to grow up to be a freak of nature, they try their best to give you a normal childhood in the hopes that you won't be too dysfunctional when you reach your adult years. They told me on my fifth Christmas Eve that I would grow up to be a wolf and that I was never to mention this to anyone, then bought my silence with some silly toy I'd circled in the Sears catalogue. They reinforced my good behaviour with painting lessons on Tuesday nights, a glossy red ten-speed for my eighth birthday, new clothes each September to celebrate the beginning of the school year. And always the unspoken rule: no one must know about the wolfishness, about the long nights my mother spent away from the house, leaving her clothes behind in the woodshed. No one must ever, ever, ever know. It would be worse than death if we mentioned it to a friend or a teacher. My father told us that, if we slipped in our silence, our mother would abandon us and never return. Can you imagine how terrifying it is, to know that your mother will vanish if you let slip the smallest whisper of the secret in your heart? Myself, my older sister and the twins, we were never to mention it to anyone outside of our little family. My mother had come from the woods, and I would grow up to go back to them.

Despite this spectre looming over the house, they tried very hard to ensure that I led as regular a life as my siblings. Hestia, my older sister, and the twins showed no symptoms of lycanthropy; only I seemed to exhibit the nuances of my mother's bloodline. The other three took after my father's side of the family, and I (lucky me) took after my mother's: a ragtag bunch of artists and drifters who split their time between the woods and the world of men. Most of them seem normal enough, perhaps more shy and demure than you'd expect from a bunch of carnivores, but Uncle Andre single-handedly undermined all of my father's attempts to construct an average household. When he visited, the Family Secret floated perilously close to the surface, because Andre didn't believe in modesty and had no flair for discretion. He hated wearing clothes; he despised the 'modern fad' of bathing; he was surrounded by the overwhelming perfume of sweat and liquor. He belched, he farted, he didn't believe in hiding what he was and what he wanted. He rarely took to two feet, but when he did, he used his booming voice to rail against some imagined enemy or conspiracy, and he delighted in the debauchery of human life: gambling, whoring and drinking until dawn. My first memory of Andre is of him showing up on our doorstep as naked as the day he was born, covered in mud up to his shoulders and raging about the Freemasons on his tail.

My father grabbed an afghan from the couch and threw it in a sweeping matador's flourish over my shivering uncle's shoulders, ushering him into the house before the neighbours called the police. We lived in a two-level log cabin on the shores of Maple Lake, a wilderness reservoir nestled deep in the mountains just north of Gilsbury Cross, but ours was not the only home to border the water. The pounding of his ham-sized fists on the weathered door echoed across the glassy surface of the water. Andre wanted to make his arrival known, and he resorted to mad, erratic yelling on a hodgepodge of subjects; you'd have to reside at the ends of the earth to avoid attracting attention with a racket like that. I was five, startled from my sleep by Andre's caterwauling, and I remember seeing the tiny square of light from the Hendersons' kitchen window—small with distance across the dark waters—flash to life.

"Andre, honey," said my mother from our front hall. "Calm down. Shush."

He huffed and puffed. He could've blown the house down. More likely, he could've had a coronary.

"Quiet, you'll wake the kids." This was my father's voice, stern and low, the sound of a patient man on the verge of snapping. You don't marry into a family of werewolves without a broad ability to accept surprises, but when it came to Andre my father had almost had his fill. And as my uncle's steps rained showers of filth over the clean carpets, my father found his empathy faltering. "Do you want a shower?"

"Shower? Goddamn, no!" he panted. "You won't catch me under any hot water."

My mother spoke gently, the sound of a spring rain in the middle of a tempest. "Here, come into the sitting room, we'll have a drink."

"Whiskey," said Andre. At the mention of spirits, he suddenly became very composed.

Their voices were muffled by the wall as they left the base of the stairs. I felt warm skin sliding into my palm and a shadowy shape looming from the bed in the opposite corner. "C'mon, dumbass," said Hestia in the darkness. "Let's listen."

"Hessie—"

"What? Scared to get out of bed?"

"No," I lied. To be afraid was to invite my sister's sadistic punishments.

She pulled me from the covers and we slipped into the hall and down the creaking stairwell, Hestia a fearless conqueror in her flannel nightgown, and I, her nervous sidekick in Spider Man pyjamas. The amber light of the downstairs lamp beckoned to us, invited us to leave the dim upper floor, and we cowered against the wall that separated the arch of the living room from the hall.

"—not really, Andre. You know this is in your head."

"Pah!" my uncle spat, fortified with firewater. "You're a fool if you think they aren't everywhere, Jack."

"I don't know what you saw, Andre, but I doubt the Freemasons have any personal vendetta against you."

My mother knew better than to doubt him openly. "Maybe they do, maybe they don't, Andre, but you're wily. They'll never catch you, whoever they might be."

"I don't know, Eve. This time it was close."

"Andre, I—"

I heard him sniffing the air. "The little ones are up."

"Hey sport!"

I looked up to my father's face as he peered around the corner. He was a kind man with an open countenance, and a life as a lumberjack had left him with weathered, tanned skin, even in the depths of winter. He smiled broadly, showing square white teeth. "What are you doing still awake? You ought to be in bed."

A quick glance behind me showed that Hessie, sensing trouble in the wind, had vanished back up the stairs without a word of warning.

"Jack, leave him alone," came my mother's voice from around the wall. "Danny? Come here."

I slunk around the corner and into the living room. On the couch sat my mother, eight months pregnant with twins, and sitting on the carpet across from her was Andre, bundled like a Turkish merchant in the purple blanket, a russet wolf's tail poking from under his behind. His brick red hair was a swirl of twigs and muck. Sweat and dirt had turned his skin from white to brown, and his eyes were emeralds set in a mask of clay.

"Hey, m'boy," he snarled, in a manner that was more feral than any of my paternal relations.

"Hello Uncle Andre," I replied, pressing my back into my father's knees.

25

"Come here, love," said my mother. She held out one hand from her swollen belly, motioning for me to cuddle at her side, and I ran from the safety of my father's shadow to the warmth of my mother's gravid bulk. She pressed a kiss onto the crown of my head. As a girl her hair had been as black as mine, but by the time I was five, it was already shot through with silver, and by my sixth birthday, all the darkness would be gone. Like Andre, her green eyes gleamed, but there was a shade of kindness in her features that Andre lacked.

She ran one hand over my own shock of hair. "Did we wake you?"

"No."

"Can't sleep, eh?" said Andre, saliva glistening on his pointed teeth. "I tell you, Eve, I can smell the changing on him already."

"Shush," she replied. "It's late. There's no need to give him nightmares." She returned her attention to me. "You should go back to bed. You have school tomorrow."

"I'm not tired."

"See? See? Insomnia. First sign." Andre pitched forward. "Are you thirsty all the time? Hey?"

"No."

"Ach, it'll come," he said.

"Andre," said my mother dryly. "Hush or I'll throw you to the Freemasons."

He snarled before hiding his lips behind the rim of his glass.

"Danny, love, don't let your uncle scare you."

"I'm not scared." Not of this idea, anyway. I was used to people and wolves. I'd seen my mother change once before,

26

and she poured herself into a new body with such grace that it made me envious. I was more afraid of sadistic Hestia, now lingering in the darkness of our bedroom, waiting to pinch me with eager fingers.

"Andre, this is all taking place in your head," said my father as he sat at my side, sandwiching me between his oaken thigh and my mother's mountainous stomach. When Andre's mouth opened, my father held up his hand to silence him. "And I don't need to hear your reasons again, but if it makes you feel better, you can stay the night here. We've got a cot in the spare room, and you're more than welcome to use it."

"I'm not sleeping on any bed," he grumbled. "That makes you soft."

"You don't have to stay the night—"

"No, no, Eve, if it makes you happy, I'll stay," he replied, shaking his head. "I don't want you worrying about where I am and if I'm safe. You don't need that kind of stress in your delicate condition."

Even as a five-year-old, I doubted that my mother's condition was the reason for Andre's reluctance to leave. When Uncle Andre came to stay, he always made a sumptuous breakfast feast, a gustatory carnival of eggs and pancakes and greasy slabs of fried ham. He left our cupboards bare.

"No, no, no," he continued, pouring another glass of whiskey from the bottle on the coffee table. "I'll sleep next to the wood stove. That'll suit me fine." The whiskey slipped down his throat, his Adam's apple bobbed, and he let out a hearty burp. "No need to worry about me. Maybe I'll stay for a few days, just to make sure I gave them the slip."

I wriggled my fingers into my father's hand. He squeezed my palm. "You ready for bed, sport?"

"I'm not tired."

"Are you sure?" said my mother. I nodded. "Did you want to sleep with us?"

"You should be sleeping on the floor, m'boy," said Andre. "That's the place for you and I. It keeps us alert. No one sneaks up on you if you're sleeping on the floor."

His words slurred together.

My mother bared her teeth, just a fraction. Living with my father had softened her wolfish tendencies. "Andre, shush. I mean it."

My father squeezed my hand. "Dan, you can sleep in our bed if it makes you feel better."

I nodded again to my father: sure it made me feel better. It meant Hessie would wait the whole night with her fingers tensed to pinch me and never get the chance.

IN THE SUMMER AFTER the twins were born, my father bundled the whole family into the blue Econoline van, which he called the 'Sulli-Van' whenever he was seized by a need to 'pun-ish' us, and we drove south to the sunny vineyards of California, to pay a little visit to a magical land of castles and cotton candy and horrific pirates surrounding a terrible ride that made me sick to my stomach. I didn't like travelling. It made me anxious. I didn't like seeing new things, or meeting new people, or leaving the shelter of our little log cabin in the woods.

The van had three rows of seats. In the front sat my parents, singing off-key country tunes that foreshadowed how embarrassed they'd make me once puberty arrived. In the back were the babies, Aiden and Erin, strapped into their government-inspected, safety-approved, Li'l Tyke pink and blue car seats, squabbling and squawking and screaming at one another in the kind of language only infants understand. Occasionally I'd look back at the pair of round mouths, dark and toothless, each surrounded by a crimson face and collared with a terry cloth bib. Erin, slightly smaller and two minutes younger, perpetually looked as if she'd sucked on something bitter, but Aiden was fierce, ruthless, and gravely insulted by the injustice of being born. He didn't cry for food or clean diapers. He raged to be returned to the womb.

That left the middle seat. Hestia sat next to me, and behind her the landscape of the Oregon coast peeled away and melted into the golden scrub grass and dry hills of the Sunshine State. I'd never been so far south; in fact, I'd rarely left the security of the forest, and I'd never visited anything larger than a town. I hadn't even ranged farther than Rosedell, and I suspected Mom hadn't either by the way she wrung her hands whenever Dad left the van to fill up the tank or grab some burgers from a truck stop. I could hear her heart beating frantically in her chest, even when she sang and looked composed.

"You okay?" he'd say upon every return.

"I'm fine," she'd reply and smile a weak smile.

"We can go back, if you want."

"No!" howled Hestia at my side, now discovering her loudest voice. At some point she lost the ability to speak in a soft and feminine tone, but, at nine, she fluctuated as if someone had control of her volume and was jerking the knob back and forth. "We *can't* go *back*! We're going to *Diz-Nee-Lan*!"

It pierced my ears. At six, my talents had already started to develop: my hearing was superb and my sense of smell was embarrassingly overdeveloped. Hestia had no ability to sympathize. She screamed and belched and stank, and if I asked her to shut up, she raised her piercing voice to the heavens. If I complained about her pungent aroma, she took my head in one of her vast, manly hands and shoved my face into her armpit. Hestia had no mercy. I pressed my palms to my ears and squeezed my eyes closed.

We continued south, into the people and the cities and the sour fog of exhaust. In the front seat, my parents continued to sing along with Johnny and Loretta and Willie, and chasing us all the way was the savage screeching of the twins.

"You and me, Lupi," said Hestia, her jet-black braid hanging over her shoulder, her green eyes flashing. "Just you and me. Wanna play a game of fish?"

"No," I said quietly. "I wanna play licence plate bingo."

"Licence plate bingo sucks *butt*."

"Hestia!"

"Sorry, Daddy," she said in a tiny voice, then leaned closer to me. I flinched, expecting a shout instead of a hissing whisper. "We're gonna play fish, got it? Now deal, or else, when we get to the next hotel, I'll cram your head down the toilet." She thrust the deck of cards into my hand.

My sister was a bully and a braggart, but she had a point. In the mean old world, where our mother had our father and the twins had each other, that left her and I as allies. I was afraid of her power, but I had no choice; she was my worst enemy and my best friend, combined into one. I dealt our cards and silently prayed she'd keep her promises of clemency, though I knew with a sense of futility that Hessie would fulfil her threat, regardless of what game we played.

AND THEN, WHEN I was ten, the Family Secret became something more than unspoken words for me.

I woke with a gasp, aware that something was different. Something was wrong. I struggled from under the bed sheets, feeling an ugly pulsing in my shoulders, and noticed that my skin had become too tight and dry for comfort. The moon shone through the bedroom window and I heard the creaking boards of the cabin as the moisture from the evening air crept through the cellulose of the logs, but these were sensations that I recognized and which gave me comfort. Underneath was another sensation, like a dull ache in my blood, like the change in barometric pressure just before a storm.

"Hessie?"

She grunted in her sleep. We still shared a bedroom, which she hated, but my father had promised us each a private room of our own when we moved into the farmhouse near Rosedell next autumn.

I put my hand on her shoulder, and she batted it away.

"Lemme alone, dumbass."

"Something's wrong."

"Yeah, you're fucking waking me up," she groaned again, giving me a hearty shove in the chest. "Go back to sleep."

I opened my mouth to persist, but at that moment an awful pain jolted through the centre of my torso, like a spear of ice and fire thrust down the core of my body. I sucked in air, doubled onto the ground, and buried my hands in my gut.

Instantly, Hessie tumbled out of bed and fumbled for the light switch. "What's wrong? What's going on?" she demanded, her footsteps all around me. She flicked the switch; the lamp blazed and the room filled with light. "Goddammit, Danny, what's—"

I rolled onto my back as she let out a howling scream.

The sight of my twisted, molten face was too much for her to bear. Hestia, who was always so bold and brave, scrambled backwards and tripped over the hem of her nightgown, falling hard against the wall. Her eyes were full of horror, her mouth gaped in terror. Suddenly, she sucked in a deep breath and screamed for help, and her voice pitched high, frantic, bestial. Over the searing bursts of pain skyrocketing through my flesh, I heard the moist galloping of her heart increase, the blood in her veins chugging like a steam engine. I tried to grab her hand for comfort—oh God, the agony!—but she kicked me away.

Changing skins hurts but I had nothing against which I could compare it, and the mystery of the process only compounded the pain. It hurt more than the time Hestia pushed me out of the tree fort and I broke my arm, bouncing off a branch on the way down. It hurt more than the stitches in my forehead after she aimed a hockey puck too high and powered it through the air with a vicious slap shot. Every quivering muscle burned and seized, every bone became a bottle rocket blasting into space. My sinews stretched as taut as piano strings, my voice snagged in a constricted throat, my wrenched ears filled with Hessie's terrified shrieks. I could barely move, but Hessie flailed backwards, flung out her arms, brandished her fists. Time stood still, washed away by the pain. Only Hestia's screams marked the passing of what could've been hours, but was more likely minutes.

She pressed her back against the door frame between our bedroom and the hall. She'd stopped screaming, but her eyes remained as wide as quarters. She looked at me with curious, fearful disgust, like she was studying the remains of a road kill.

I wanted the light turned off. I wanted her to turn away.

"Don't... watch... you... bitch—"

I grabbed a shoe and threw it at her, but my arm wasn't working right and the throw went wild.

"Mom!" she screamed down the hall. "Hurry!" Her voice was like iron but this was a thin disguise. The terror in her expression hurt my vanity more than any of her other abuses, and I could read it in her features: 'Thank God it's you and not me.' I filled with shame. I wanted to hide my ugliness from her. I didn't want anyone I loved to see me. I tried to drag my disgusting form under my bed, but I only managed to flop against the carpet. As I struggled, she took a fearful step forward; her gaze was that of a sideshow guest staring at the pathetic beast behind the bars.

I heard heavy steps as my father raced up the stairway, followed by the shush-shush of my mother's slippers on the landing. He pushed Hestia aside. "Wait in the hall, honey," he said. "Make sure the twins stay in bed." Then he turned to me; I'd never seen my father afraid, but he reeked of fear, and his eyes were filled with revulsion. He faltered, paused for a heartbeat, just long enough for my mother to push past him.

She fell to her knees next to me. There was nothing but adoration in her face, and she wrapped her arms around me, struggling to pull my pyjamas over my head. My clavicles had changed and I was now unable to lift my hands over my shoulders.

"Hurts," was all I managed to say. I tried not to look at my father.

"Of course it does, Danny," she crooned back. "First changes always do. It'll get better."

"How... long?"

She kissed my forehead, now itchy as the guard hairs tore through my skin. "Relax. Don't fight. You take after my side of the family, nothing to be done about it." She glanced over the back portion of my body, now unrecognizable under an inky blue-black pelt, and smiled the same way that she did at Hestia's piano concerts or Aiden's soccer games: matronly proud. "This probably isn't a complete alteration, Danny. You're still too young," she added as she held my stunted hands and looked me in the eyes. "Take a deep breath. The pain will pass."

I glanced towards the door. Hestia was clinging to the threshold, her face grey and waxy, my father standing behind her. I could smell them both. The musky scent of panic clung to the walls and the curtains.

Mom could smell it too. "Jack? Turn off the light and take Hessie to wait in the kitchen."

"I'll call Andre," said my father in a measured, forced tone.

Hessie gasped. "He's *ugly*."

"You better mean Andre, Hestia, because I would hate to think that you were insulting Danny to his face." My mother's underlying sentiment was clear: yes, your brother may be a warped monster halfway between man and beast, but he can ` still hear you and understand you, and you better be respectful. Mom aimed her fiery eyes towards her eldest daughter, still loitering in the doorframe, still staring at my shivering molten body on the floor. "Hessie? Go wait in the kitchen. Now."

"But—"

"Kitchen, Hestia Anne."

The use of two names. My mother's interpretation of a warning shot over the bow.

I heard Hessie running down the stairs after our father.

God, it hurt to breathe. It felt as though great hands had prized my sternum apart and now pulled each side of my ribcage open on the hinge of my spine. I took shallow, stilted breaths. "Turn… back… ever?"

"Don't be afraid, love," she said to me with a sly grin, holding up my pyjama shirt. "Keep this close, and when you want to come back, put it on. The action of something so human, so familiar, will remind your body where to go. It's your safety net."

35

I reached out with one curled hand, fingers stubby and shrunken, to touch the fabric. I wanted to turn back right now but no longer had a voice to express it. Instead of words, a low whine escaped.

"Twice a year you have to be a wolf, but only for a few days. Keep your clothes safe and they'll help you return. The rest of the time you are free to wear whichever body you choose, but for those two times, you have to get the wolfishness out of your system." She kissed my nose. "Don't be afraid."

But I was, and not for any reason that my mother would guess. I'd known I was going to be a werewolf for my whole life; I'd shown all the preliminary signs, and it had only been a matter of time before the change came upon me and I was forced to learn to live as a beast. I'd seen my mother change in the dark of the night, her silver fur bright and luminous under the light of the moon, and I'd never been afraid because she transformed with the smooth precision of a dancer, flowing like water into her second body.

But Hestia was my partner in crime, my role model and everything I wanted to be, even when I hated her. The twins would always have each other, and I couldn't imagine my parents separated, but Hestia was my match, and as painful and agonizing as that was, I'd accepted my lot. My sister could make me laugh and torture me at the same time. She'd sit on my head and fart in my face as I struggled for freedom, both of us giggling uproariously. She'd lock me in the closet and only let me out if I promised to dress in her Wonder Woman Underoos and run through the adults' dinner party. Together, we'd watch Saturday morning cartoons at the break of dawn, eat entire boxes of Sugar Pops and then chase each other through the silent house, squealing like piglets. She knew more about the world than me, and if I needed protection, I went to her.

In this terrible twisted body, with my snout half formed and my fur sprouting in ragged patches, I curled on the ground and discovered that I'd lost the ability to weep. My sobs sounded like heaving coughs, more like a bark than any expression of sorrow. All I wanted to do was cry, but even that human ability was gone.

I couldn't explain to my mother that Hestia's fear of me was more than I could bear. It upset the balance of our manic friendship. She would always look at me with distrust, secretly happy to be unaffected herself. It meant, more than anything, that I was truly, truly alone.

3

"SO YOUR SISTER HATED you."

Sullivan gave this statement some thought. "No. She didn't hate me. At first she was afraid, but that passed in time." He grinned. "She didn't want to sleep in the same room as me anymore, so Mom and Dad finally gave Hessie her own bedroom. She appreciated that."

"She didn't become all wolfy?" Caufield took a swig from his mug of coffee.

"Hestia doesn't change her skin but she can still be a bitch," Sullivan laughed. "When we were kids, she took great delight in reminding me how different I was from everyone else."

"Like what?"

Sullivan shifted in the wooden chair, leaning back and crossing his arms. "Stupid things, really. She gave me a dog collar for my fifteenth birthday; yeah, *that* was appreciated. She'd pull my tail, yank on my ears, complain about wolf hair blocking up the sink. For a while, she started calling me 'Chewbacca', but Mom put a stop to that."

Caufield grinned. "It sounds like she made your puberty a living hell."

"Mom claimed Hessie was jealous, but I don't know," Sullivan said, giving an absent shrug. "It always seemed to me that she was relieved to be normal, and tormenting me was a way of reminding herself it could've been worse. I mean, even when we were adults, she'd let little things slip."

Caufield motioned to the leather chair by the door. "You want a more comfortable seat? There's a cushioned one over there. Feel free to move it."

"Thanks," Sullivan replied as he stood and dragged it closer to the desk.

"So, what do you mean, little things?" said Caufield as Sullivan took the other mug of coffee.

"Let me think—" he said, and after a pause a wince crossed his features. "There was one time, in my second year of college, when she was particularly cruel in that fleeting and unthinking way of hers."

I LAID THE CHISEL aside and breathed lightly over the surface of the maple block, pushing the last persistent curls of wood with the pressure of my breath. They fluttered and fell to the sides. Two more lines remained to be carved, two sweeping curves to complete the intricate Islamic design, and this hunk of old wood taken from the back shed would be transformed into a cherished relief. I'd spent most of the afternoon tracing the design in pencil, measuring the angles, ensuring each swirl and arabesque mirrored perfectly. I'd tensed my fingers and paced back and forth, finding the courage to mar such a lovely block of wood with a gouge that might go wild, but luck was with me. I'd hit no knots, I'd made no unsightly cracks. My hands were miraculously free of slivers. Once I'd finished these final strokes, the block would be ready for printing, and my grade in Middle Eastern Design 201 would be assured.

Plucking the chisel from the table and feeling its weight in my hand, I set it to the commencement of the line and pressed into the soft, yielding wood.

"Dan?"

The blade skipped, the carved line jumped. I yanked my hands back, pushing the heavy block across the dining room table, knocking over a chair.

"Hessie will be here any minute, Dan."

Oh no, oh please, not now, not…

I scrambled forward and pulled the maple block towards me, examining the surface and terrified by what I might see. I let out a ragged sigh; the block was unmarred. Yes, the blade had skipped and cut deeply where it landed, but fate had smiled upon me, and its unintentional bite corresponded with my pencil marks. When the block was completed, no one would ever know I'd slipped.

But where the block had skittered across the table was a long and visible groove, a pale yellow scar against the red-brown finish. I'd left a scratch of mammoth proportions in my mother's oak table.

Shit.

Her voice from the kitchen shattered my stunned silence. "Can you please, please, clean up the mess in the dining room? Please?"

"In a minute, Mom." I pulled a piece of newspaper over the scratch, furiously devising ways of fixing it. I'll put down a tablecloth, grab some wax out of my supply box, smooth down the edges of the groove with fine sandpaper. Tonight, after she goes to bed, I'll sneak back in here, she'll never see the damage, I'll pour all my knowledge from art college into masking the scratch...

"Daniel—"

She stood in the arch between the dining room and kitchen, arms crossed, staring with restrained horror at the table which in an hour would support a Thanksgiving turkey bigger than the dog.

Had she seen? I rubbed the back of my neck, staying calm. "What?"

She tried without success to keep an angry face. "This is your homework? It's a mess!"

"Fine Arts, Mom," I replied.

"Ah yes," she nodded sagely. "I spend good money for my child to doodle and cut pictures out of magazines."

"It's called *photomontage.*"

"Of course. Photomontage."

I mirrored her grin. "And I'm finished with the photomontage. This—" I said as I waved one hand over the disaster area, "—this is woodblock printing."

"Ah. On my cherished antique table." She disappeared into the kitchen. "As long as it's gone by dinner, I'll be happy."

"Mom?"

"Mmm-hmm?"

I wasn't sure how to phrase the question. After glancing to ensure she was out of sight, I bundled the newspaper with its burden of wood chips and stuffed it into a garbage bag, letting the crinkling and rustling obscure my silence while I thought. Grabbing a folded tablecloth from the linen drawer, I tossed it over the offending mark, smoothing the edges and crossing my fingers. A quick glance from a step back proved it was hidden, and I asked, as casually as possible, "Erin said Hessie is bringing a guest?"

"Yes."

"What kind of guest?"

I heard her set a pan on the counter and push the chopping block aside. She poked her head through the threshold that joined the kitchen to the dining area. "A young man. His name is—" She squinted slightly, thinking. "Vincent Garzoni. She met him at a conference in Seattle."

"Seattle." I kept my head down.

"He's a med student. Finishing his internship."

"Ah."

She slumped against the doorway. In her left hand she held a wicked cleaver splattered with poultry innards. "Penny for your thoughts."

I glanced at her sideways, then back to the table. "It'll just be… odd, that's all. To have a stranger in the house."

"Well," she began, ever tactful. "I think it'll be nice to have someone new to talk to, now that your father's gone." She took a deep breath; it hadn't been long enough since his death for her to speak of him without a stab of pain. "And Andre hates

42

family gatherings, and your cousins had other plans. I thought this might be a very lonely Thanksgiving, so I'm pleased."

"I see."

"You don't sound so pleased."

I looked towards the doorway. She was already prepared for tonight, dressed in a modest black sweater and khaki pants, every hair in place and a conservative shade of brown to colour her lips. My mother had been stunning as a younger woman, and she was still very beautiful, strong willed and independent, but her looks had mellowed and softened after Dad's accident. His death had left her diminished, duller. Eve Sullivan had lost her vibrancy and now spent her evenings alone. Erin had told me that Mr Deaver at the Rosedell mini-mart had asked her out for dinner last Wednesday.

My mother had politely, but firmly, refused.

Her statement ran through my head. "What's that supposed to mean, that I don't sound pleased?"

She wiggled the cleaver in my direction before thumping it down on the chopping block and returning to the dining room. "I mean that you and Hestia have always been close."

"And?"

"She's busy with her own life now, and this will be a lonely holiday for you, one way or another. Oh Danny, don't be so depressed." She threw her arms around me and squeezed me close. "When did my little boy get so tall?"

"Do you ever feel—" I fought for words, pressed my chin onto the top of her head. "That there's no one in the world that understands you?"

She laughed and let me go. "Daniel, you're an art student. I thought that was a prerequisite." She motioned for me to take one chair as she sat in the other. "You're twenty-one. Of course no one understands you."

"No, I mean with… you know… the lycanthropy."

She rolled her eyes. "You spend three weeks a year in a different body. You can't blame the malaise of the other forty-nine on being a werewolf, love." And before I could answer, she said, "Look at it this way: the change is something you *can* count on. The rest of the world might be unreliable, but at least you always know where you'll be in six months."

"I can set my watch by it," I said, slumping back against the wooden chair. "October and April. Midterms and finals."

"Always nine nights?"

"Without question."

She tipped her head. "Andre's changing is all over the map. Sometimes ten days, sometimes five. And sometimes he chooses to stay as a wolf and doesn't come back for a month or two." She reclined in the chair. "I've lost the stamina for running through the woods. I miss my goose down pillow and my tea and my talk shows every afternoon."

"But do you ever feel like you're disconnected?" I leaned forward and rested my elbows on my knees. "That you don't belong in this world at all?"

"God loves every one of His creatures," she replied. "Even the humble lycanthrope."

"Don't bring God into it," I groaned.

"You brought God into it," she replied with a pointed finger. "We belong here just as much as anyone. Don't let them tell you otherwise."

"Yes, but—"

"The church knows that metamorphosis is possible… the church is founded on the idea. What else is Communion?" She rocked back in her chair. "When the bread and wine cease to change, Danny, then I'll suspect that God's forgotten about us, but until then I know He's watching over me."

"But they don't *really* change—"

"Yes they do. You don't have the faith to taste it." She plucked a curl of shaved wood from the carpet and spun it between her fingers. "When did you last confess?"

"I don't go to church anymore, Mom. God doesn't exist."

She shook her head. "I still stand by the belief that we are as much a part of creation as anything else. There's no need for you to feel disconnected, Danny."

But I did, very much. I didn't say anything, but she saw it in my features and smelt it on my skin.

"Danny," my mother sighed. "I don't argue with your atheism; your faith is your own. But you've been depressed for so long—"

"I'm fine."

"You are not," she replied, concerned. "Perhaps you should give up school and spend a year or two in the woods. Find a pack, hook up with them. You wouldn't be the first werewolf to prefer a life on four feet to a life on two."

"I'm not leaving."

"But you aren't happy here."

I scowled. "I'll finish my degree first. Dad would've wanted that."

"Your father wanted you to be happy," she replied. "That's why he asked to have the company sold and the money divided, instead of forcing you to take over the business." She waggled her finger at me. "I was married to Jack for twenty-five years. Don't presume to tell me what he wanted." She parted her lips to say more, but the rumbling of a car in the driveway caught her attention, and her face brightened. "We'll talk about this later. Hessie's home."

The dog began his volley of barking. Erin tumbled down the stairs in a flurry of limbs and we followed her into the main foyer of the vast, turn-of-the-century farmhouse. Monty, a matted mongrel who looked more like a shag rug than a hound, scratched at the door and implored my mother with passive yips to open it for him; he'd been hit by a car at the age of six which broke his hip and left him old, but when his kingdom was invaded by a rumbling vehicle, he perked up to proclaim his dominion in thundering, gravely houfs. I pushed him aside and opened the front door, spilling Erin and my mother out before me. Monty limped after them, but I lingered in the hall, wary.

"Is this a boyfriend?" said Aiden as he joined me. My brother could not change his skin but he walked with unnatural silence. He's the only human with the ability to startle me. I reeled back and he cast me a dour, if self-satisfied, smirk. "You're walking on eggshells, aren't you?"

"I scratched Mom's table."

"She doesn't know it?"

"No," I admitted. "And I'd rather keep it that way."

We both looked towards the driveway, where our oldest sister had jumped out of her Volkswagen van, wearing old cut-offs and a sweatshirt with her black hair pinned on top of her head. Hestia crushed both Mom and Erin in an unforgiving hug. The three of them began chattering like magpies.

"She hasn't brought any of her other boyfriends home," I said.

Aiden was fifteen and almost as tall as Mom. He grimaced, a lock of black hair falling over his features. "Think she likes this one?" he grunted.

"She must."

"Huh." He watched the three women squealing and hugging, his adolescent face already exhibiting the gruff cynicism he'd display as an adult. At fifteen years old, however, Aiden still spoke to me, and hadn't yet dismissed werewolves as something to be ignored. He and I were allies in a house full of girls, and his question contained an element of camaraderie that would be gone by next summer. "D'ya wanna play a game of one-on-one?"

"Later," I replied. I caught a whiff of Hestia's perfume on the air, followed by the scent of a stranger. Male, late twenties or early thirties. Nervous as hell. Wearing cotton and wool. Drank too much coffee and ate spicy chicken wings for last night's dinner.

Hestia caught sight of us lurking. Her lips turned up in a joyous smirk. "What? Are you hiding? Get over here. Give me a hug, dammit! Vinnie, these are my brothers. Dan, Aiden— Vincent Garzoni."

Vincent fumbled his way out of the driver's door, struggling with the latch and the lock, and when he was finally free he crossed the driveway in three quick steps and extended one lanky arm towards me. The visual impression was not far from the one given by his scent. He wore a dark suit and blue tie, the complete opposite of Hestia's slovenly outfit, and he was losing his hair, making him prematurely conservative. "Ah, Daniel, I've heard a great deal about you," Vincent said as he took my hand in a strong grip. But he was a thin wisp of a man, and I had the sudden impression that I could reduce him to pulp if I tightened my fingers. "Fine arts, yes? Hestia talks about you all the time. And Aiden, who snowboards, yes? Hello. Hello." He shook Aiden's hand formally.

I caught sight of Hestia studying my reaction. I threw Vincent a cautious smile and asked, "How was the drive?"

"Fantastic countryside," he replied. Then to my mother, "I love British Columbia in the autumn. What a delightfully beautiful house and garden. Is the place old?"

"It is, but we replaced the wiring and plumbing a few years ago. It looks old on the outside but it has the heart of a teenager. A bit like me." She laughed lightly, and instantly Vinnie's scent lost its pungent nervousness. She took his hand in hers. "Come on in, I'll give you a tour." She guided him past me and into the entrance hall, and when his back was turned, she mouthed the words to me, "Be nice."

Erin clung to Hestia with long, skinny arms. "Are you staying for the whole weekend?"

"Yep."

"Wanna go shopping tomorrow?"

"I thought I'd take Vinnie up to the old cabin at Maple Lake," she replied. "Sorry Erin. I live in the city. It's nice to get out into the woods when I can."

"Can I come with you?"

"Sure, sweet pea." She disentangled herself from Erin's arms. "You want to come too, Aiden?"

"Ungh," he grunted with a shrug. It could have been yes or no, but it was Aiden's style to be noncommittal. "C'mon, Erin. One-on-one."

My younger siblings retreated to the flat of concrete in the backyard and Hestia sidled close as they rounded the house, out of earshot. "Are you home for the whole weekend, or are you going back later tonight?"

"Like you said, it's nice to get out in the woods when I can."

"How're ya doing, Lupi?"

"I'm alright."

"Still living the monk's life?" she said, pinching my arm.

I glared at her, but instead of answering, I asked, "He's not quite your normal choice, is he? Bit skinny for your tastes. Bit too intellectual."

"Jealous?" she said as she elbowed me in the ribs. "Looks are deceiving. He used to be in a band in Seattle."

I narrowed my eyes; I didn't believe her. "And then he became a doctor."

"Shut up, he's fun," she said. "Really." Hestia leaned against the door jamb and ran her hand over Monty's scruffy head; the dog gazed up at her with adoring eyes. "In fact, I've got some news to tell you. Promise you won't say a word to Mom?"

"Okay," I replied with caution.

"Vinnie and I are getting married."

I blinked twice. "You're joking."

Hestia shook her head, beaming with happiness. "I'm in love, Lupi. He's had a job offer in the south of France—France!—so I'm marrying him and we're moving in January. Please don't say a word. I want to tell Mom after dinner."

"To France?"

She nodded rapidly. "Isn't that great?"

I was speechless.

"And," she continued as I leaned against the opposite wall, "Vinnie doesn't know all that many people here, and so we hoped you'd be the best man."

"I... I guess so—"

"And maybe," she began, then paused and looked to the ground. "With Dad gone, maybe you'd give me away?"

I swallowed but couldn't answer.

"Think about it," she said. "I know it's tough without him here. It hasn't been very long." Hestia took my hand. "It would mean a lot if you walked with me down the aisle."

"Of course then."

She flung her arms around me and pushed a fierce kiss onto my cheek. "Thanks Danny! I was so scared you'd say no! Damn, look, I'm all weepy now." She smeared the tears from her eyes and laughed. "You'll like Vinnie so much. He's witty as hell and we just hit it off. Don't roll your eyes, dumbass, it was like we were made for each other."

"I'm happy for you, Hes. You seem really... taken with him."

"You think he looks stuffy."

"What does it matter what I think?" I replied. "I'm not the one who has to sleep with him."

"You *will* like him," she said, and it sounded more like a command than an assurance.

As we ate dinner, I said little. My mother glanced often in my direction but all I could think was how far away Hestia would live with a man about whom I knew nothing. Her life was her own. My life was mine. Dad was dead and I was taking his place. Everything changed so quickly.

"Do you feel alright?" said Mom after we'd reduced the turkey to bones and scraps. Erin and Aiden started to clear the dishes, Vincent and Hestia leaned towards each other and snickered at an unspoken joke, I reclined in my chair considering how swiftly my life was altering. I shook myself from my introspection to see my mother staring intently at me. "You look... I don't know... a little stricken, Danny."

"He's just surprised by my news," said Hestia, off the cuff, laying her fork down. She brushed a few speckles of wood dust from the edge of the tablecloth.

My mother raised one eyebrow. "News?"

Hestia took Vincent's hand and they shared a coy smile between them. "Well," she started slowly, taking a deep breath. "Vinnie and I are getting married."

There was a long heartbeat of a pause.

Then, with the same explosive jolt as a thoroughbred leaving the starting gate, my mother leapt from the table to hug them both before beginning to cry. "Married! My Hestia, married! What a brave man!" She threw her arms around

Vincent and kissed his cheek. "That's wonderful! Absolutely wonderful!"

"When?" said Aiden, returning to his chair next to mine.

"January fifteenth," said Hessie.

"You knocked up?"

"Aiden!" scolded our mom, but he shrugged.

"Could be," he replied in his own defence. Vincent looked unnerved, but Hessie laughed.

"No," she said once she'd regained her composure.

My mother rested one hand on Vinnie's shoulder and fixed Hessie with a piercing gaze, her exuberance mellowing into a restrained joy. "Will you have children?"

Hestia pursed her lips. "I think so," she said as Mom returned to her seat. "We've discussed that possibility."

"I'd love kids," said Vincent. "Once my practice is settled and we have a house and some land."

"Hmmm—" Mom nodded slowly, thoughtfully. "Then you should tell him."

"I will," said Hestia. She wasn't anxious. Her answer was measured. "I've told him that there's a condition that runs in your side of the family. I've told him I might carry it, and I might not."

"Ah."

Vincent leaned forward. "Hestia's been very discrete about the nature of your illness. She's been extremely respectful, Mrs Sullivan."

"Please, Vincent, call me Eve. And really, it's not an illness. It's more of a way of life."

He nodded, folding his hands. "I may be a few months yet from beginning my own practice, but I hope you'd allow me to discuss your symptoms in the greatest of confidence. Is it blood related? Digestive? There may be some research being done, somewhere, that I could—"

"I doubt it," she interrupted, smiling kindly. "It's extremely rare. In our immediate family, only Dan and I exhibit symptoms."

I raised my eyebrows. "Mom, we hardly know him," I said. This was a lesson I'd learnt early, that lycanthropy was not the sort of thing one discusses with strangers.

"He's almost family," said Erin.

"Almost but not quite," I snapped.

"You want me to wait until after we're hitched, Lupi?" said Hessie with her brows drawn down and her face as dark as thunder. "You want me to spring this on him after the first kid's born?"

"No, but—"

"Or how about," she added, fiery, "when he finds our first son writhing in agony on the bedroom floor? Christ, I know what kind of shock *that* is. I remember the noise you made. The screaming, the crying—"

"Hestia," said my mother, and she would have said more, but I lurched forward.

"You had no right to say anything to him."

"I have every right." She crossed her arms and glared.

"You should have asked me first."

"Dan, calm down. Sit."

I ignored my mother and said to Hestia, "This is my life, Hes."

"Well, this is mine," she snapped back, louder than me. "And I need to tell him what he's in for. It's only fair."

"You don't just tell whoever you happen to be fucking that—"

A sharp slap caught me unaware across the back of the head. My mother lowered her hand and growled, deep in her throat, to remind me that she was first amongst us. Erin and Aiden looked away, Hessie lowered her gaze. Even Monty, lying under the table, sensed the tension between us and ceased to beg for scraps.

"You do not go against me, Daniel," she said in a low snarl. "You do as I say or I'll rip out your throat. Understand?"

Vincent's jaw dropped and his throat hitched.

"Yes." I lowered my gaze.

My mother's expression softened as she turned to our guest. "I'm sorry, Vincent. My son is not having an easy time at school, and he's still reeling from the death of his father. He's a bit depressed."

"Oh," said Vinnie, eyes wide. "Sorry to hear that."

I glowered as I returned to my seat.

"I think, in light of your concerns, Danny, you should be the one to discuss our lineage with Vincent."

"Me?"

"I don't want your relationship with him sullied by your immature display. Besides," and she ran her finger over the tablecloth, pushing the fabric into the deep gouge underneath, "you tell him, and I may just forgive you for this."

I swallowed.

"Why don't you three retire to the rumpus room, and Dan can answer your questions and tell you what he deems necessary, no?"

Her eyes bore into the side of my face. I cast her a sideways glance. "But—"

"Aiden, Erin and I are capable of cleaning up," she replied. "We'll have dessert when you get back."

With her mischievous, lopsided grin, my mother looked like the lovechild of Martha Stewart and the devil. If I'd held my tongue, she'd have told Vincent about our lineage and history, but if I was going to act like a spoilt child at the dinner table, then I'd have to prove I was an adult by indulging his curiosity myself. I growled back and she heard. She only smiled wider.

So we moved into the basement, through the library filled with my father's books and past the pool table in the corner, and Vincent sat on the couch next to Hestia. I paced back and forth, grinding my teeth. "Well?" Hestia said after a few minutes of silence.

"What?"

"Can I tell him, or do you want to?"

Vincent folded his hands in his lap and leaned towards me. In a flash I saw the kind of doctor he'd be: aloof, curious, considering his patients as specimens rather than souls. He cast a reserved and clinical smile, kind but distant, and said, "If this is an uncomfortable subject, I don't mind waiting. We just met, Daniel, and you're obviously not happy about this situation. Regardless of what your mother said, this discussion can wait."

"No it can't," Hestia replied before I had a chance to answer. "May as well get the truth on the table right away, and give you an opportunity to back out of our engagement before—"

"There'll be no backing out," he said with a tense squint in her direction, bewildered. "I don't care what condition you're carrying. I adore you, Hestia." He kissed her as if her lips were the petals of a delicate peony. She flushed slightly. I'd never in all my life seen my tomboyish sister act so sickeningly feminine. It was unnerving.

But I couldn't ignore it; they really loved each other. They displayed the same bright joy in being with one another as my parents once had, and through my jealousy and indignant rage I was also happy for Hestia, happy she'd found someone who matched her so completely. If he didn't mind marrying into a family of werewolves, I suspected their relationship would last forever.

"Dammit, alright!" I said at last, unbuttoning my shirt. "May as well show him."

"Thank you Lupi," she cheered, squeezing her eyes and smiling wide enough to show all her teeth. "I promise I'll make it up to you. An extra big Christmas gift."

"Save your money, you harpy," I grumbled as I kicked off my shoes.

"There's no need for a physical," Vincent started as I pulled off my jeans, shuffling his hands back and forth with my sudden nudity. Let's face it, it's not every Thanksgiving that your future brother-in-law pulls off all his clothes. Modest for a doctor, he looked away as he said, "Dan, you can just tell me."

"No he can't," said Hestia as the last of my clothes fell into the pile. "He's a werewolf, Vin. He can tell you all you want, but you're not gonna believe it, so he may as well show you. Damn, Lupi, you been working out? You're not the stick insect you used to be."

I stood on my toes and stretched my arms above my head.

"I beg your pardon?" said Vinnie. He must have been positive that he'd misheard.

"Werewolf," I said. "Yes, harpy queen, I have been working out. Mostly swimming, a bit of weights."

"And you got a tattoo," she laughed, pointing at the words scrawled just below my navel.

"Don't tell Mom," I replied. "It's new. She'd flip out."

Hessie peered closer at the black words emblazoned on my skin. "Is it Latin?"

"Mmm-hmm."

Vinnie was sorting out my previous answer. "There's no such thing as—"

"Did it hurt?"

I shrugged. "Not much."

"Liar! I see it in your eyes. I bet you cried."

With a chuckle, I said, "Compared to changing skins, it was a walk in the park."

"Did you say—"

Hestia put her hand over Vincent's mouth. "Give me a copy of your exercise routine, Lupi. I need to drop a few pounds before the wedding."

I hunched over and laid my hands on the carpet, and took a deep breath that reached to the bottom of my lungs. "He won't talk?"

Vincent's eyebrows knit together. "There's no such—"

"What are we, the fucking mafia?" said Hestia. "Of course he won't talk."

"Better not," I replied. "Or I'll run him down and drop him like a deer."

If he'd had a glove in his hand, Vincent would have slapped my face with it. He thought I was crazy, that was evident enough in the self-effacing compassion in his eyes, but he wasn't about to let a delusional crackpot threaten him. "Daniel, I promise that anything you share here with me today will be treated with the strictest confidentiality, and you can implicitly trust—"

"Dan, I swear to God, he won't say a word," Hestia replied. Her expression was sincere, her voice was softer than it had been in decades. "I promise. Don't threaten him, just show him."

I lowered my head and let the change sweep over me. I breathed deeply through the familiar pain as the rasp of fur swept like a dark tide over my naked skin, as my skull squeezed my eyes into a wider alignment, as my fingers shortened and my thumb drifted up the back of my wrist. And when the pain receded, the full glorious world of smells unfurled before me, as breathtaking and beautiful as a map unrolled with a flourish: sensual layers of mildew, rot, grease, skin, carpet, wood, leaves, food, blood, salts, sweat. I closed my eyes, drank in the heady fragrances, and when the transformation was done, I shook my head and stretched forward, arching my back.

Vinnie, his face now the putty-coloured pallor of a corpse, was taking small, shallow gasps.

"C'mere, Lupi," said Hestia. Over the years, she'd seen it many times, and it was no longer a big deal. "I remember you saying the hair coming in was itchy as hell."

"holymarymotheragod!" Vincent whispered.

She ran her fingers over my back and scratched along my spine. When she hit the ticklish spot over my hips, I whined and thumped my foot against the carpet. "This is my little brother, Vin."

He reached out with one trembling hand, wary and afraid. I snapped at his fingers. Hestia whipped her hands around my snout and squeezed it closed. "Hey! Don't bite! Just 'cause you're grumpy about changing for a stranger doesn't mean anyone needs stitches." Her fingers still encircling my nose, she said, "Go on, Vincent. Keep your hand away from the pointy end, but he won't bite or I'll bite him back. Got it, Lupi?"

I responded with a low, unhappy growl.

"Why didn't you say something, Hestia?" he asked. To be fair, he was taking it rather well. He sounded amazed and a little afraid, but nowhere near as unglued as I'd assumed he'd be.

"Does this alter our engagement?"

I heard a quiver of fear in her voice.

"Of course not, Hes."

She exhaled and her grip on my muzzle slackened.

"Do you do this too?"

"No," she replied. "Just Dan and Mom. The rest of us are normal."

My heart sank in my chest to hear her say that. I shook my head until she let go of my nose, and backing away from Vinnie's outstretched palm, I curled up and cast off my wolfish body. I coughed to clear my throat of the last growls.

"I'm stunned," Vincent said quietly as I pulled my clothes back on. "I had no idea... are there many of you?"

"Just one of me," I replied.

"No, I mean—"

"I know what you mean," I said bitterly. "Us and them. No, Vincent, there aren't many of us in the world." Us, who are monstrous and grotesque and who inspire instinctual terror in the hearts of those who know our secrets. I glared at Hestia. "There are very few of us, and we keep mostly to ourselves."

"How can I not know about this?" He appeared completely bewildered by the idea.

"I'm sure there's lots you don't know about, Dr Garzoni," I replied.

His eyes ranged up and down, all over me. "You look so... so... normal."

I bowed my head and gritted my teeth.

"It's not like he goes crazy under a full moon, Vinnie," said Hestia quickly, seeing my embarrassment. "Those old stories are just a bunch of bullshit."

"Yes, but—"

When I stepped forward, he instinctively shrank back.

"Is it contagious?"

"No," I replied. "You can't become a werewolf unless you were born into a family of werewolves. And even then," I glanced at Hestia, "even then, you might be lucky enough to skip it."

"Dan," she said. "It's not a case of being lucky or unlucky—"

"I'm going outside," I said, dismissing her statement with a wave of my hand. "You can answer the rest of his questions, Hes."

I retreated to the back garden and watched the moon rise with Monty at my side. Me and the dog. I'd never felt so depressed, so thrown aside by the rest of the world. There was no one who would understand me, I suspected, and I was doomed to live a life alone. I heard happy conversation and laughter in the living room, and I wrapped my arms around my knees and stared at the heavens.

"How does she do it, Monty? How does Mom reconcile her lives?"

Monty, destined to live a mute life by virtue of his genes, wagged his tail at the sound of his name.

"You know what I think?" I said, staring at his grizzled nose and amber eyes. "If there is a God, Monty, He doesn't care a rat's ass for you and I."

Monty pressed his shoulder against my chest before the sounds of a vole in the ferns demanded his attention, and he limped away, gurgling and snuffling for the trail.

When they married and moved to Carcassonne, I was almost relieved to see Hestia go.

SULLIVAN NARROWED his eyes, quizzical. "What's wrong?"

Caufield knew he had a peculiar expression on his face but he couldn't hide it. A laugh threatened to bubble over and spoil his attempts to remain serious. "I've got a question."

"Sure. What?"

"Werewolves are Catholic?"

Sullivan rolled his eyes. "It's a long story."

"Hell, I've got time. That's one tale I want to hear."

"No, trust me—"

"Is the Pope? I always thought there was something sneaky—"

"God, no," Sullivan answered, grinning in response. "And this is making you think I'm even crazier, isn't it?"

"Loopy as a rollercoaster, my friend," Caufield replied. "Next thing I know, you'll be telling me the Beatles were all werewolves."

"Only one," Sullivan said, with a straight face.

ANDRE TOOK GREAT delight in retelling the history of our family. He seemed to celebrate the bloodshed and horror, like it was a badge of honour that we'd lasted so long, even though our numbers are small and scattered.

And he never included my siblings in his sweeping generalizations. It made me feel better, to be with Andre. It made me feel special in a powerful way, not in an ugly way.

"We gotta stick together, us wolves," he'd say as he slipped a dollop of scotch into my milk at family dinners. This particular gathering must have been sometime around Christmas, because I recall the delicious musty smell of fig pudding and the whispering sounds of the pine needles from the tree in the corner of the living room. Andre and I sat on the carpet next to the wood stove. No comfy chairs for him, or for me, when he was around. "You're what, twelve now?" he said, one eye squinting. "Old enough to drink like a man."

I didn't like scotch—I still don't—but at twelve I didn't have the courage to refuse his alcoholic gifts, given quickly whenever my mother's back was turned. My father and Aiden must have been bringing in the firewood, for Andre would never have dared to spike my drinks if Jack was nearby. Like any self-respecting territorial animal, he acknowledged my father's authority in the house.

"See, m'boy, we come from a long and illustrious line. We were once the fiercest fighters, the most courageous soldiers, and kings and noblemen scrambled to have us number amongst their armies, because with a werewolf leading the campaign, they knew they'd never lose. We fought till the death! Till every drop of our blood was squeezed from our bodies! Till every half-turned limb had been severed from our corpses!" His voice grew progressively louder, his grimy face flushed. He pulled at the collar of his shirt, which had once been my father's and fit him poorly. "And our enemies cowered and quaked in their boots to hear us howling on the frontlines, thirsting for their deaths, eager to taste their throats between our jagged teeth. We were mighty, unstoppable, a hurricane of terror—"

"Andre, honey, calm down."

"But we were, Eve," he insisted, as she headed into the kitchen to help Hestia with dinner. "We were the scourge of the Hun and of the Infidel. It was the church who encouraged us. Who used us to try and steal back Jerusalem during the Crusades."

My mother gave me a look that I instantly recognized— don't believe everything he says—before disappearing into the kitchen.

"And when the schism between the Church and the wolves came," he continued in a theatrical hiss. "And the witch hunts began, it was the Franciscans who took us in, sheltered us from the storms, started to burn the records of our existence. They knew we still had use, they wanted us to lead their missionary campaigns in the New World, and they shipped us here by the dozens. Who better to live in the harsh conditions and convert the heathens, hey?" he cackled. "But they didn't bank on us finding a place here. Here, we were as free as any full-blooded wolf, without the priests and the bishops and the inquisitors to remind us that we ought to feel guilty for our bestial side, for the very same beast that helped them win all that money and land. No, m'boy, they didn't realize we'd like it better here than under their thumb in the old country, and we slipped quietly away into the vast forests, living with the full-blooded wolves, easy as pie."

"Really?" I said, eager for more. The living room seemed to be swimming in and out of focus, and I felt warm and drowsy.

"True as rain!" he said. "Us werewolves, we don't need any fancy church to worship the God who made us. That's as true as rain."

"Didn't the inquisitors try to find us?"

"Oh, they tried—" he sneered, his teeth pointed. "But you know as well as I that once you're in the woods, ain't no one can track a lycanthrope! Smart as a man and silent as a shadow, hey? Hey?" He punched me roughly in the arm. With another quick glance to ensure my parents were out of sight, he poured another mouthful of scotch into my glass. "Eve says you've been changing. Says it's starting in patches: you wake in the night with a tail 'tween your legs, or your backside all covered in fur."

"I almost changed the whole way to a wolf, three times," I said with pride. "And I can kind of control it too, see?" I pulled up my sleeve and gritted my teeth together, and a shadow of fur rippled over my right arm. But it didn't last; the scotch made it difficult to concentrate for very long.

"Well, I'll tell you what, Danny, m'boy. When the summer comes, I'll take you into the mountains, and I'll teach you the art of being a wolf."

The thought of it was frightening and exciting, all at the same time.

"No summer holidays for you, m'boy," he continued, his eyes flashing. "We'll be too busy hunting and tracking and learning how to be kings of the forest." He licked his lips. "And, I dare say, the wolf women will enjoy making your acquaintance—"

"Andre."

Mom stood in the dining room, one eyebrow raised, arms crossed. She looked very displeased, and I lowered my glass of amber-tinged milk out of her line of sight.

"Well they will," said my uncle with a licentious grin. "Look at him, Eve. He's got the wild blood in him, as they say. He'll be a brute, big as a bear!"

"He's my son, and he's twelve," she snapped. "And you'll keep him away from the wolves until he's older."

Andre growled but didn't argue.

When my mother returned to the kitchen, he dipped his head close to mine. "You gotta watch the wolf women, m'boy, even your mother. They got teeth to 'em. They got spirit, like in that story… y'know the one… Eleanor and St Francis." He gave a curt nod.

I didn't know much about women, except for Katie King, who pinned me down on the playground until I bit her hand and brought blood to the surface of her skin. She'd gone running, wailing, to the school nurse. She didn't seem to have much spirit, and I told this to Andre.

"Ah, now y'see, that's what you'd call a ruse," he said sagely. "They reel you in, looking all helpless and frail. Then, just when you're ready to woo 'em, they turn and snap at you." He pulled down the collar of his shirt to reveal a pattern of tiny white scars, teeth marks from past encounters. "You gotta be careful around wolf women."

"But Katie, she's just a human," I said. It was wonderful to say that word, 'just', as if Andre and I were something greater than everyone else, instead of repulsive gargoyles forced to live in secret.

Andre laughed and laughed. "That don't matter, m'boy. Equally mean, equally crafty." His laughter mellowed and he took another deep swig of his bottle. "Naw, it don't matter the species, m'boy, it comes with the gender. A she-bear and a moose cow, they're just as devious in their own ways." He tapped his finger against my chest to accentuate his point. "If it's got nothin' between its legs, watch out!"

"Yes sir," I replied. When I glanced through the dining room to the kitchen door, I saw Hestia cutting into the roast with a gleaming knife, throwing her weight into the blade with her shoulder, teeth clenched. Erin stood on tiptoes beside her, lips bloodied, hoping to steal another morsel of rare meat before it was laid upon the serving platter. I shuddered. "I'll be careful."

"ELEANOR AND ST Francis?"

Sullivan smiled at Caufield. "Look, that's a whole other story."

67

"I know who St Francis is, but who's this Eleanor?"

"I guess you don't know the story of St Francis and the werewolf."

Caufield shook his head.

"Let me think. It's been ages since my mother told me," said Sullivan, reclining in his chair. "St Francis came upon a beautiful woman in the woods, wearing nothing but the mantle of her red hair, and asked her why she loitered in the wilds, so far from home. She replied that this wood was her home, and he was free to walk in it if he offered her no threat. "Many a man has come this way with foul intentions," she told him. "And he that raises a hand against me never leaves the shade of my forest." Francis assured her that he wanted no touch of her flesh, for he was a man of God and above the bestial impulse of lust. "Bestial?" she replied. "Does the beast feel lust? The beast knows only to procreate, as the Lord bid Adam and Eve in the Garden. Lust is an impulse of man, sir, for if it were not, I'd have no trouble with men in my forests." Francis was pleased by her words. She spoke with such candour and assurance, and he asked her to walk with him, never looking once upon her body but only upon her face. "I will walk with you," she replied, taking stride at his shoulder and not a step behind. "And you may call me Eleanor." They walked together for a day and a night, and when they reached the edge of the wild spaces, Francis asked her to join him on his journey, and he would grant her as safe a passage through the world of men as she had granted him through her forest. Eleanor agreed, and they walked together for many a long month, he in the shape of a man and she in the shape of a wolf. He took her counsel and admired her wit, and their friendship endured until the last of their days. That's why St Francis's emblem is the wolf." Sullivan tipped his chin to one side, eyes downcast. "Well, a werewolf, actually, but seeing as how we're in hiding, we let everyone think she's a wolf."

"So which Beatle?"

"Sorry, Morris, but I can't tell you that," said Sullivan. He set his empty coffee mug on the table. "It was one of Andre's claims, and I wouldn't want to reveal anyone's secret without knowing if it's true or not. Besides, it has nothing to do with my divorce."

"But it's interesting," said Caufield. "Most of my clients come in whining about adultery and money problems. I've never had anyone tell me he's leaving his wife because he's a wolf."

"No, I'm leaving my wife because she tried to kill me," said Sullivan, his brow furrowed. "Twice."

4

IN THE YEARS FOLLOWING her marriage to Vincent, Hestia sensed she'd broken my heart and bruised my pride, worse than ever before. She knew that my depression was linked to her, and she strove to do all that she could to remedy my lonely life, but she had no understanding of exactly how she'd contributed to my sorrow. I guess she felt guilty, because almost overnight the quest to cure my solitary ways became her hobby. Mercifully, she never attempted to set me up with anyone; she was living in Lyon, and we simply didn't know anyone in common anymore. But she would phone me every few weeks, whenever her busy schedule allowed. Hestia never missed an opportunity to call and check on me; she was determined to root out the underlying reason for my unhappiness.

One evening, the phone rang. I picked it up.

"Hello?"

"Are you still a virgin?" she blurted. There was no 'hi' or 'how are you?' to buffer it.

"Huh?"

"You heard me, Lupi," she said. "Are you still unschooled in the bedroom arts? Are you an innocent? Have you done the nasty—"

"Jesus, Hessie! What the hell?" I glanced at the clock in the kitchen and did a little time zone math. "It's got to be the middle of the night where you are. What are you doing, calling me at this hour?"

"You're changing the subject," she said. "You been with a girl, Lupi?"

I groaned and rolled my eyes. "Yes, Hessie, I have."

"Good. I was worried."

"Everyone else would tell you it's none of your business, you know. What time is it there?"

"A little after three in the morning. John needed to be fed. I was sitting here, thinking of you, and I figured maybe your problem is that you haven't done it yet, and you just don't know what you're missing." I heard the baby snort in the background, and Hessie shifted her weight. "So I thought I'd call and ask. No harm in asking, right? So tell me, how many notches do you have above your bed?"

"Hestia—"

"I'm just curious."

She wouldn't let it go. I knew her well enough to recognize her tenacity. "One, Hessie. At least, one on two legs."

I'd hoped that would shut her up, but no luck.

"Who, that Sylvia girl from college? The one with the Lisa Loeb glasses and the funny nose?"

"Mmm-hmm." I was shutting down, going onto autopilot. Something in the quality of her tone told me this lecture might go on for half an hour so, holding the receiver to my ear but not really listening, I grabbed a pencil and a sketchbook from the den. I wandered into the living room, sat down on the

71

floor, and began sketching. I figured I may as well do something productive while she harped about my sex life.

"That was, like, years and years ago!"

"Yep."

"You're a monk, you know that? Seriously, I worry about you, Dan. I mean, Jesus, you've got to have some sort of urges, don't you? Healthy men are supposed to have an active libido. Have you had your prostate checked?"

I shuddered. "Sylvia just wasn't my type, Hes."

"According to you, no one's your type," Hestia said. "You don't make many friends and I know you don't go out. Do you do anything socially?"

"Nope."

"Doesn't your roommate ever introduce you to people?"

"Ethan?" I laughed coolly. "Of course not."

"Why not?"

I set the sketchbook on my knees as I sat on the hall floor. "Because I don't want him to, Hessie."

"He's a crappy friend, Dan. I'm going to have to talk to him and tell him to take better care of you."

The pencil bit into the paper with more anger than I'd intended. "Leave Ethan out of it."

"But Lupi—"

"Hes, why are you always meddling in my life?"

Her voice dropped to a harsh whisper. "Because I don't want you to end up like Uncle Andre. The man is insane, Dan, because he shuts himself away from both people and wolves. I don't want that happening to you too." She sighed resignedly.

"Has he ever told you his theory of chicken farming and population control and the Knights Templar?"

I smirked and drew a caricature of a chicken in chainmail. "I can't say he has."

"Andre is seriously disturbed, Dan, and his condition goes way beyond lycanthropy or alcoholism." She whistled low. "A fucking nut cake, that's what he is."

"Well, I promise I won't end up like Andre."

"You better not, Lupi, or I'll have to fly home and kick some sense into you." I heard a small gurgle as John fussed and resumed feeding. When Hestia spoke again, her words were pleading. "Find a girl, Dan. Find someone to love. I mean, you need someone who can take care of you."

I rubbed my fingers against my brow. "I didn't ask you to take care of me, Hes."

"I know, I know," she said in lieu of an apology. "But you can't possibly be happy with your manuscripts and your paintings. C'mon, I'm your big sister. Can't I be a little concerned?"

"If you start sending me money for prostitutes, I'll only send it back."

"How about some porn? Some of these French magazines show a lot of skin."

"Hestia. Please." I put the pencil aside and stifled a chuckle. "Y'know, Ethan's sister doesn't pester him about sex."

"Of course not. Where's Ethan right now?"

I chewed my lip. "Out."

"Out with who?"

"Some girl named Heather."

"See?" And before I could interject, she said, "Wolves are social. People are social. That means you should be doubly so."

"You're a snoop, Hes."

"And you love me for it," she replied. "When Ethan moves out, you'll be alone. What'll you do then, Lupi? You'll have no one to talk to. I mean, you have your job, but beyond that—"

"It may not be as time consuming as being a nurse or a mother, Hestia, but I scored another contract with Warley's studio. I'm happy to work, and come home, and read a good book. Besides—" I tried to blanch the envy in my voice, and the words came out mechanically. "Ethan *is* moving out. He got a supervisory position at Warley's."

"Ethan's your boss now?"

"It's not that bad," I replied, although I couldn't hide the jealousy in my voice. "But I figure it's a conflict of interest if we share a house. I think he's moving in with Heather."

"Well, I guess it's kind of a blessing," she said pensively. "I mean, it's your house. You should be able to be… y'know… be yourself when you're at home."

I glanced around my living room, which boasted a big window overlooking Victoria Drive, pitted wooden floors, and a narrow staircase leading up to three tiny, drafty bedrooms. There were pizza boxes on the side tables, a pile of laundry at the base of the stairs, and a stack of guitar magazines flanking the old fireplace, all of which belonged to Ethan. Most of the furniture was his too, so were the posters on the wall. When he left, this old house of mine was going to look very empty.

"If you're alluding to the fact that I'm a nonhuman pretending to be human in a very human world, then yes, it'll be nice to have my house to myself." I doodled a savage black wolf lunging at the comical chicken. "I'll be free to eat raw meat and wander around with my tail out."

I didn't want to admit to Hestia that it was going to be quiet without Ethan here. He was loud, boisterous, a little too rambunctious when he'd been drinking, and certainly he lacked any sense of cleanliness, but he'd been a good friend. During my first year of art college, we'd shared a table during Colour Theory class, and his sly, stealthy commentary about our absent-minded, Birkenstock-shod professor provided me with hours of amusement. In second semester, he was kicked out of the dorms for hosting the kegger of the century. Since he needed a place to stay and I had an extra room, I invited him to move in. We'd been roommates for almost five years now, and while he didn't always pay his rent on time, I'd grown accustomed to having the swaggering, swashbuckling braggart around.

"Well, Lupi—" I could hear her shifting John's weight from arm to arm. "If you ever need someone to talk to, day or night, you can always call me."

Ah, Hessie. Even after pressing all my buttons, she always knew exactly the right thing to say.

"I doubt all you wanted to know was my score. Why this call?"

She became very quiet. "I talked to Mom. Aiden decided to live in Toronto."

"Oh."

We were both silent for a moment.

Then, in a rush, Hestia said, "She's all by herself in that big old house and I worry about her, y'know? She had to put Monty down last week—"

"Monty's dead?"

"She didn't take it very well, but the vet said he slipped a disc in his back and he was in so much pain—" She faded away, then gave a little cough. "Well, she told me over the phone that it was an awful thing to do. And now Aiden's got a job back east, closer to Erin. Mom'll be completely alone."

"Poor Mom."

"That's all you can say?"

"She loved that stupid old dog. Christ, he stank, but she adored him." I lowered my sketchbook and reclined heavily against the wall.

"I'm worried she's going to leave us, Lupi. Just switch her skins and never come back."

"Oh, Hes, she wouldn't—"

"How can you say that?" Hestia replied. "Why wouldn't she? There's nothing else holding her here. Dad's gone, and for all intents and purposes, so are we."

I scoured my palm over my face. "I'll drive up on the weekend to check on her."

"Thanks Dan." She gave a small, homesick sigh. "I miss you, Lupi."

"Hes, even if she does go," I started, unsure of how to phrase my answer. "No matter what she does, she's still our mother. I won't hold her to a life that she doesn't want to live anymore."

"Yes, but alone in the forest—"

"Not alone. And after putting Monty down, I wouldn't blame her for wanting to leave." Poor old Monty. What a terrible way for him to fizzle and vanish, erased from his existence by a needle's prickling. A wolf's philosophy revolved around the thrill of the hunt and the tang of blood on the back of your teeth. Death should find you howling out the last of your soul, not ushered into oblivion on a drowsy raft of sedatives.

Hestia paused. I heard the baby sputtering in the background, beginning to gurgle and sob. "I've got to go, Lupi. John needs to be burped."

"Give Vinnie a great big smoochie kiss from me."

She laughed sardonically. "Save it for when you see him at Christmas. Surprise him with it when we get off the plane."

"Oh, and Hessie?"

"Yeah?"

"You can send over some of those magazines. I won't send them back."

I heard her laughing as she hung up.

I sat on the floor for a long while, staring at the blankness of the opposite wall with my sketchbook on my lap. Hestia wouldn't understand, but I did. If Mom left for her other life, my siblings with their human perspectives would never comprehend it. They'd hate her for it, be angry at her for abandoning us, but why wouldn't she go? And they'd hate me for not stopping her, but I couldn't hold her here.

I picked up the phone.

It rang twice, a silly musical trilling far, far away.

"Hello?"

"Hey Mom."

"Danny?" she said joyfully. "How are you? I just hung up the phone with your sister."

"Hestia thinks you're leaving for the hills."

"Now?" I imagined her looking towards the garden through the kitchen window. It was a spring evening; she'd have dirt on her jeans and be holding her gardening gloves in one hand. "I'm not going anywhere, love. At least not until later in the week. Andre and I are planning to run on the far side of Petersburg Valley, to pull down a moose if we can find one and have ourselves a good old blood-soaked feast. Would you like to join us?"

"I'd like to, but I'm busy with work these days."

"You were talking to Hestia?" I heard the dawning in her voice. "Ah, Hessie thinks I'm going for good."

"Apparently."

"Aiden might come back," she said. "Especially once he realizes no one else will do his laundry. Don't worry, love. I'm not giving up a life on two legs just yet."

I let out a little sigh of relief.

"And Hessie, did she ask you about a girlfriend?"

My sigh of relief became a groan.

"Hestia's concerned, that's all, but it doesn't matter. There's a girl for you somewhere, Danny, and she'll find her way to you one day. Of that, I have faith."

CAUFIELD SCRIBBLED shorthand on a yellow pad as Sullivan spoke, and at length Sullivan stopped and watched him finish a sentence.

"What are you writing down?"

"Trying to keep track of these women!" he replied. "Damn, between your sister and your mother and all their meddling... worse than a pack of hyenas. I'm only keeping notes for later."

"For my wife's case."

"To tell Helen when I get home," he said. Then quickly amended, "Of course for your wife's case. Don't get all huffy. Keep going, keep going."

THREE YEARS LATER, I was twenty-seven, living alone and working quietly, and the autumn was bitterly, strangely, unforgivingly cold. To carry out my change, I went to the old cabin at Maple Lake, and found the waters locked behind a thick fortress of hard blue ice. The barren woods hibernated under blankets of snow, and the alder trees were naked of leaves. The resident pack, hungry and desperate for the sun's warmth, wanted nothing to do with me, so I kept out of the valley and wandered in the higher elevations for nine long, starving days.

When I came down out of the mountains on the last evening, I found piles of powdery snow around the tires of my rusted blue Bronco that reached as far as the running boards. I'd taken care to park it in the shadow of the old cedar on the south side of the cabin, offering it some shelter against the elements, but an early storm had swept through and buried everything in its path. I dug out the tires, tongue lolling and front paws sore with the cold. After shaking the lacy snow from my coat, I rambled towards the cabin and took a few sniffs of the air to test for trespassers, but I smelt nothing. The dilapidated building squatted at the terminus of a pitted dirt road, three miles into the woods off of an old logging route, and the building was obviously abandoned.

My father had willed me a generous share of his fortune. The logging business had left him a wealthy man, and my bank account was sizeable, but this cabin was the only thing that I'd desired. All the money in the world couldn't match how dear it was to me.

I came to this place when the onset of the change became so excruciating that I couldn't bear to ignore it, and the cabin offered me a haven from the smells and sounds of the world of men. It gave me a place to hide my car, to stash my clothes and to rest after my return, but it was also a place where happy memories of childhood abounded. From the back door led the path to Maple Lake that Hestia and I would race every summer morning. If I held my ear to the breeze, there were times when

I thought I could hear her squealing still, begging me to let her win as she was older and thought this meant victory was her right. To the side of the path were the ruins of the woodshed, which, through neglect and heavy rains, had toppled over two summers ago. Now, nothing but bare timbers poked up through the drifts. Beyond this was the patch of earth that had once been my mother's garden, splendid with ferns and jasmine, gardenias and crocuses, but which had now returned in steady paces to its wild state.

Mom rarely came up here anymore. She had her own gardens to tend at the farmhouse. Sometimes I caught the scent of Andre or my cousins in the grass, but not today.

The only smells in the air were the musky perfume of a half-starved mule deer and the fetid remains of a raccoon carcass, sweet and thick but muted with the cold temperature. I considered it as a snack before heading back to the city, pausing in the shadows of a maple tree's bare branches and gauging the rumbling in my stomach. The sun was low in the west, the shadows had grown more indigo than azure. Night was coming and I had appointments to attend: at 8.30 tomorrow morning, I was expected at the Adua Gallery to discuss the work on the Italian exhibit. I hated meeting with the board. The simple thought of it created a low growl in the base of my chest. Coffee, donuts, and notebooks to jot down instructions. A host of stuffy collectors preening and parading before us, explaining in very small words their expectations of our work. Roy Warley sitting in the back, offering personal jabs when a lag in the conversation allowed. "Not like last time, Stella. Get your colours right." "I expect you to keep to schedule with this show, Chris." "Are you awake, Mr Sullivan? If we're boring you, Dan, there's always the door."

To the owners of the exhibit, we were art janitors, nothing else.

I paced as I worked out the schedule in my lupine head: an hour to get the vehicle back to the road if the snowfall hadn't mired it too badly, then another two back to the city, then a big meal at Raj's All You Can Eat Indian Buffet. For nine long days, all I'd caught were emaciated mice. Honest to God, I could devour buckets of mattar paneer, with a ton of garlic naan on the side.

And then, after dinner, a few hours of sleep before a dreadful appointment with the board.

No, there was no time for rotted raccoon. I decided to save my hunger for Raj's.

I crossed the yard and mounted the back steps, and pushed the door open with my nose. Nothing smelt disturbed. The cabin was empty, the air was stale and cold, and not a single creature had entered since I'd left it. I crossed to the fireplace in the corner of the kitchen and, seizing the canvas sack in my teeth, pulled it out of the flue. It fell to the stone hearth with a puff of dust that made me sneeze, but I'd left the zipper open, and my shirt poked from the bag as if taunting me. 'Time to go home,' it mocked. 'Back to work until next April.'

Ever paranoid, I glanced around once more.

Then I took a deep breath.

The dark hairs receded in a pattern that began just below my navel and swept up my sides, over my back, down my legs and arms with that maddening itching. And even before my bones had ceased to crackle and set back into place, I was dragging my fingers over my limbs in a desperate attempt to quell the loss of my winter coat. As soon as my voice returned I was cursing and swearing at the cold. I rooted through the sack as swiftly as humanly possible for underwear, jeans, a sweater, socks. My boots lay at the door. I threw them on as well, driving out the chill with layer upon layer of cotton and wool. My cell phone was in the bottom of the bag, but the only number it had recorded in nine days was Ethan's. I gave another low growl. He knew I was on holiday. He was excited about working on the Italian collection, but couldn't he at least wait until tomorrow to portion out our assignments?

I threw the sack into the rear seat of the Bronco, turned the key until the engine sputtered to a start, and switched on the heater as soon as I was able. I punched out Ethan's home number and coughed to clear my voice.

It rang once, and a cheerful voice greeted me. "Hey buddy! I've been waiting for your call."

"Why the hell are you interrupting my holiday, Eth?" I said, grinning.

His laugh was confident, mischievous, and almost a little sinister. "Oh, Danny boy, you are going to like what I have to tell you."

He paused for dramatic effect.

"I'm waiting—"

But instead, he asked, "How was the ice fishing?"

I paused. Is that what I told him this time? I was almost certain I'd said I was going snowboarding at Whistler. "Oh, it was fine. Of course, I caught nothing."

"You're awful for someone who fishes so often," he said.

"If you're going to tell me the news, you'd better hurry, Ethan," I said, looking up through the trees to the billowing clouds. "Service up here is spotty and I'm going to lose you if the weather shifts. What's so important that it can't wait until tomorrow?"

Ethan's voice adopted a sombre tone, and I could see his boyish face in my mind, pulled down long and thin in an expression of serious efficiency. Somewhere between working as my equal and joining the levels of upper management, Ethan had decided that it didn't pay to be frivolous when talking about business. Once, he'd been swashbuckling, but three years in management had made him stodgy. "You know the book exhibit at Adua?"

"It's why we're meeting the board tomorrow."

"Well, a few of the items," he said, taking a deep breath, "were damaged in transit."

My heart beat a little faster. "What? Not the Venice transcripts. Please, don't say the Venice transcripts."

"Ah, they're fine. You think they'd ship those without a mile of protective packing?" He snickered at the thought as that old levity crept back into his voice. "No, those are worth way too much. The Venice transcripts are perfectly safe."

I let out a small sigh of relief. "As long as those are okay, we can fix the rest." And my heart resumed its quick pace, but now with excitement instead of fear. "So which books were damaged?"

His voice slowed. "Some of the bibles, a few medieval manuscripts, but the best of all… if you can say that—" He chuckled. "The best of all was the 1489 Apuleius incunable."

"Really?" I could barely contain my glee. "That's great!"

"That's not what Roy said," he exclaimed. "One of the dolts on the tarmac dropped the crate when they were bringing it off the plane, and when we opened the crate and saw how badly it was all mangled, Roy nearly shit his pants. Those Italian owners would string him up by the balls if they knew what happened to their precious books."

I slumped against the driver's seat, grinning. "How badly were the items hurt?"

"Well, Stella took a preliminary glance at the *Metamorphoses* edition, and she said there's a fracture on the binding and a bunch of folios are torn, with some damage to the gilding in three of the illuminations."

"So you're taking it?"

"Me? I wish!" he said. "No, Roy's got me arranging the insurance claims, so he asked me who I thought was most qualified to take it. I put in a good word for you, Dan. I said I couldn't bear the look on your face if he gave it to someone else, considering your love for gold and vellum." After a pause, he said, "Are you still there?"

"I'm speechless."

"It's a big contract, Dan. It's got to look as good as new, or else it's Roy's reputation on the line."

"A 1489 incunable… I've never worked on anything so old. Are you sure Warley wants me to do it?"

"Look, can you do it or not?"

"What if I screw up?"

"Then the Italians string you up by your balls and Roy gets off scot free. Well? What do I tell Warley?"

I grinned. "I'll take it."

"I knew you wouldn't let me down," he said. "Clear your schedule, buddy; you've got plenty of work to do. The show goes up next Friday, and you're damn lucky your fishing trip ended now, or else you'd have missed the opportunity of your lifetime."

I tapped my foot against the gas pedal to keep the engine from stalling. "Thanks, Ethan. I owe you."

"Yeah, you do. But I'll warn you now, Danny: Stella really had her heart set on this one. When you come to the meeting, I recommend bringing her a box of gourmet chocolates. You know the ones from that little place in Kitsilano? Nothing less is going to do."

I laughed. "Got it."

"See you in the morning."

The phone hung up with a chirp. I smiled and scratched at a patch of fur that hadn't yet receded on the back of my left hand. Ethan's voice rang through my thoughts, 'opportunity of your lifetime'. This could vault me into better contracts, more challenging restorations. I might even slip Warley's outfit and start freelancing, pick up some work with the National Gallery or the Royal Academy of Art. This begged for a celebration! I deserved to treat myself to that half-buried raccoon carcass in the vale. I left the Bronco running while I trudged through the snow to find it, all the time thinking of Apuleius' text, graceful lines of Latin words printed on smooth, ghostly vellum, waiting for my eager hands to fix it.

5

G WEN CAME INTO MY life so quickly and completely that
our relationship, even from the first moment, seemed
scripted.

It took an entire day to assemble the restored exhibits for
'Beast of Burden: The Horse Through History', the Adua
Gallery's much-anticipated winter show, and on every wall the
clocks ticked towards the hour when the doors would open, the
invited guests would arrive, and our work would be displayed
to all the world. Roy Warley spent half the afternoon pacing
and the other half complaining, and I watched him examine the
manuscripts and incunabula as they were fitted under Plexiglas
plinths and lit to accentuate their features. He spent an
agonizing eighteen minutes scrutinizing the *Metamorphoses*, and I
loitered at the door to the gallery with arms crossed, waiting for
him to find fault with my work.

Eventually, he beckoned me over. His brown suede jacket
and slicked grey hair, parted precisely in the middle, gave him
the appearance of a university professor, but there was nothing
welcoming or educational about the hard lines of his face and
the flinty coldness of his eyes. He vultured over the display
with more predatory focus than any teacher. Warley did not
provide instruction; he provided assessment and, if we were
found lacking, discipline and ridicule. It was not uncommon for

young female interns to leave Warley's employment after only a month, running from the building in tears. I'd heard that a few young male interns had left the same way.

As I neared, his head pivoted towards me, and when he frowned the creases at the edge of his mouth deepened until they flanked his chin. "Mr Sullivan," he said in his English accent, which I'd often suspected was as fake as his smile. The fingers of each hand were held stiff from his palms, his elbows were perched away from his torso as though repelled by the body that sprouted them. "What's this?" He jammed a stubby finger against the Plexiglas top, leaving a grease smear.

"What?"

"Right there." He traced an outline over the top corner of the binding. "See? Is it foxing?"

I looked closer and saw a rusty tinge to the upper quadrant of the illumination. "This is too old for foxing," I said. "It's vellum, Roy—calfskin. There's no iron in it to cause foxing." And now I peered closer, grinding my teeth, an element of desperation tainting my words. "It might be discoloration from the sizing, but I can't fix that. It's not current damage."

Roy fumed. "This is a private contract."

I continued to stare at the book, aware of the disappointment in his sentence and unsure why it was there. From between clenched jaws I said, "I'm only hired to fix current damage. I don't fix the wear and tear of ageing. Hell, Roy, I may as well illuminate a brand new manuscript if you want something clean and shining." I immediately regretted my words. Roy was owner, dictator, lord and master of all he surveyed. He ruled the only art restoration outfit west of the

Rockies, and if I wanted any work at all without moving east, I was forced to stay on his good side. You didn't speak ill of Roy Warley without finding yourself on your butt in the snow and the gallery door slammed shut behind you.

One sarcastic comment to the touchy bastard and I threatened my place in his studio as well as anywhere else. "Sorry," I recanted. "I didn't mean that. But I was hired to fix current damage. The binding, the chipped gilding—"

"Not with a private contract," he replied as he pushed his glasses higher on his nose and cast me a sideways glance that was full of venom. "Public artifacts, yes, you don't fix anything but current damage. But private collections, you tart them up, as good as new. You knew this was a personal artifact, didn't you? I thought I was fairly explicit in my instructions during our project meeting. Most of the show is on loan from the Musei Vaticani and the Uffizi, but the *Metamorphoses*, the 1680 King James and the *Tetrabiblos* are all privately owned."

Scowling, I said nothing.

"I should have given this to Stella," he said, crossing his arms and glaring at the book as if it were a crumpled, ketchup-stained napkin. "I can rely on Stella. She wouldn't make me look like a fool with a lazy bit of poor workmanship."

That was unfair. I hadn't slept in two days, and that crossed the line. "If your reputation is relying on this contract," I snapped, "you should've damn well done it yourself."

He took a sharp breath and regarded me with a look of utmost surprise. "If you wish to leave my employment, Mr Sullivan, that can be arranged."

I raised a hand to my forehead. "Sorry sir. I've been up all night fixing those illuminations. I didn't mean—"

But he was unimpressed. "We'll talk later. You're only a first-level employee, Mr Sullivan: please keep in mind that I still consider you expendable."

I swallowed and lowered my chin but held my tongue.

"Right now, Mr Sullivan, I have more pressing items to consider than your future at my establishment," he said. "Come to my office tomorrow and we'll have a little chat about your responsibilities here."

"If you'd told me—"

His back was turned. "Excuses tomorrow," he said dismissively, before sauntering towards the back of the gallery to examine the other restorations.

I glowered at *Metamorphoses*.

"Is his holiness displeased?" said Ethan, peering into the display from behind my right shoulder.

I ground my teeth and remained silent.

"Don't let him get to you, Dan. It's in his nature to be a prick. He really can't help it." Ethan studied the text. "Roy didn't see it when they brought it in off the plane. I think you did a bang-up job."

"No offence, Ethan, but it's not you I need to impress."

"You don't need to impress anyone, Dan. You said it yourself, you aren't here for the money."

I winced. Once, when we were roommates, Ethan asked me how an artist like myself could afford to own a house in Vancouver. "And you're not even a good artist, mate," he'd added. "How'd you get so lucky?"

And feeling slighted by the idea that I, a monstrosity trapped between two worlds, could be considered lucky by someone as successful and talented as Ethan, I admitted that my father was dead and had bequeathed to me a huge share of his fortune. Ethan asked more questions, I started to boast, and before I knew it, he was leafing through my bank statements with a look of amazement. He admired me, if only for a moment, and I hadn't noticed my lack of discretion until it was too late.

Whenever he mentioned my wealth, which was far too often and always in public places, I cursed my loose tongue. At least, I consoled myself, I'd told him about the money and not the Family Secret. Thank God for small miracles.

Before he could say anything else about my financial situation, I asked him, "How'd the insurance claims go?"

"Pah," he shrugged. "Paperwork! I didn't go to art school to fill out forms, but it looks like I have a knack for it. There won't be any difficulties, once we pay the deductible, and that'll be a pittance compared to what Adua pulls in for this gig. Roy's pleased he won't be out of pocket for this venture." He rubbed one hand over his short brown hair, shrugging again. "And look, if I can put a good word in with Roy for you, I will. Public or private, you did a nice job on this one." He rocked back on his heels, hands thrust in the pockets of his jacket. "It's three hours before opening. They're putting up the rest of the displays and we'll just be in the way. Wanna grab a bite to eat?"

"I'm exhausted. I think I'll head home."

"Come on, I want to introduce you to someone."

I took one more glance at the manuscript with a feeling akin to vengeful hatred burning in my gut. I shook my head. "I need sleep."

"You aren't coming to the opening, are you?"

"Of course not."

"You have the worst case of social anxiety I've seen," he replied. "Especially amongst the antique and art dealer set. You'll get nowhere if you don't network."

"Leave that to Stella," I said. "Roy destroyed any desire I might have had to attend tonight, especially if the owner of the collection drops by. I don't need him accusing me of poor workmanship too."

"You take your work too much to heart, Dan. That's why they eat you alive." Ethan beckoned to someone on the opposite side of the gallery. "Here, meet Gwen. She'll cheer you up."

When I followed his gaze, a lithe blonde woman was sprinting across the gallery floor towards us, a sizeable camera bag slung at her waist.

Ethan held out his hand to her. "Gwen Herve, photographer. This is my friend Daniel Sullivan. He's one of Warley's slaves."

"You're a limner?" she said brightly. "Warley hired me on to catalogue the show." She took my hand in hers, small and frail as a sparrow, and shook firmly. "Nice to meet you. You've got callused hands for a painter, Mr Sullivan. I would have guessed you were a sculptor or a carpenter."

I took my hand back, embarrassed by the comment for no reason other than her notice. "Grinding gold and honey, to

93

repair illuminations. It's hard on the hands." Plus running for nine days on the flats of your palms over rocky hills can really build up your calluses, but that, I left out.

Perhaps I answered her a little too quickly. She smiled with a tinge of polite blankness, absolutely charming but unfamiliar with the art of gilding. She tipped her head towards the display.

"This one?"

"It's called the *Metamorphoses*," said Ethan, nonplussed by her radiance. "Or, by its alternate title, *The Golden Ass*."

She giggled. "Seriously?"

Ethan grinned at her mistake. "Not 'ass' as in 'bum', but as in 'donkey'. In the story, this poor guy falls in love with a witch and is turned into a donkey for a year. It caused a bit of a stir back in the day, raising questions about whether or not animals have souls." He smiled at her with enviable familiarity. "I've got a good translation at home, if you're interested in reading it."

She screwed her face into a playful frown. "I prefer glossy magazines, thanks." She tipped her heart-shaped face down and gazed at the book through golden lashes. "But good work, Sullivan. It's beautiful."

Roy's comments melted away.

"Dan and I were just heading out to get a bite to eat," he said to her. "Do you want to join us?"

"Oh no, thanks," she said. "I'm here early to photograph the exhibits before they let in the crowds. But I'll be here tonight." And she looked at me, smiling. "I'll see you then?"

I nodded, quite speechless.

She left without another word, pulling out her camera and checking it under the light of an exhibit before heading into the concourse.

Ethan watched her go. "I met her at a seminar last year at the university."

"You and she—"

"Are you joking?" he said. "No, she's not interested. But damn, I tried."

"I applaud you. I'd never get near enough to ask her." I let my eyes linger on her figure through the archway, moving with the slow grace of a willow swaying in a summer breeze. Her jeans clung to her hips and flared below her ankles, accentuating the lean length of her legs. "She's married, isn't she? Or she has a girlfriend. Or she's committed to the convent." I chewed my lip, entranced. "Something that lovely can't be available."

"She's free," he replied. "C'mon, Dan. I'll buy you dinner."

6

"I CAN SEE IT IN THE way you say her name," said Caufield as he set the pad of paper aside. "Gwen's the one you married, hey?"

Sullivan nodded and stared out the window at the darkening sky.

"Real looker?"

"As beautiful as a pre-Raphaelite painting." Sullivan shuffled off the dullness in his eyes, the sorrow that seeped into his voice when he mentioned Gwen. He took a steady breath. "But she betrayed me, Morris, and it's easy to fall out of love when you're being shot at."

"I guess, buddy," he replied. "I can't say I've had that experience."

"ISN'T IT PAST YOUR curfew?" Stella ribbed me when I finally arrived at ten after ten. I was already breaking out in a nervous sweat, wringing my hands. Underneath my grey suit, a small patch of fur had sprouted at the base of my spine, a reaction to the adrenaline in my blood. It refused all efforts to make it disappear.

"Don't taunt me too much, Stella. I'm liable to turn tail and run home."

The gallery was packed with hundreds of artists, historians, dealers, spectators; it was the biggest show of the winter season, having come all the way from Italy and even boasting a few pieces that had not previously been allowed to leave that country. A sea of people flowed through the hall, but as Stella approached, her flamboyant wardrobe offset the conservative group with the same impact as a peacock amongst pigeons. Tonight, she was wearing a slinky lavender leather dress that revealed every bulge and curve of her body, with only a cobalt blue boa to keep her warm. Stella had many, many bulges and she was proud of every one. Most women would slap a man who asked her how many months until she was due, especially if she wasn't pregnant, but Stella had simply giggled at me and planted a rosy kiss on my forehead. "It's lucky you're so damn cute," she'd said as I'd scrambled to apologize on my first day of work. "Or you'd be on the floor, buster, with a shiner the size of an apple."

She never failed to surprise me. We nurtured a friendly rivalry at work, but she had a kind and generous heart. I suspected she'd been waiting for my arrival, just to ease me into this social situation, and for that I was grateful. She held out a second glass of champagne for me. "Toast," she said simply.

"Alright."

"To urban hermits and whores of the modern Babylon. May your tux remain in the closet and my mascara never run."

I tapped my glass against hers and drained it in one gulp.

"You never come to these things," she said, leaning forward. "I didn't think we'd see you again after Roy tore apart your work."

I shrugged. "He was critical, but it's an exaggeration to say he tore it apart."

"Not in front of you, he didn't, but you should have heard what he said to the owner," she replied, and when she smiled, her cherub face grew ruddy. "Don't take it personally. We've all been on the receiving end of Roy's backstabbing." She took a long sip. "He's hauling you into the office for the responsibility lecture? Don't let it worry you. He's a prick, but he's harmless."

"It's in his nature. Yeah, I've heard."

"How was ice fishing?"

"Fun," I said. "Caught nothing, but I'll go again next year."

"You're going to have to take us all up to this cabin of yours. Maybe a summer barbecue? A little camping?" She finished her champagne. "It must be a beautiful spot for you to go up there so often."

"It is," I replied, scanning the crowd. There was an awkward pause, for which I felt a pang of guilt, and thought, 'How can I be so terrible at casual conversation?'

Stella's gaze followed mine. "Who're you looking for?"

"No one in particular." My voice trailed away.

"But if you were, would it the lovely Miss Herve? I see that randy gleam in your eye."

I smirked. "Is she here?"

"Oh, she's around somewhere. I'm assuming you want to try and gild her golden ass?" She gave a delicate belch, the champagne hitting her stomach, and she held a gloved hand to her mouth and laughed. "I have my sights on him." Stella tipped her glass towards an older gentleman in a tweed suit, his peppered hair brushed back from his forehead and a pair of wire rim glasses perched on his hawkish nose. "I want to wake up next to him tomorrow."

"He's old enough to be your father."

"I like 'em with experience," she said. "He accompanied the shipment from the Vatican. I want to see if he'll bend to temptation."

"Stella, you're going to go to hell for flirting with a priest."

"You think so?" She peered closer. "Is he a man of the cloth? God, they shouldn't be allowed to wear street clothes; it puts my soul in peril."

"If you want my opinion—" I continued. "—go with him." I motioned to one of the burly bodyguards flanking the door. "Better suit. Expensive shoes. Less chance of eternal damnation."

"If we're swapping opinions on partners," she replied, "give Gwen Herve a miss. She's not the most gracious of women to walk the face of the earth."

"Why would you say that?"

"Call it a hunch," Stella said.

Another crush of people came through the entrance, and we were pressed towards the back hall. When we passed through the archway, a delicate hand laid itself on my arm, and when I turned, there was the figure of Gwen, standing with a glass of champagne the same colour as her hair, and my breath caught in my throat. The gesture wasn't lost on Stella.

"I'll leave you here," she said, casting me a look of warning.

"No, don't," I said, perhaps a little too desperately.

"I didn't think you'd make it," said Gwen, glancing once at Stella and then back to me. "It was Ursula, right? Or Helga?"

"Stella."

"Oh, that's right. I knew it was a fat girl name."

There was an unmistakable coolness to Stella's tone, but her face remained cheery. "Actually, it's Latin for 'star', not 'fat girl'," she replied. "But I can see your confusion: both are big, powerful and heavenly. My dear Danny," Stella's smile grew warmer when she spoke to me. "I've a few other people I want to chat up before the night is over, so if you'll excuse me." She flung me a quick wink and sauntered back into the main concourse.

I thought briefly of bolting for the exit, but Gwen kept her hand on my arm. "God, what an odd girl. She's got awful taste in clothes."

"Stella's wardrobe? It's pretty spectacular," I replied.

"I wouldn't be caught dead in an outfit like that, even on Halloween," she said in return. "Some people just don't believe in modesty." She watched Stella from a distance. There was disdain in her eyes, but it vanished with the return of her smile. God, she was absolutely gorgeous. A thin jaw, round eyes the colour of hazelnuts, hair that moved with a life of its own. She leaned forward and I smelt peppermints and wine on her breath, saw the plump swell of her breasts through the neckline of her sheer dress. She spoke as if she had a secret she could only share with me. "Can I ask a favour?"

"Sure."

"Can I take your picture?"

I fought to keep my breathing controlled. "Now?"

That light, lovely laugh again. "No, not now. Next week, maybe. There's something unique in your face; I can't put my finger on it."

"Of course." I shrugged.

Another awful, terrible, guilt-laden silence. Why did Hestia have to get all the loud-mouthed traits in the family? She could talk a hole through a wall, if she didn't have to stop yakking to sleep and eat.

Gwen took a sip of her champagne and watched me fidget from over the rim of her glass. "You don't get out much, do you?" she said when the pause in conversation became too much to bear.

I rubbed one hand over the back of the other. "Sorry, no. These kinds of functions are not my thing."

"Well, let's ditch it then, and go back to your place." She pulled on my arm. "You game?"

Her forthright nature startled me. I thought, at first, that I'd misunderstood. "Pardon?"

"If a conversation's awkward, you may as well skip it and get straight to business. I'm attracted to you, and I want to spend the night with you," she said, in a low voice as smooth as silk. "Are you game?"

It took a heartbeat for me to realize that, yes, a beautiful woman was actually propositioning me, and I was not, in fact, dreaming. I put my empty glass down on top of the plinth protecting the *Metamorphoses*. "Alright."

And that was that.

7

GWEN AND I WERE married two months later.

Hestia pulled me aside before the wedding and dragged me into the nursery room, behind the chapel, where the bridesmaids were prepping. Crumpled nylons, shoes, make-up bags, and vanity magazines littered the carpet. The other attendants looked up with horror to see the groom being dragged in against his will, but when Hestia scooted them out, they didn't argue. My sister has a tongue of steel and a spine to match.

"Out! Shoo!" she said. They scattered like pink and tangerine crows. "Out out out!"

"Hes, I have to—"

"Ethan will take care of everything. That's what a best man does," she snapped as a parade of Gwen's friends filed out. John sidled close and took his mother's hand, and Hessie bent down to straighten the little boy's tie. She said, "Can you do a favour for me, sweet pea?"

John nodded, his thumb in his mouth.

"I want you to tell your new Auntie Gwen not to come in here. I need to have a chat with Uncle Daniel," said Hessie gently. "Can you tell her that?"

Clinging a little tighter to his mother's hand, John shook his head. "Effrayante," he said around her thumb.

Hestia sighed.

"I don't speak French," I said. "What did he say?"

"He said 'scary'. John can speak English, but he refuses to, no matter what I say. Stubborn as a mule." Hestia bent down again and took both of her child's hands. "Ask your Auntie Erin to tell your new Auntie Gwen not to come in here. Can you do that for me?"

"Oui," he chirped, and scampered out into the main hall of the church. The door banged shut behind him.

Hestia leaned against the worn piano bench, crossing her arms. Her hair was streaked with silver and her skin was tanned by the Mediterranean sun. The coral bridesmaid dress looked terrible against her colouring but she wore it with such rugged determination that no one dared speak ill of her. Hestia had a square jaw, strong arms, muscles that jumped under her skin like bundles of wire.

"So?"

I looked away, towards the fur coats hanging in the closet and the luggage by the door. "What?"

"Have you told her?"

"Um—"

"You're marrying the girl and you haven't told her you're a werewolf?"

"I didn't think it was important."

She looked at me in shock. "Not important? Not fucking important?" Hestia drew her lips into a snarl and her eyes grew thunderous. "Did you think she wouldn't notice? What about when the change hits you? You have to tell her you're a werewolf, Danny."

I slouched against a fold-out table and looked at the floor. "Hes, it hasn't come up."

"And it won't be bloody likely to, will it?" she replied. "Not unless you sprout your tail and she wonders why your pants don't fit."

"Hessie—"

"I've never seen you with such poor judgment," Hestia continued, but lowering her voice. "This woman is unbelievable! I fly all the way home for my brother's marriage, to discover that a self-aggrandizing, greedy, spiteful Medusa is about to become my sister-in-law? She's cruel, Lupi. She already screamed at John for eating a tart from the buffet table; what kind of cold-hearted monster yells at a three-year-old?"

"She's a cold-hearted monster. She was made for me." I muttered back.

Hestia was not amused. "I swear to God, you're so afraid of being a monster, you've become a gutless wimp." She clenched her teeth. "I don't care what you think of yourself, Dan, but I believe you are way too good for her."

"I didn't like Vincent when you married him."

"You still don't like Vincent," she replied. "But I love Vincent, and he loves me, and that's what matters. She doesn't love you... she doesn't even know you."

I started to protest, but Hestia held up one hand.

"If you thought she was perfect for you, you would have told her about the lycanthropy long before now." She laughed sharply and threw up her hands. "Long before now... you've known her for what? Three months?"

"Two."

Hestia rolled her eyes.

"I can't tell her, Hes."

"Why not?" pressed Hestia. "Do you think she'll leave? Because honest to God, Daniel, that would be a goddamn blessing!"

"She won't believe me."

"This woman has reduced you to a timorous wimp," she spat, and the door opened a crack. Erin poked her shaved head through the door. "Look at you!" she shrieked with a smile that split her head in two, bouncing on her toes and clapping her hands together. "A tuxedo! On Danny! How freakin' weird is that?"

Her shrieks of delight were met with Hestia's silence and my scowl.

"Sweet corn a' Christ, Dan," she said to my stony expression, my crossed arms, my stormy eyes. "I told Gwen to stay out, but what's up? Did someone die?"

Hestia spoke. "Can you fetch Mom?"

"Yeah, sure," she said, retreating to the hall. I said nothing until Erin returned with my mother in tow, who looked wholly confused and mildly intrigued. "I hear that someone might be dead?" she said as Erin closed the door behind them.

"No."

My mother looked at Hestia for an explanation. "Well? What's happened? Is he getting cold feet?"

"He hasn't told Gwen about the lycanthropy."

"Really?" said Mom as her eyebrows arched. "Is that so?"

"Fuck, Dan!" squealed Erin. "What the fuck?"

"Language, missy," said Mom. "You're in a house of God."

105

Erin bit her lip to keep her obscenities from tumbling out. She'd assumed I would've disclosed my talents to my own fiancée. I could see her playing back her conversations with Gwen in an effort to determine her own slips.

I cast my eyes to the floor. "She'll leave me."

"And so?" said Mom. "Let her go. That woman is vile."

"Mom!" said Erin. "You can't say that!"

"I can say what I please," she replied.

"Gwen won't leave," said Hestia for my benefit, throwing a look of astonishment at my mother.

I studied the floor, feeling outnumbered. "I suppose it's not fair for the groom's side to be aware of its genetic aberrations while the bride's side remains blissfully ignorant."

Hestia rounded on me. "I'm not saying you have to tell her whole goddamn family! Christ, the lot of them are narcissistic fuckheaded prats. But at least—"

"Hestia Anne! Language!"

"Mom, I think God will forgive me in this instance. I'm sure He agrees."

"What God thinks of Gwen Herve is not my concern," she replied. "All I know is, that woman doesn't have a single gracious bone in her body."

"I agree, Mom, I do," said Hessie. "And I don't like her any more than you, but it's not our place to break up a wedding—"

"It doesn't matter what either of you think," shouted Erin. "For Chrissake, it's up to Dan—"

"Erin, that mouth of yours is your ticket to hell—"

"Mom, I'm old enough to say whatever the fuck I want—"

I backed away from the three of them, leaving them engrossed in their debate. I almost reached the door before they noticed.

"Where're you going?" said Hessie blackly.

The triad ceased to bicker and stared at me, six feral female eyes boring into my soul.

"I'm going to get married," I replied in a thinly veiled growl.

"You'll tell her?"

"No, Mom, I won't."

"Then nothing but trouble will come of it," she warned, and I knew in my heart she was right. Still, pride and loneliness are a volatile combination.

"I'm not backing out."

"When you have children—"

"There won't be any, Mom," I said. "Gwen doesn't like children. She's already told me so."

A flicker of sorrow crossed my mother's features before the anger returned. "I suppose I should be relieved that *that's* worked out." She fiddled with her wedding ring. "But if you marry that woman, Daniel, I refuse to stay here any longer. I cannot bear to watch her make you even more unhappy."

"Mom?" said Erin, running one hand over the russet stubble of her scalp. "What're you talking about?"

"Danny asked me, a few years back, if I'd ever leave this life and go back to the woods. I confess, lately, I've been considering the idea." Her eyes never left mine. "I think the time has come for me to go."

Erin shook her head. "You can't just go!"

107

"I don't want death to find me, an old woman with no teeth and children who ignore her." She broke her gaze from me to look at her eldest daughter, and still she turned the ring on her finger, back and forth. "Hessie, I already transferred the farmhouse into your name. Rent it, sell it, do with it whatever you want."

"But Mom—" Hestia started, stricken. She clasped her hands to the base of her throat. "Mom, you can't go. It doesn't work like that!"

"Yes it does. Hessie gets the house, so I'm sure you'll feel as though she got the better deal, but Erin, I want you to have this." She took the liberated ring from her hand and dropped it into her youngest child's palm. "Your father was a wonderful man. I loved him with all my heart, and of all of my children, Erin, you remind me most of him. You are courageous, and silly, and not afraid to play."

Erin stared at the ring as if it were leprous.

"The car is yours as well, sweet pea. The boat will go to Aiden. I should have given it to him years ago. I mean, a boat? What do I need a boat for?"

"Mom," I said. "You can't leave."

"Danny," she replied, her voice leached of anger now that her intentions had been said. "I can't stay here and watch you crumble under the strain of this union. I've worried about you long enough." She took my hands in hers. "You're an adult now. You make your own mistakes and you live with them."

"It's no reason for you to abandon us."

"Do you love this woman?" she replied. When I balked, she said, "It doesn't matter. Regardless of what you do, Dan, I suspect you'll be lonely for the rest of your life." She kissed the base of my neck. "I'm not abandoning you. I'm just not needed here any longer."

Tears had begun to spill from Erin's eyes, and Hestia looked remorseful but composed. My mother wiped the tears from Erin's cheek with the thumb of her right hand.

"My mind's made up," she said and tipped her head to one side, the silver curls brushing the collar of her lapis dress. She looked peaceful, pleased and oblivious to the desperation on the faces of her daughters. Instead, she looked directly at me. "I've begun to miss running through the forest again, Danny. You understand, I know you do." Her lips kinked into a wistful smile. "I miss your father, and I'll never find another man like him, so it's best if I stop looking and go home to the woods. And don't worry about me, girls, I'll be fine. The wolf's way was my first life, and it's like riding a bicycle. You simply can't forget it."

"Mom, I'll move back here, into the farmhouse, and if you ever want to return—"

"Of course I'll visit, Hessie," she said. "Perhaps this is all a ploy to move my grandchildren back into this country where I can keep a watchful eye on them." She pressed a kiss to Hestia's cheek. "I've got to get back to my seat. Fifteen minutes until the ceremony starts. Come on, Erin. We'll sit together and tell Aiden the news."

Erin slid her hand over Mom's elbow, her head down. They walked out, arm in arm, and as they passed through the doorway into the hall, Erin aimed a glance at me that was as thin and sour as vinegar.

For a heartbeat, the room was still.

"You clinging scrap of rabbit shit," Hestia muttered at me.

"I didn't want this."

Hestia screwed her eyes closed and clenched her fists. Between gritted teeth, she admitted, "I know you didn't put that idea in Mom's head."

"Erin thinks I did."

"I'll try to explain to her." Hestia crossed her arms and stared out the window. "But both the twins will be angry. They don't understand you like I do, Lupi."

I slumped against the table and put my hands to my forehead. "I'll call it off."

Hestia shook her head. "Tell Gwen the truth, Lupi. Whatever happens, happens." She sidled close and laid her head on my shoulder. "If she loves you, truly loves you, she'll stay."

"She'll think I'm insane."

"Change for her."

I shuddered. "I can't "

"Why not?" Hestia's question was an arrow.

"Remember when you first saw me changing? I was... what... ten?"

"I remember," she said in a careful tone. This memory was burned in her mind, never to be erased.

"I'd rather die than see Gwen look at me like that."

She took a breath and shook her head. "I was thirteen. I couldn't sleep without the hall light on and the bedroom door open. Andre told us ghost stories that made me pee the bed. I was young and impressionable and you can't compare that to

110

telling a grown woman." She rolled her eyes, exasperated. "A woman who yells and rages and orders everyone to do her bidding, even Father Quinn."

"But you knew what I was; there was no question in your mind that we were werewolves." I swung my hand to the door. "Gwen lives in a world where no such creature exists. She won't see me behind the wolf."

"Lupi, I never meant to hurt your feelings—"

"I know you didn't, but… are you smiling?"

An amused grin had appeared on her face. "That first change of yours… I was such a little coward. I must've looked like an idiot, screaming my fool head off."

"Yeah, you did," I said. "You looked like the monster had finally escaped the closet."

She laughed at that. "It was ages ago. I kinda hoped you'd forgotten. I hope I didn't scar you permanently."

"You left me with a lot of scars, Hessie," I said, touching my fingers to the little white mark on my forehead, curved in the same degree as the edge of a well-aimed hockey puck. "Not all of them were visible."

"Well Danny," she replied. "If it's any consolation, you left a few marks on me." She laughed. "I love you, ya jerk. And you're certainly no monster.

"*A werewolf is neither man nor wolf, but a satanic creature with the worst qualities of both.*"

She drew her brows together. "What's that from?"

Half-ashamed, I muttered, "*Werewolf of London.*"

Her levity vanished. "How dare you quote bad horror films to justify your own depreciation? What, do you sit alone at

111

night, watching cheap movies to make yourself feel worse?" My sister gave a short harrumph of disapproval, almost amused disbelief. "Lupi, you're a nice guy. You deserve better than Hollywood's opinions, and you certainly deserve better than Gwen."

"She speaks her mind, but she's not a bad person."

Hestia raised one eyebrow and said, "Vinnie likes her."

I looked to the ground, thinking back to my first meeting with Vincent five years before. "He took the lycanthropy well. I don't like him, but he impressed me."

"He's a doctor, Lupi. When he works the emergency ward, he gets to pull Pepsi bottles out of perverts' butts." She grinned at me in that unabashed tomboy way she had when we were children. "It takes a hell of a lot to shake Dr Garzoni's steely nerves."

"Gwen doesn't have that kind of strength."

"That gorgon is the farthest thing possible from a delicate flower," she said. Then, in a sympathetic tone as she took my hand in hers, she added, "But love really is blind, isn't it? You're completely lost in her."

"Hes, I won't tell her. I can't." When she stepped away from me and rested her palms on her hips, I said, "Promise me, Hes, that you won't say anything."

Asking Hestia to keep a secret was like asking the ocean to rest or the sun to take a day off. She flinched, fighting all her instinctual urges to gossip. "Not even a little something?"

"Nothing."

She wrinkled her nose. "Dammit, Lupi. I promise."

"Thank you."

She studied me with her jaw clenched and her eyes dark, the waves of her black hair casting deep shadows over her strong face. "It's your life, Daniel. If you can't own up to your own biology, it's your problem."

"I'm sick of being by myself."

She looked at me with pity, with the same sadness she'd afford a bird with a broken wing. "I want you to be happy, Dan," she said. "But I don't know how to help you and I don't think you'll be any happier with her. If you always have to hide, you'll only be more alone than before."

"Why wouldn't I be happy when I'm with Gwen? She's talented, intelligent, beautiful—"

"It takes more than a great ass to make a wife," said Hestia. "Believe me, I know. I lost mine after pregnancy and I still haven't found it again, but Vinnie's still the same wonderful husband as he was before."

"I'm not marrying her for her looks."

"Then why, Lupi?"

I looked away. How could I admit that being with Gwen made me feel... well... normal?

"Oh God," she groaned. "You've become a romantic fool." She reached up and grabbed my chin. "But Mom's right: you're an adult now, and you make your own mistakes. Don't say I didn't warn you." Hestia pushed her disappointment away and replaced her sad expression with a mask of happiness. "Right then. Let's get this circus underway."

Within the hour Gwen Herve became Gwen Sullivan, and I became a shadow of myself in my own home.

PART II

"Then the king, in too changeable and irresolute a mood and too devoted in his affection for his wife, explained to her how the manner stood. To this his queen replied, 'You ought to have no secrets from your wife, and you must know for certain that I would rather die than live, so long as I feel I am so little loved by you.'"

Arthur and Gorlagon (14th Century)

1

SHE WAS A DEMANDING woman, this is true.

It became clear, very quickly, that Gwen required nothing less than the best money could buy. Because she refused to be seen in a vehicle that was more than three years old, we purchased a red convertible that swallowed petrol like a sprinter gulps air, and my faithful blue Bronco was banished to a storage garage. With the same unquestioning sneer, she also refused to live in my house.

"It's way too small," she said. "And dark. And the neighbourhood's terrible."

So we bought a split-level condominium in Jericho Bay at the edge of the university district, a spacious two bedroom with den and a spectacular vista of the mountains and ocean. Once our new residence was secured, my furniture proved to be too shabby for Gwen's taste and, with credit cards in hand, she found suitable furnishings for every room: a sepia leather couch, marble end tables, her massive photographic portraits of various people framed and hung on every wall. Somewhere in the move between my old east side home and our new west side condo, my beloved comic collection vanished without a trace.

I rooted through boxes and cupboards, letting my nose guide me, but found not a single whiff of old paper and ink. I paused in the living room and scratched the back of my neck, bewildered. "Can you help me look, Gwen? I mean, I've had them since I was five."

"Oh for God's sake," she said, screwing up her nose in disgust and not even bothering to look up from her magazine. "Grow up."

She wouldn't abide a studio in the condominium, and even though there was a spare room where I could have set up my drawing table, Gwen strictly forbade it. "Daniel!" she barked when she discovered me bolting the legs to the tabletop. "You'll get dirt and pigment and marks on the carpets. We didn't just spend a king's ransom on this place so you could splatter paint everywhere. Honestly, I wouldn't think you'd need me to tell you to rent a studio. Do you need me to do that? Do you?" She snorted, arms crossed. "This is our home, not some warehouse where you can spread your junk all over the floor. What were you thinking?"

So I rented a studio.

I found myself drowning in her. She was insatiable; the more I did to please her, the more she required, but if I dared to question any of her requests, she pouted and threw her arms around my neck and kissed me. "I love you so much," she said. "I want us to live a decent life together. We can't do that in a smelly, dark little hole in the wall with ugly furniture and a single truck between us, now can we?" She tipped her head back and laughed as if the idea was beyond implausible. "Next you'll want us to live in a shack and eat baked beans out of the can."

"No, but—"

118

"Good," she said. "Because I'd rather die than live like that, Daniel." She kissed my throat again and pressed herself close to my chest. "Horrid. Absolutely horrid. I don't know how anyone can bear to live in poverty."

"You know, Gwen," I began, wincing at her words. "Before my father started Sullivan Timber, we lived in an old cabin in the woods and didn't have two pennies to rub together."

She wrinkled her nose a fraction, almost invisibly. She didn't like to be reminded of my impoverished past. "Oh Daniel, you were only content with that because you didn't know any better." She kissed me again and added, "You can't argue that our lives are happier now."

This, apparently, was reason enough to spend vast amounts of money on frivolous things. It made her happy. I sighed and left the discussion at that. I mean, I loved her, didn't I? Why wouldn't I want her to be happy?

The first change began three months later.

For most of the time, I have full control over my shape. If the evening was moonlit and clear, I could hop in the Bronco and drive over the Lions Gate Bridge, and spend the night on a wolfish run through the North Shore mountains; when Ethan used to turn up his stereo and invite friends over for drinks, the forest was often where I'd seek quiet solitude. Most of the time, I have choice.

But twice a year, for nine days in spring and nine days in fall, a fierce agony in my bones forces me into my alternate shape, and I am helpless to ignore it. If I try to remain on two legs, my muscles burn and my bones warp, I grow anxious and agitated, and the alluring scent of the wilderness is too strong for me to

119

resist. The drive to be a wolf is so strong, so overpowering, that my return to human shape requires more than simple will—after nine days in my lupine body, I need something to remind my flesh of its human form. The touch of clothes, the feel of fabric against my skin: my mother had made it clear that, without a reminder to kick-start my change back, I would forever be trapped. There's no worse reminder that I am powerless in the face of my transformation. For any other time of the year, I can choose to be whatever I wish, and my lycanthropy has little consequence on my everyday life. But by the end of my wilderness exile, when I can't help but be a beast, the feeling of utter helplessness that seizes me is almost more than I can bear.

In the fourth month of life in our new home, I awoke in the middle of the night with a thirst that no amount of water could slake and a boundless frantic energy that kept me from returning to sleep. I spent the early morning hours bounding up and down the stairwell, trying to work this persistent longing out of my bones. Clothing was restrictive and uncomfortable. When, on the third consecutive night, Gwen awoke to the sound of thumping, she rose to find me jumping stairs two by two with my pyjama pants in a heap at the bottom.

"What the hell are you doing?" she shrieked. Then, before I could catch my breath to answer, "I have a photo shoot in the morning. The Vagabonds for the cover of Saturday Night. I'll look awful if I don't get a decent sleep."

I covered three stairs to the top landing in one leap. "Then go back to bed."

"I can't sleep with this racket!" Her pretty face was pinched and mean, and she clung to the banister with her hands clenched into angry claws.

"Well," I said, wiping beads of sweat from my brow. "I'll go for a run."

"It's four in the fucking morning!"

"I know."

She gave a frustrated squeal, dropped her shoulders and retreated to the bedroom. I heard the lock click.

At dawn I headed to Warley's studio and resumed my contract from the day before, but I couldn't concentrate on work. I unwrapped the eighteenth-century book of prose and laid my tools along the edge of the desk, but as I studied it for damage, I knocked a bone folder to the floor and cursed as it cracked in half.

I took a deep breath and ignored the rising urgency in my blood. With my hands tensed into fists, I tried again to focus on my work.

The flyleaf was torn from spine to edge. I unwrapped a razor blade and began to shave fibres from the surface; mixed with glue, they'd make an invisible paste to patch the damage, but in the course of dragging the razor over the back page, I slipped. The blade bit deep into my thumb. I cursed again, more loudly this time, breaking the ecclesiastical stillness of the conservator's lab.

"Y'alright?" said Stella as she looked up from her desk. It was just after seven in the morning and we were the only ones in the building.

Examining the damage to my thumb, I nodded my head.

"Need stitches?"

"No, no, I'll live," I grumbled, sticking the bloodied gash in my mouth.

"Time for you to be going fishing again." Stella laughed at my surprised expression. "It's April, Dan. You're like clockwork."

"I didn't realize I was so obvious," I replied around my thumb. The taste of blood only aggravated my body's desire to turn. I'd already postponed my departure for two days, and I knew I couldn't fight it much longer. "You're right, Stella, it's time to leave."

"Taking Gwen?"

I shook my head, dragging a leaf of tissue paper over my book and keeping my injured hand away from the table. What good is restoring a book only to bleed over it?

"She's not going to take it well."

I didn't care. The changing was as frustrating as a stone in my shoe, or an itch under my skin beyond the reach of my fingers. Imagine an urge to urinate even though the bladder's empty: multiply it by a million, and you'll start to understand why my patience was flagging. I paced my breathing and pinched my own forearm to distract myself. "Can you take on this contract? Roy won't care which one of us does it, as long as it's finished."

Stella looked at her own work, gauged how long it would take to finish her own restorations. Finally, she said, "I get your commission and you buy me a martini when you get back. Deal?"

"Fine."

"Come here. I've got a first aid kit in my desk." She laid her brush aside, and began to root through the side drawer. "Can I ask you a personal question, Dan?"

"Mmm-hmm."

"Why do you even work here? You don't have to be here, do you? I heard a rumour that you're as rich as Croesus."

"Um, no, not Croesus," I replied. "My father owned a timber company. It was sold off when he died, and I received a share of its value."

She whistled low. "Sullivan Timber? I've heard of it."

"Yes, well, that was my father's." I pulled a stool close to Stella's desk and sat. "How'd you know about my money?"

She paused for a moment in her search. Her desk contained a whirlwind of papers, string, notes, scraps, phone numbers, pins, tubes of hand cream. As she rested her elbows on her knees, I smelt old perfume and powder, and her hair held the scent of last night's conquest. Every Monday, Stella smelt of a different man.

"Ethan was blabbing over a couple of beers, last week after work." She scratched at her throat and from under the collar of her white lab coat slipped a frill of black ostrich feathers. "He was pretty drunk, and he told everyone that you fell into a fortune." She grinned and a blush crossed her cheeks. "It was a bit of a surprise to me, y'know? You don't dress like a millionaire."

My jeans were spattered with acrylic paint, the hem of my old t-shirt was frayed, my work boots were battered and beaten. "You know me, Stella: comfort before style. Beside, with the

123

way Gwen likes to spend, I don't want to waste money on my own clothes; I might soon have to work for a living again."

"Well, I'd probably develop a passion for shopping too, if I was in her shoes," she said. And then hastily added, "Oh, for Pete's sake, I'm sorry. Forget I said that. I mean, who am I to talk about your finances, hmm? That's not my place."

"Which pair of shoes?" I said. "She's got over a hundred now, and the total is still rising—" I clenched my teeth, frustrated, wondering how many people had heard Ethan's claims. Although she heard my complaint, Stella was too polite to pursue that topic of conversation further.

"Ah, here it is," she said instead, pulling out a roll of bandage. Stella cut off a length with her small brass scissors and bound my thumb in gauze. "How are things between you and Gwen?"

I grunted.

"That bad, hey?"

"She's not… well—" I chose my words with care. "Let's say she doesn't like my family all that much, and they don't call anymore."

"Oh dear," said Stella.

"It doesn't matter," I said, shrugging. "My mom moved away, and my siblings and I were growing apart. These squabbles between Gwen and I will work out. We just need time."

She tucked the bandage back into her desk under a drift of papers. "Look, I'll tell Roy that you'll be back in two weeks. Call him when you're ready to come back."

"He'll have my head for disappearing."

"No, he won't. I'll convince him it's for the best," she said with a puckish grin. Tipping her head to one side, she added, "You're all fidgety and you look like you haven't slept in days. If you ask my opinion, I think you need a holiday from Gwen more than you need a holiday from the city."

"Thanks, Stella," I said, standing. I planted a kiss on the crown of her head to show my appreciation, and she threw me a wink as she blushed. Stella replaced her latex gloves and bowed her head to her work again.

She'd be able convince him, this was true. If I wasn't mistaken, it was Roy Warley's scent that was thick in her hair.

CAUFIELD HELD UP HIS hands, waved his fingers back and forth and shook his head. "Wait a sec, wait a sec."

"What is it?"

"Your father was Jack Sullivan? The rich old bastard who made a mint in the lumber business?"

Sullivan nodded.

"Did he know that you thought you were a werewolf?"

"Of course."

Caufield clasped his fingers together and thought of a delicate way to phrase his next question. "Didn't he seek any sort of medical assistance for you? Send you to a few doctors, see if they could cure you?"

"Of depression? Or lycanthropy?"

"Of... of—"

Sullivan tipped his head back and smiled. "Ah, of delusions."

"Well yeah, actually. I mean, the man was rolling in money after the lumber markets opened up. He financed half of the building projects in this city from the 90s onwards, and he was one of the top entrepreneurs. He could've afforded the best medical care for you, couldn't he?"

"My father knew what I was, and he knew there was no cure," Sullivan replied. "And I doubt my mother would've let him cure me, even if he could. Like she said to Vinnie, being a werewolf isn't a disease, it's a way of life." He paused and a smile spread as slow as oil over his lips. "Don't tell me that my father's reputation is making you question your opinions of me, Morris."

"I still think you've got a screw loose."

"You don't sound so convinced."

Caufield shrugged. "I met Jack Sullivan and his wife once, at a charity function. Nice couple. Very—" His voice trailed away.

"Very what?"

Caufield rubbed the crown of his head as he sorted through his thoughts. "Most rich people in this town are showy as hell, Dan, but your parents were different. Generous, but very quiet. They didn't want any attention. They kept as far out of the spotlight as possible."

Sullivan smiled and gave a small, almost imperceptible nod.

WHEN GWEN CAME HOME from her photography shoot to find me packing an extra set of clothes in a canvas sack, she didn't take it well.

"You're what?"

"I'm going camping for a few days."

"Where?"

"North."

"Where?"

"My father's cabin."

"Where?"

I dropped the sweater into the sack and zipped it closed. "Does it matter? I'll be back in nine days."

"Where is this cabin? You've never taken me there," she said, blocking the bedroom door with her slight frame. "Why didn't I know you owned a cabin?"

"Would you want to sleep in a dilapidated shack in the woods?"

She screwed up her face.

"I didn't think so," I replied.

"Is this because of me?" She said this harshly, without any sense of remorse.

"Of course not."

"Do you still love me?"

"Of course I do." But the urge to return to the woods was driving me mad, and the words came out with less passion that she'd desired.

"Are you seeing someone else?"

I pushed past her, into the hall and towards the front door. "Of course not."

Gwen began to cry.

I came back like a dog with its tail between its legs, and gathered her into my arms. With a deep breath to calm my voice I said, "I'm not seeing anyone else. Work has been demanding. I want to get away from people for a while."

She sobbed and shook against my chest for a long time, and as I waited for her to collect herself, I counted to a hundred and shifted my weight from foot to foot. At last, when her breathing began to slow, I said, "I have to go."

"You've never just left before. I don't understand."

"I'll be home soon, Gwen." Before she could say another word, I rushed from the front door. Two hours to Gilsbury Cross, another one to my father's cabin, and I'd be free from my life as a man for the next nine days.

2

THREE TIMES THIS happened, and each time was the same. Gwen stood in the door and sobbed, accusing me of being heartless and cruel, of abandoning her for another woman or, worse, another man. Each time I'd stand in the door and assure her there was no one else, but she didn't believe me. She watched me go with distrust and depression, her arms folded across her breasts, her hips swayed to one side, and her eyes tumescent from crying.

Always the question: "Where do you go?"

And my answer: "My father's cabin." But that wasn't good enough. She wanted to go there with me, and I always denied her request.

When I came back, it was the same too. She'd pull me into bed and we'd fuck as if sunrise marked the end of the world, and sex was always better after a week amongst the wolves. I suppose, technically, there were other partners in my life, but they ran on four legs and couldn't compare to Gwen's angelic body. She moved like the sea, slow and rhythmic, pulling pleasure from my flesh with each rolling undulation, and every time we finished, she'd lie in my arms and beg me not to leave again.

3

I N ALL THESE MONTHS, there was only one aberration in this pattern.

Early in the summer I returned from the mountains; the hour was late and I threw my bag under the dining room table before rooting in the kitchen cupboard for something to eat. My stomach lurched and grumbled, displeased with everything my eyes saw. Gwen had a love for food that was as bland as cardboard, designed to keep her waist slender and her skin smooth, but obviously not built for taste. Granola. Rubbery oatmeal cookies. Rye crisps. The paper packaging looked more appetizing than the product. I shut the cupboard with disappointment and wondered if I should climb into bed or drive to an all-night supermarket to buy ice cream and instant pizzas. I jingled the keys in my hand, thinking, and decided to wait until tomorrow.

I vaulted the steps to the upper floor in four strides.

Gwen was asleep, her hands folded under her chin and her eyes closed, her dark lips parted and her chest rising in shallow breaths. I sat on the edge of the bed, watched her sleep, and examined her beauty. The moonlight through the open window gave her flawless, porcelain skin the pallor of milk, and her hair spread over the pillows with the same lines as wind over a field of wheat. I leaned down to kiss her, but before my lips connected with her cheek, I paused.

A scent on the pillow, masculine and familiar.

Ethan?

I should explain that Ethan's scent was quite often all over the house, because he spent most Saturday nights on our couch, watching sitcoms or goading me into playing video games. I didn't mind. If he was here, he wasn't out drinking with Warley's staff, and I could keep an eye on him. Besides, having him hanging around, eating dinner with us, telling ribald jokes, it reminded me of our college days in the east side house.

But here, in my bedroom, I'd never detected Ethan's smell before. I turned and sniffed the air, brow furrowed with concern as I caught another hint of his skin on a draft from the window. This chamber was a private sanctuary, and yet his musky simian scent lay thickly on my pillow and sheets.

"Gwen?"

"Hmmm?" Her eyes fluttered. "Home?"

"Was Ethan here?"

She rose to one elbow. "Now? No." She sounded sweetly confused.

"I just—" How do I ask without sounding paranoid, without explaining that I could identify a human scent over a mile away? I traced a finger over her cheek. "I thought I smelt Ethan's cologne."

"You probably do." She flopped back and giggled at my confused expression. "He drove me to Haverwood's today and I bought new sheets. He carried them out to the car, then he stayed for lunch and helped me make the bed. God! I couldn't get rid of him. Poor guy, he's so lonely." She tsked and, twisting slightly, stretched her spine like a cat, raising her languid arms over her head to arch her back. Her movements were graceful and seductive, she seemed to glide over the surface of the bed. "Next time you see him, Dan, tell him he wears too much cologne." She stuck out her little pink tongue. "Disgusting, cheap stuff."

I brushed a kiss over her lips.

"Did you think I was having an affair?" she said with a jolt. "With Ethan? Eww!"

"No," I replied. "Of course not."

"I love you, silly. Even if you take off on me to go camping. Bleurgh." She kissed me back. With enough zest to leave us panting, we broke in the sheets.

When we were finished, I expected her to ask about my absence, but instead she ran her hand over the space between my navel and my right hip. "What a bizarre design."

I looked at the tattoo.

"What is it?" And, before I could answer, she read it aloud.

S A T O R
A R E P O
T E N E T
O P E R A
R O T A S

"It's a medieval talisman, a good luck charm, but it's much older than that," I said. "You can read it backwards and forwards, up and down, and it's always the same."

She never asked what it meant; she'd never shown much interest in other languages. But she dragged her nails over it, eliciting shivers, and she laughed as my muscles jumped under the sensation.

"I'm so happy to have you home," she said. "Please, Daniel. Don't go away again."

But I made no promises.

"ALRIGHT BUDDY, LET'S see this tat of yours."

Sullivan paused. "What?"

"Come on, come on," Caufield said, a toothy grin breaking his face in half. "I got one in Cambodia, see?" He rolled up his white shirt to reveal a poorly executed tiger slinking towards the inside of his elbow. "We did it with a guitar string and a sewing machine motor. Christ, hurt like a bitch! Swelled up like a sausage, burned for days." He chuckled at the memory of blood poisoning as if it were a ride in an amusement park.

"I didn't think lawyers had tattoos."

"We're all broadening our experiences today, aren't we, wolfboy?" he replied. "C'mon, let's see it."

Sullivan pulled back his shirt from his stomach to reveal the square of letters. "Ethan and I got tattoos after finishing our first year."

"That's a prissy little parlour job!"

133

"So?" Sullivan laughed back. "Ethan had a friend who worked in an ink shop on Hastings Street and he gave us each a deal. We were art students; we had no money to spare, but we still managed to scrape together enough to get tattoos. It was two weeks before my father died. He never saw it."

"It reminds you of him?"

Sullivan lowered his shirt. "It wasn't meant to. It was supposed to be a celebration of finishing our exams, but the timing was bad. It used to depress me, to look at it and remember how tough that summer was without my father." He patted his hand against the flat of his stomach. "But it saved my life, Morris. I owe this little patch of ink everything."

WHEN OCTOBER CAME AND the impulse started afresh, slight and persistent, I began my preparations to leave.

As always, Gwen asked, "Where are you going?"

This time I looked at her with disbelief. "You know exactly where I'm going."

"I don't know exactly. You're very good at keeping your secrets."

"Gwen, you know I'll come back."

She sat in bed with her silk nightgown falling in shimmering violet folds around her curves, her hair mussed. The morning sunlight, still warm from summer but thin with the promise of winter, fell in a perfect square over the white carpet. "But where do you go?"

I rummaged through the walk-in closet. "Camping. To the woods. Hiking. What more do you need to know?"

"Why?"

She'd never asked this before. It gave me pause, and she misinterpreted my surprise as a minor victory.

"Well, Daniel? Why do you leave me every six months? I want to understand."

I slumped against the wall of the closet, closing my eyes. "I don't think you can."

"Why?"

I stepped back into the bedroom. "Gwen, please don't ask anymore."

"Alright," she said with resolution.

A silence descended over the bedroom.

"That's it?" I asked when I'd rediscovered my voice. "You won't ask?"

"No, I'm done with asking," she replied. She clamped her arms across her chest and tipped her chin upwards. "Daniel, if you won't tell me, I swear to God I'll stop eating, and by the time you get back in nine days, I'll be dead of thirst and starvation."

I scowled. "You can't be serious."

"I can't live the rest of my life married to a puzzle," she replied. "So yes, I'm quite serious."

"Don't be childish, Gwen."

Bright rage flared in her eyes. I'd always pandered to her.

"I've been more than patient with you, Daniel. Go ahead. Leave and come back after your mysterious little holiday, but I won't be here when you get home," she said. "I'll be dead and buried, and all the blame will be on your conscience."

I sat on the edge of the bed. "I won't leave for a few more days. You'll come to your senses as soon as it's dinnertime."

She pursed her lips and looked at me with hooded eyes. There was a fire there to match Hestia's and it startled me.

"We'll see, beloved," she said. "We'll see."

GWEN DIDN'T EAT ALL that day or the next. On the dawn of the third, her skin was grey and her eyes dull, and she phoned her assistant to cancel all of her appointments for the next week. There would be no photo shoots or business luncheons or brunches with prospective clients. Gwen curled into a ball in our bed and refused to rise, groaning whenever the cramps forced her to clutch at her stomach. Purple shadows ringed her eye sockets. Her fair hair lost its bounce and lay in tangled, greasy snakes around her head. The scent of our sex on the sheets faded under the sour stench of her sweat.

I brought her plates of food, but nothing tempted her. I begged her, I pleaded, I threatened to call a doctor. Her answer was always the same.

"One thing will make me eat again," she said. "It's your choice."

Despite the aggravation of my change, I stayed home and paced back and forth; I couldn't leave, not under these circumstances. She knew that something more than my concern for her was working in her favour, for the longer I stayed, the more desperate I became, and the itching blossomed into a searing pain underneath my skin. I took showers to relieve the tension in my muscles and the relentless ache in my joints.

At last, on the morning of the fifth, I buckled.

"Gwen?"

She didn't open her eyes, but turned her face towards the sound of my voice.

"Hmm?"

"I'll tell you where I go, and why."

I swear, she didn't move a single muscle in her face, but somehow a look of victory crossed her features. "Go on," she said in a whisper.

With my hands clasped in my lap, I took a deep breath.

"For nine nights, I run through the woods of my father's property in the form of a wolf. I have to. I can't help it. It drives me mad if I stay in this body for longer than six months."

She didn't stir.

"Did you hear me?"

"I did."

"Well?"

Her eyes opened, not fully but enough to stare at me with anger.

"You think I'd believe that?"

I cast my eyes down. "It's the truth. You can phone Hestia. She'll verify it."

"You're lying to me."

I shook my head. "I swear, it's true. I'm a werewolf. The trait runs in my family." I looked at my hands and found them trembling. "I wouldn't lie to you, Gwen. If I was going to fabricate a story to explain my absence, would I bother to concoct something you wouldn't believe?"

She struggled to rise to her elbows. "Why is it always nine days?"

"I don't know—my mother claims it's a flux in hormones. It's not exactly something I can see a doctor about," I said weakly. Gwen's face remained stern and she looked at me so fiercely that I wanted to cower and hide, but I continued. "For nine days, I can't change back at all. The wolf takes over, and even if I try, I can't stop it. It's my biology—Hestia used to tease me that it was my version of menstruation."

The faintest hint of a mocking smile graced her lips. "You're a wolfman?"

"Don't say it like that. It makes me think of Lon Chaney."

She touched my face gingerly. "I don't know what to think." And she rose to one elbow. "Show me."

But I shook my head. I remembered the way Vincent had stared, the way he immediately separated 'us' and 'them', and I couldn't bear the thought of Gwen looking at me with contempt and fear. "If I change now, I'll be stuck for nine days," I said. "No, not here, in the city. There's nowhere I could go, I'd be trapped inside. You don't want a shaggy black wolf in the house, getting hair on the furniture."

She dropped her chin and bared her teeth at me. "Do you think I'm a fucking idiot? Like, you're just going to spin some stupid fairy tale and I'll fall for it? You're a liar, Dan, and not a very good one either."

"I swear, Gwen, I'm not lying."

"If you're not going to show me, then why should I trust you?"

I swallowed my fear. "I'll tell you something, but you must promise never to tell another living soul. I'll trust you, and you'll trust me. Do you promise?"

"I do," she said as she softened. "Daniel, I'm your wife. Have I ever lied to you? Have I ever given you any reason to distrust me?" Her expression melted from anger to affection, and she took my quaking hands in her own. "You can trust me implicitly."

I searched for the right words. "When I change in October and April, I have to hide my clothes in a safe location. After my body's purged itself of its wolfishness, I need them or else I can't come back; the change is too strong to overcome with just willpower. If I don't have the items which I wore before the change, my body won't remember what to do."

She raised one eyebrow.

"I swear, it's true," I insisted.

"And your clothes—" she began. "You hide them in your father's cabin?"

The anger in her face was gone. Her eyes were full of curiosity and delight without a hint of disbelief. Her hands were warm, soft, and comforting, and she caressed my face with her palm. I'd expected her to think I was crazy, but now she'd accepted my claim without fear, and I was so relieved that I blurted the answer without hesitation. "It's north of a little town called Gilsbury Cross, halfway to Whistler. Three miles past Gilsbury, there's a junction to a deserted logging road that leads to Maple Lake. My father's log cabin is at the end of that road. Inside, on the main floor, there's a stone fireplace, and to the side of the fireplace is an iron hatch to the flue. And that's where I stash the canvas bag of clothes."

"What happens if you lose them?" She laid her hand on mine. "Or some of them go missing? If you just leave them there, anyone could steal them."

"It's so remote, there's no one around, and I hide them well," I said. "I've never lost them before. But Gwen, you have to promise never to tell anyone. Please. This is my life I've put in your hands."

"Daniel," she said, and clasped my fingers tightly in hers. "I love you with all my heart. I'd never betray you."

"You don't hate me?" I swallowed. "You don't think I'm a monster?"

She shook her head. "I love you more for trusting me with this. For the first time I feel like I really know you." She pulled my face to hers and kissed me with more desire than I'd ever felt from her body, and she pressed my hand to her flat stomach. She whispered in my ear, "Will you stay long enough to eat with me before you leave for the woods? I'm absolutely starving."

4

WHEN SULLIVAN PAUSED to take another sip of his coffee, Caufield scratched at his chin and said, "Helen can be like that. Whining for this, crying for that. Kills me."

Sullivan didn't answer. He continued to stare out the window, lost in thought.

"Hey," Caufield prompted. "You okay?"

"Yeah, yeah, I'm fine." Sullivan sighed and leaned his elbows on his knees. "That moment was… to remember it—" He glanced up at Morris, his mouth curling up into a remorseful smile. "Well, it was the happiest I felt with Gwen. You have no idea how much effort it takes to keep a secret."

"I'm the one being blackmailed, buddy."

"So you pay some money, buy yourself another month of security," Sullivan replied. "But you haven't lived with it your whole life, have you? Haven't jumped at shadows and built walls around your innermost thoughts as long as you can remember. And you chose to follow the path that led to your secret. You had choice."

"I didn't have a choice to be blackmailed," said Morris. "That just came out of the blue."

"You have no idea who's pinning you?"

Caufield drew up his shoulders, puffed out his chest like a walrus. "I got an idea—"

"No you don't," Sullivan replied. "I smell it on you."

"Like Warley on Stella's hair?"

"Exactly."

"Must be a pain, hey?" he said with a wry grin. "Smelling everything?"

"A pain?" said Sullivan, and he gave a laugh. "It's how wolves communicate, Morris, and it's a better method than fallible sounds. Your scent never lies."

"Yeah, well, when it came to Gwen, it seems your nose was as blinded by love as much as anything else."

Sullivan returned his gaze to the window. "I've been here for ages. You probably have other clients. I should come back next week."

"Sandra knows to cancel my appointments if I'm still with a client," Caufield replied. "She's a snappy old turtle but she runs the office with an iron fist, and God have mercy on your soul if you get on her bad side. Trust me. I moved a stack of papers once, nearly lost my head. No, you sit right there and keep telling me what happened."

"You believe me yet?"

"Not on your life, buddy."

Sullivan reclined in his chair. "After I told Gwen what I was, I felt liberated. I felt like the prison doors had been thrown open and I was finally free." He laughed. "It's a two hour drive to Gilsbury Cross, but I turned up the radio and sang along to whatever came on, and it seemed like I arrived at Maple Lake in no time at all. I didn't want to admit it, but Hestia had been right all along—I realized that, all this time, the struggles and the arguments could have been avoided if I'd been honest with my wife from the start."

"Gilsbury Cross?"

"Mmm-hmm."

"You mentioned it before."

"It's the closest town to the old cabin," Sullivan replied. He gave a sly smile. "You're familiar with the place?"

Caufield nodded and said slowly, "I know a few people in Gilsbury Cross."

"I told you," Sullivan said. "I was given good references for you. Did you think I made that up to get my foot in the door?"

"After you mentioned the blackmail I didn't know what to think of you, buddy."

Caufield pressed the receiver of the intercom, and after the box buzzed like a hornet in a plastic cup, a sharp voice crackled. "Yes, Mr Caufield?"

"Bring in some hot coffee, Sandra, and a few of those cookies from the lunchroom."

The intercom beeped off. Within the space of five minutes, the tepid cups were refreshed, ribbons of steam drifting from their inky contents, and joined by a saucer of dry sugar biscuits. "Go on, have a cookie," Caufield urged, pushing the plate towards Sullivan. "And tell me who we know in common."

"Because you want to know who'd refer a crackpot like myself to you?"

Caufield tipped his head to acknowledge the truth in that statement.

143

GILSBURY CROSS HAD seen better days, but not many.

In the mid-1800s, the discovery of mineral riches in the colonial West had drawn European miners like Tolkien's dwarfs. The men bought passage on steamers to the port of Victoria, coaxed to the harsh landscape at the edge of the Pacific by flyers and unscrupulous businessmen, fuelled by dreams of finding prosperity amid the ancient forests and precipitous peaks. Like the tragic quest of Ponce de León, they were driven by constant, unrelenting promises: of a place to stake their claims, of wealth and happiness, of glory and riches at the farthest reaches of the New World. Most came for gold, but some came for timber, furs or coal, and all came for a better future than they could find in the slums of the Old World.

In 1872, an enterprising Englishman named John Gilsbury stopped in Victoria en route to the newly purchased state of Alaska, where he hoped to establish a series of brothels, but a rousing game of rummy in a decrepit boarding house left Gilsbury with a curious prize—an unseen plot of land amid the mainland mountains where, the previous owner claimed, there sat a rich seam of coal. Gilsbury wasn't one to ignore a business opportunity, illegal or otherwise. He decided to forego his Alaskan adventure in lieu of building a coal empire, like James Dunsmuir had done before him. The fact that Gilsbury had little education, less money, and no connections didn't dissuade him; with his smooth manner and persuasive showmanship, he won the confidence of a group of twenty Welsh miners, fresh off the ship from Aberystwyth, and convinced them that God Himself had sent them to dig his coal.

So Gilsbury and his band travelled to the British Columbian mainland, first by ship, then by mule train, and into a secluded valley between three fierce mountains. At first glance, the plot of land seemed to be little more than a cleft in the savage terrain, but Gilsbury saw that the dark soil glittered with quartz fragments. Yes, he decided, fortune had truly smiled upon him. This valley, surrounded with ground on all sides for their pickaxes to plunder, would make them rich beyond their wildest dreams. They built square houses and planted plots of vegetables, familiar to their eyes and tastes, and they raised a crooked Anglican church with a bright red roof. How they must've looked up from their doorsteps and squirrelled their hands with glee, eager to pull their wealth from the ground. How the mountains must have looked down at them, these tiny foreign men with ruddy faces and tweed caps, ignorant of the ruthless forces that faced them.

It must be said, however, that Gilsbury (whose business prospects had included rum running and prostitution, but very little by way of coal mining) was not a man to trust. The miners laboured and burrowed, using mules to pull carts of greasy black stone from under the earth, but the mountains of Gilsbury's winnings were charlatans. Instead of profitable, the coal beds turned out to be false and shallow. Within five years, both the seams and the men would be exhausted.

Perhaps it was a mixed blessing that John Gilsbury was the first to die on the expedition, succumbing to the vicious winter of 1872, the very year he'd won the land. If the elements hadn't killed him, the desperate miners with their pickaxes would've gladly done the job.

Penniless, destitute, but ever resourceful, the Welsh pioneers attempted to farm the weak soil, but this venture proved even less successful. Nature intended to reclaim her valley. With the coal boom finished and the farms faltering, nothing remained to hold the starving men to the land, and one by one the abandoned houses fell into ruin. Some hardy individuals, as stubborn as their mules, refused to be dislodged and planted fruit trees, but the climate proved too wicked for orchards. The industrious 1920s brought prospects of logging, and in a fit of capitalist excitement, a mill was built where the rushing Trent River met the deep, iron-coloured waters of Maple Lake.

Still, it didn't last. It was too difficult to move the lumber to market, far down a winding dirt track to the Squamish inlet. The brief timber industry stumbled and faltered like an old dog until, weary of trying, it crumpled and died.

By the Depression, the future of Gilsbury Cross seemed hopeless. The last few families eked a meagre existence raising sheep or goats, the only animals that could navigate the harsh terrain with ease, and Gilsbury Cross seemed destined to fade away.

But when it looked as if all hope was lost, opportunity arrived in a dubious disguise—Britain declared war upon Germany, taking her colonies with her to battle, and the war brought orders for wool and milk. Slowly, cautiously, Gilsbury Cross ceased to shrink. Gilsbury wool, known for its resilience and warmth, was suddenly in demand around the world, and for a few decades, buoyed by a fashion industry that loved fine sheepskin and woollens, the population held steady.

In the 1970s, urbanites discovered the hamlet. It was a haven far from the bustle of Vancouver but close enough to reach in a day's travel. Here, the rich and athletic could hike in the summer and cross-country ski in the winter, and the old town had a quaint charm that delighted tourists. Summer homes sprang up where the old square houses once had stood, and Gilsbury Cross, for the first time in a hundred years, began to grow.

By its physical nature, Gilsbury Cross will never be large. The mountains hem in too close, the winters are too savage, to allow a sizeable community to flourish here. Like a line drawn in the sand, the town ends and the wilderness begins. The tiny valley cradles a main street with two restaurants and a hotel, a school, a library and a post office, and a few gravel roads fan from the village towards outlying farms. There are no stoplights, no frills, and absolutely no nightlife, except for raccoons and the occasional cougar. A gas station doubles as a general store, the scant library is housed in the basement of the red-roofed church, and the hardware store opens at ten and closes at five. The entire village remains shut on Wednesdays in true Welsh tradition.

John Gilsbury was buried on the slopes of the southern mountain with a granite cross to mark his resting place. It seemed to me that the death of the expedition's leader was a portent of bad luck from the beginning, and naming the town after a tombstone didn't help to raise anyone's spirits. The cross is long gone, worn into gravel by the elements, but an air of isolation remains.

While most residents found Gilsbury Cross to be quietly depressing, I thought the desolation was perfect. Gilsbury Cross is the kind of town where 'rush hour' is bringing the herds in from the fields, where a car accident is the news for the month, where it's not uncommon to see a moose grazing at the side of the street. People mark the years with weather occurrences: the Big Snow of '73, the wind storm that blew over Leary's chicken coop, the flood that washed out the Trent River Bridge (or, in knowing company, the Trent Flood, which took place between 1980 and 1985, depending on who's telling the story). It's a tiny place in the middle of nowhere, the literal End of the Road. Most of the forty-odd families raise sheep or goats; there are no vast pastures for wheat or corn and the steep terrain makes mechanized farming an expensive hassle, but here and there are hints of previous attempts at cultivation. Fruit trees pepper the area from old, forgotten pioneer orchards. Knotted apple trees and bowers of pears hunch in the sheltering lees or along the edges of properties. Twisted tangles of grapevines cling to the sides of houses like drowning men flailing for flotsam. Maybe it sounds like a cliché to say the march of time has forgotten Gilsbury Cross, but it's all too true.

Don't mistake my description for idealism. Yes, it's peaceful and quiet, but there are problems in any community, and Gilsbury Cross is no exception. Folks keep their little ones in

148

on Friday nights, when the restless teenagers grab their rifles and six-packs and head for the hills. Throughout the decades, settlers had attempted logging, mining and farming, all with little success, and the community had teetered on the precipice of full unemployment for so long that the spectre of poverty and isolation had become part of the ambiance. Nothing is new in Gilsbury Cross. Everything has a patina of age and neglect, and even the stop signs are speckled with bullet holes from gun-slinging drivers.

As I drove through its sparse Main Street at five o'clock in the evening, every store was closed and the lonely length of sidewalk was utterly deserted. A few mud-caked vehicles cruised through the side streets on their way to outlying houses but the town was vacant, and even as I turned left at the north end of town, towards the beginning of the logging road that led up through the valley to Maple Lake, I saw no one. Purple twilight muted the colours of the day and turned the fields into depthless shadows. Naked limbs of alders and elms scratched at the October sky.

The roads were bare of snow until I reached higher elevations, and even here, only a scattering of white dusted the grass and the pines. I maneuvered the vehicle up the old driveway, threw it into park under the shelter of the cedar's branches, and locked the doors.

The old cabin smelt cool and musty. I tossed the sack to the floor and disrobed, feeling the gooseflesh ripple over my skin; it was barely winter and already the temperature was too close to freezing for my comfort without fur. I took off my wedding ring, slipped it onto my key chain, and buried it deeply into the bag with my cell phone and wallet. The jeans, shirt and sweater I stuffed in without folding, and then the whole sack was stashed into the flue.

The urge to change could no longer be ignored. I bent down and tucked my chin to my chest, laid my hands on the hardwood floor, and succumbed to the relief of my shifting. The first prickling hairs spread across my back, down my spine, over my arms and thighs. The bones of my feet cracked and bent, my fingers shortened and my thumbs travelled up the length of my forearm to their position as dew claws. My skull lengthened and my teeth grew. I shut my eyes to the pain of the transformation and fought off the agony with speed. My first full transformation at the age of ten had taken an excruciating two hours, but I had been changing my skin for almost twenty years now, and in less than a minute I'd left behind my birth body. The first thing I did, once the change was complete, was to roll on my back to ease the itching, paws in the air and tongue lolling.

I pushed out the back door and stood for a moment on the porch.

It was beautiful to be back in this form. The sounds of deer in the vale below, the scent of wet earth and fallen leaves thick with mould and decay. I stretched my legs before me and yawned, absently wondering where the resident pack would be at this time of year. The alpha male didn't like me all that much, but the alpha female was always happy to see me, and she had far more sway in the politics of the group than a male could hope to garner. I loped down the stairs in a single, easy stride, acclimatizing myself to the sensation of falling head first with every step.

Without further hesitation, I dashed into the trees, and the dark evening woods swallowed me whole.

I caught a whiff of the pack's scent at the side of the river that flowed from the lake, but it was faint and old. More recent was a grizzly's passing, and the thick, heady smell of a wolverine as it waddled close to water to drink. I paced up and down the side of the river in the giddy pursuit of intriguing smells; the sandbars along the shore were palimpsests of sensations and it was a joy to sort through them. Eyesight has no comparison to the rich texture of smell. A coyote, a herd of elk, a few dead fish that were now nothing but silhouettes of stench in the gravel. I waded into the water and lapped at the surface, dashed back to land and ran with abandon through the ferns.

To a casual observer, I was nothing but a black wolf that had gone crazy with play.

When, at last, the journey of the day and the exertion of the shift caught up with me, I curled into a ball between the roots of a red cedar and covered my nose with my tail. The thin sliver of the crescent moon had appeared through the branches, and it shimmered with an intensity that the city skies muted and disguised. I watched it for a while, breathing peacefully, allowing sleep to find me. When I finally dreamt, Gwen's face pervaded every image in my mind, and my dreams were accompanied by a feeling of perfection such as I had never felt before.

The scent of smoke wrenched me awake.

Sometimes, in the spring, the wood smoke from the valley would drift into the mountains on drafts of warming air, but even then the smell was faint and cheery, not thick and choking like this. I started awake and stood, instantly alert, listening.

Footsteps and voices at the top of the hill, close to the cabin.

I flew up the rise on silent paws, hearing my blood beating in my ears.

At first, I didn't recognize her in jeans and a thick white sweater, her hair bundled onto the top of her head in a ponytail, but Gwen's fragrance was unmistakable. She stood back, the canvas sack at her feet and my clothes in her hands.

Addled with shock, I didn't understand what I saw. It took a moment to become clear.

Flames wreathed the cabin, fed with gasoline and dry tinder from the remains of the woodshed, and a curtain of rose tinted smoke billowed upwards and hid the sun. The top level was already gone, the roof had collapsed, the stone chimney had blackened into a besieged tower. At Gwen's feet sat an empty red gas can. She lingered at the perimeter of the inferno's heavy heat, and she held up each item of clothing, identifying them as mine. As she sorted through them, she tossed each piece into the fire, one by one.

If I'd still possessed a human voice, I would have screamed, but all that escaped my throat was a sharp, strangled bark.

Gwen looked towards the underbrush as the last item, my white t-shirt, left her hands and fell into the blaze. It was held aloft on a draft of heat before flames tore through the fabric and turned it to ash.

"Daniel?" she called out, her voice quizzical, her smile malicious. "Is that you, love?"

What do I do? Frantic, I circled the outskirts of the clearing, the smoke stinging my nose and lungs, and stared as she bundled the empty sack under her arm and surveyed the trees. The cabin crackled and popped, the blackened spine of the stairway visible between the timbers. My father had built this place with his own hands. He'd met my mother here; we'd lived here until the twins were born, then visited every summer after that. Gone. Destroyed. Stolen from me like she'd stolen my body.

"Holy shit," she said.

I had, in my distress, edged closer to the fire, and now stood half exposed from the underbrush. Gwen stared, her grin growing into one of utmost curiosity, and she crouched down and held out her hand. "Come here, Daniel." She gave a little whistle, as if I were some pitiful dog under her command.

I laid my ears flat and drew back my lips in a snarl.

"It is you," she hissed. "C'mon, come here. Don't you want to kill me?"

She seemed so assured, so solidly cruel. Her features were illuminated by the flames, flickering orange and white, and as she reached out her hand I found myself terribly afraid of her, this creature who'd effortlessly manipulated both my mind and my flesh. Gwen was no delicate flower. She was a succubus, a siren, a foul devil who played my impulses against me. I smelt no fear on her flesh, only surprise surrounded by the acidic perfume of burning gasoline. I prowled forward with teeth bared, but she didn't back away. She remained on one knee, her back now to the fire, her slender eggshell hand outstretched.

"I thought you were insane, Dan, but I decided to humour you." Her grin was a skull's maw. "Certifiably crazy. I never dreamed you were telling the truth." She paused to gauge my reaction. "C'mon, Daniel. If that is you, surely you're angrier than just a little growl or two."

I lowered my head and studied her for some hint of her purpose. She seemed to be waiting for me to spring. She wasn't afraid. I looked past her, to the fire, and felt my knees weaken. Gone. All gone. My entire life, utterly destroyed.

A bang split the air in two, and an explosion of dirt sent pebbles flying inches from my feet. I scurried backwards into the ferns.

"Goddammit! How can you miss? He's massive," she screamed, standing and reeling towards the driveway as she dropped the bag, and for the first time I saw Ethan's car parked behind my own. He was leaning across the hood, using it to brace his elbows for a better aim, but the end of the rifle shivered violently. Gwen dashed to the car, grabbed the gun from his hands, and took aim.

I turned and fled, but not before Gwen managed one shot in my direction. A searing spear drove itself into my right flank and I felt muscle and skin tear away. She shrieked in triumph.

They crashed through the underbrush in pursuit. I ran as swiftly as I could manage, but back legs give power while fore legs give direction, and I was dragging my right rear paw and leaving long smears of blood in the dirt. Another gunshot echoed up the valley as a blossom of wood shards and twigs exploded above my head. I dodged left, stumbled, fell to the ground and scrambled to my feet again. There was no pain, only an intense heat and the pulse of adrenaline in my muscles, and I raced for the river with little thought other than my own survival. They were closing the distance. Gwen shouted, and I heard Ethan's muffled cry from higher on the ridge.

I splashed into the river with the intent to cross it.

Get to the other side, up the opposite ridge.

A single, ridiculous and desperate thought rang through my head. *Gwen won't want to get her shoes wet.*

I plunged up to my chest, and holding my head high, the water surged around me as I struggled to keep my footing. Throwing one quick glance back, I saw her burst onto the sandy shore. When she spied me in the middle of the open water, she raised the rifle butt against the crook of her shoulder. A sly smile of victory crossed her lips.

But the river bottom was paved with boulders the size of pumpkins, each one polished smooth by centuries of friction and all of them covered in algae. I found no secure footing. A swell hit me and the water swept my feet from under me. When I disappeared below the surface, the current grabbed me and tossed me against rocks and deadfalls. Battered, the breath was knocked from my lungs in a line of silver bubbles. I felt a rib snap against a submerged boulder.

When I finally struggled to the surface, gasping and panting, the rapids had carried me far downstream and Gwen was nothing but a distant speck on the shore. She searched the river but, not looking far enough downstream, her efforts were to no avail. The water coursed too quickly for her to run alongside,

155

and as the swift current took me around a curve in the river, I saw Ethan join Gwen on the banks and take the gun from her hand.

My heart, broken, was far more painful than any bullet wound or bruise.

"SO THAT WAS THE first attempt?"

"Mmm-hmm."

"That's where you got the scar on your ass?"

"Yep."

Caufield reached for another cookie. "I can't help but feel sorry for you, if it's all true. I don't normally take sides in this kind of thing, but she sounds like she played you like a violin."

"That's a kind way of saying it," Sullivan replied.

"I'd hate women too, if I'd seen what you've seen." He leaned back in his chair and glanced out the window at the evening skyline. "Probably pretend I was a dog too, just to get away from them."

Sullivan narrowed his eyes, frowned. "I don't hate women."

"Sure you do," said Caufield. "Listen to yourself."

"No, I really don't. I've had bad luck, but I don't hate them all."

"Name one woman in this story that hasn't been a right bitch to you, hasn't ruined your life or tried to do you in. Go on, name one." Morris jotted a note on his yellow legal pad and underlined it twice. *Still in the closet.*

"Stella," said Sullivan without hesitation.

With a grunt, Caufield said, "That's only one."

"My little sister Erin. My niece Brittany."

"Alright, alright, so you like women," Caufield replied, scratching out his note. "So you like three women."

"And Soph."

"Soph?"

The right corner of Sullivan's mouth curled up in a smile, and he said, "I'm getting to her."

I DRAGGED MY BODY from the water to the opposite side, my right leg numb and useless. The sun was high in the west, brushing the tops of the willow trees and casting stubby shadows as it eased its way towards late afternoon, and with my head low, I finally collapsed on a rocky promontory. The swelling had caused the bleeding in my thigh to slow but every breath was agony, and I knew that if I stayed by the river I was as good as dead. The grizzly I'd scented earlier would find me. It would come to the smell of my blood and tear me to pieces, limb from limb.

The river led from the lake towards Gilsbury Cross, and when I hauled myself up the small embankment, I saw wide pastures stretching out before me, portioned out with crooked wooden fences. Herds of sheep and horses dotted the fields. The outlines of distant farmhouses seemed hazy in the autumn mist. I saw these things as if I were in a dream, and realized that the forests I knew were far behind me. But the risk was too high: I'd never approached Gilsbury Cross as a wolf, and now I looked over the vista of farms as if they were the landscape of an enemy territory: unexplored, dangerous, forbidden. I lay down momentarily on the crest of the embankment, weighing my options, before struggling to my feet and limping slowly, painfully, forward.

I needed to rest, and with my fur soaked to my skin and the loss of blood, I was frozen inside and out. I needed a place to lick my wounds and warm myself.

Everything was gone.

The thought swam through my mind like a carp, lazy and slow, under the surface of the pain in my haunch and chest.

I stumbled, pitched drunkenly forward before finding my footing. The closest building was a tiny ramshackle barn on the opposite side of the field, and I set my eyes on it with resolution. It took most of the afternoon to reach it, creeping on my belly between the fences, but once there, I pushed aside the door and shuffled inside, taking care to close the gate behind me. I collapsed in the first pen and buried myself in the hay.

The scent of lanolin hung in the close and stuffy air, and as soon as my heart slowed and the blaze of my wounds diminished, I heard the bleating of ewes disturbed in their evening meal. I looked like a wolf but I didn't possess a wolfish

158

odour, and sheep are extremely stupid when it comes to an intruder in their midst. They examined me from a safe distance as they huddled together, muttering and groaning, debating my threat to one another like suspicious old hags. But while I looked like a predator, I smelt more like the farmer that brought them food. I closed my eyes and laid my head upon the floor. The simple act of breathing was agony. They edged closer, and before long the bravest ewe was pushing her grey muzzle against my neck to satisfy her curiosity. I lay still to let her determine my purpose, and when she finally decided that I offered no threat, she went back to her trough to finish her oats.

With difficulty I licked the wound on my thigh while they ate. The bullet had grazed across my skin and cleft a deep abrasion through the muscle, but had passed over my body without lodging itself in the flesh. If I grabbed my right foot in my mouth I could feel a distant sensation, but the limb was still numb with shock and refused to move or bear weight. Once the gash had been licked clean, I was confident it would heal well, but now I grew more concerned with my chest. I'd broken a rib, maybe two, and each breath sent shards of pain through my torso. Neither lung was punctured, but there was nothing to guarantee that a bone fragment couldn't worry its way through soft tissue with every movement. If I lay still, I was fine.

The warmth of the animals began to chase the chill from my body. At length a couple of ewes entered the pen in which I had taken residence and lay down beside me. The heat of their bodies served to warm me further, and while I recognized that they slept here out of habit, and not out of any assistance to me, I snuggled my head into the wool of one and breathed a ragged sigh of relief. If I could stay here for just a little while, just long enough to dry off and grow warm, maybe I could figure out what to do.

5

I WOKE AS THE EWE under my head lurched to her feet, bleating and stumbling forward.

"Oh my good God," said a lilting voice, hushed with surprise. "Maddy, go get your father. Go on now."

Groggy, I blinked my eyes. I lifted my head to remind myself of where I slept, and the sharp pain in my ribs tore through my confusion.

A woman in a tartan flannel shirt and brown corduroy pants stood in the entrance to the sheep pen, her hand grasping the top beam of the gate and her gumboots braced. She had pinned her chestnut hair loosely on top of her head, but tendrils had broken free and tumbled down to her shoulders to frame a round face as pale as the moon. She studied me as the ewes brushed past her until only I remained in the stall. I tried to stand. The throbbing pain in my chest returned as soon as I shifted my weight, forcing me to collapse again.

We stared at each other, neither one daring to blink, for long minutes.

She had a small frame, but the labours of farming had made her strong and solid. Her shirt had been cut to fit a large man; the sleeves were rolled up to her elbows and the hem reached halfway down her thighs. Her grey eyes were inquisitive and wary but without a hint of fear. As we appraised each other, she brushed the dirt from her hands on her faded pants, then ran her fingers through her hair to tuck the stray strands behind delicate white ears. Each was pierced and adorned with little silver stars.

I pricked my ears up as I heard the tap of hard soles on concrete. A large man rushed into the barn, but he came to an abrupt halt when he saw me and gave a low whistle. "Jesus, look at that!" he said, drawing close to her side. He wore a pressed shirt, slacks and a tie slung over one beefy shoulder, and his blond hair was clipped short with government precision; you could scrub a floor with that scalp. He jerked his head in a tight nod in my direction, and asked, "Did it kill anything?"

"It was sleeping between Parsifal and Lamerocke."

"You gotta be joking, Sophie."

"No, it's true. Curled up between them," she said, not once taking her eyes away.

"I'll go get the rifle. You move the sheep out."

He rushed back outside. I heard his steps disappearing towards the farmhouse.

"Come on girls," she said to the sheep. "Into the pasture. Time for a midnight feeding." She stepped away, refusing to turn her back to me, and began to close the gate of the pen.

I tried to stand, but when that didn't work, I dragged myself forward by my front legs. At this sign of slow movement, she stood still, watching, and when I laid my head on her foot, she gave a little gasp, but she didn't pull away.

I gave a small sigh of pain.

"Oh, you poor thing," she said.

162

The man returned to the door. I heard his hurried steps on the concrete floor of the barn and the click of the safety on his weapon.

"No, Simon, wait," she said. "Look."

In an appeal for mercy, I wrapped my paws around her rubber boot and licked the corduroy of her knee.

"Back up, Soph," he replied. "It'll take off your leg."

"No, look!" she said again, and crouched down with her hand gently pushing my head to one side. "It's already been shot. It came here to die."

"Then I'll put it out of its misery," he replied. "Get out of my way. Get the sheep into the pasture."

"Put the gun down, Simon," she insisted.

Please please please put the gun down, Simon. I don't want to die.

I felt her hands on my chest, on my neck.

"What if it's rabid?"

"It would have attacked me right away," she replied. "It's eyes are clear. It's not rabid."

He drew closer but still held his rifle at the ready.

She pushed my head to the ground and began to prod the wound on my back leg, waiting for me to snap at the pain and visibly pleased when I gave no resistance. "Go call Gloria. See if she'll do a house call. This'll need stitches."

"We don't have any money to pay a vet for stitches, Sophie," he said.

"Simon? Please?"

He grumbled more, but unintelligibly, and she chose to ignore it.

"Hey, wait. Come back here."

163

"What?"

She beckoned him closer. "Look at this."

I whimpered when she tried to move me onto my back, but there was no need. The fur on my stomach is lighter than elsewhere, and where I'd been tattooed, the hair never grew in as thick as before. She pulled it aside. I felt her fingers against my skin. Under the finer fur, the dark marks against white flesh had caught her eye. "It's a letter. I think it's an A."

Simon squatted next to her, pushing more roughly. "What do you know? Somebody's marked him."

"What's it say?"

There was more poking, more prodding, but I whined when the throbbing in my chest became too great to bear.

"Maybe it's a registration number. Ask Gloria," said Sophie, patting my head and scratching behind my ears. She smiled kindly, and I leaned into her warm, loving touch as Simon slipped back into the yard.

SULLIVAN PAUSED AS Caufield's eyebrows vaulted towards his receding hairline.

"Simon and Sophie Rawlins."

With a nod, Sullivan took the last cookie from the plate.

"You… the little girl… what's her name?"

"Madeleine."

164

Caufield drew his brows together. "You saved her? You?"

"So now you believe in werewolves?" Sullivan asked, and when Caufield continued to stare at him, his eyes boring into the odd and persistent man across his desk, Sullivan smiled knowingly and answered for him. "What a silly question. Of course you don't."

GLORIA EXPLORED THE extent of my injuries with her leathery hands, and her touch was neither gentle nor forgiving. I yelped twice when she hit the ribs, and she held her ear to my chest and rapped on the bones, listening for my torso's reply. "The stitches are nothing," she said in her slight drawl, and I noticed curlers still entangled in her peppered brown hair. "He's got two ribs cracked. Someone beat you good, didn't they, sugar pie?"

"Can you do anything for him?" said Sophie, sitting on the top of the pen's gate.

"I don't know if I've got a sedative strong enough for him," said Gloria, as she hovered over me, examining my haunch under the harsh glare of a portable construction lamp. "You said it was a wolf in your barn, but he's a brute." She rose to her feet, clapped her hands together to knock the dust and hair away. "But he's certainly someone's animal. I don't see a single parasite on him."

165

"But that's a bullet track, isn't it?" said Simon.

"Yup."

"He's so friendly, why would anyone shoot him?" said Sophie.

Martin, Gloria's teenage son and veterinary assistant, hawked and spat into the next enclosure. He was late into his teens and thin as a whippet, with a disdainful expression under a prominent brow ridge. He smelt of frightened cats and cheap beer; I suspected he'd spent the afternoon drinking and terrorizing the neighbours' pets. An odd choice of assistant for a veterinarian, I agree, but he'd been born into the position and didn't look pleased with the arrangement. His lipless mouth was pulled down in a sour grimace, his thumbs were hooked into the pockets of his denim jacket, and he watched his mother work with thinly-veiled boredom. He stifled a yawn and said, "Wouldn't you want that pelt on your wall? Betcha you could get five thousand bucks for a pelt like that." The mere thought brought a little glimmer of interest to his eyes. "Y'know, Mr Rawlins, you should get Mac Simmons to skin him and tan the—"

"Martin!" said Gloria.

"Well, if it's gonna die anyways—" he said, trailing off.

She rocked back on her heels. "Damn it, Martin, if you're going to talk about animals dying, I'm not bringing you with me on house calls. No one wants to hear that their pets are going to *die*."

"The boy's just being practical," said Simon, now leaning against the fence next to Sophie's knees.

"Well, this one's not going to die," she replied sharply. "At least, not if I have my way."

"What can you do for him?" said Sophie. "Stitch him up? Give him antibiotics?"

Gloria took another look at the abrasion. "I can put a few stitches here, but I doubt he'll need antibiotics; as far as I can tell, he's healthy as a horse. Clear eyes, well fed, and other than these injuries, I don't think he's ever been maltreated. Whoever owns him loves him."

I collapsed my head back into the hay and sighed piteously.

"What sort of cost are we looking at?" said Simon.

Gloria stood up. She was a lanky woman, with long limbs and a bony neck, and the light of the construction lamp cast deep shadows over her narrow, sallow cheeks. "Martin, go get my bag from the truck." As the boy hunched over, jammed his hands deeper in his pockets and lurched out the door, she said, "Night call, examination, stitches. I'll have to charge you two hundred dollars, at least."

Simon slumped forward. He was a proud man foiled by the void in his wallet.

Sophie stepped in. "Can I give Elsie her next three violin lessons free, plus a hundred dollars, and we call it even?" she said. "We're short on cash these days, Glo."

The veterinarian gave me a quick glance. She chewed her lip thoughtfully and wrung her hands at the small of her back, and with a quick look at Simon, judging his reaction, she nodded. "I'll tell you what: give me four lessons for free, and we're square."

167

"Thanks, Glo," said Sophie with relief. "We really appreciate it."

"And—" she added, raising one crooked finger. "You throw in a batch of those huckleberry muffins. Two dozen."

"Fair enough."

"Glo, you're a doll," said Simon, kissing her cheek. He was a big man, broad in both shoulders and girth, but Gloria matched him in height.

"But don't you tell anyone. Not even Martin," she warned, waggling her finger and exposing a picket fence of crooked teeth. "I can't start giving away my services for baked goods and music lessons." She crouched down and took my head in her hands, and I caught a whiff of cold tobacco, beer and steak sauce on her clothes. "Then again, you probably weren't counting on another mouth to feed either, and this one—he's gonna eat a lot." She looked in my ears again, causing a shiver to run down my back. I shook my head free of her grip. She rocked back on her feet, crossing her arms. "I want you to keep him inside where it's warm. You're going to have to watch the wounds for infection."

"We don't let the animals in the house," said Simon.

Sophie threw him a quick glance. "We can make an exception this time."

"I don't think—"

"If you leave him out here, he's going to catch a chill," said Gloria. "Put your fingers through his coat—it's thick, but he's damp right through to his skin."

Simon snorted. "He stays in the sitting room then." When he saw Sophie smile, he added, "And you keep an eye on him."

"We're gonna have to move him. He's not going anywhere himself," said Gloria. "I've got a horse blanket in the truck but it's gonna take four or five guys to lift him."

"I'll go next door to see if Knut and Jan are awake."

"And, Glo, we wanted ask you what this is," said Sophie, leaping down from the gate as Simon left to round up the neighbours. She patted me lightly on the side and ran her fingers over my exposed stomach. "Ah, here it is. What does it mean?"

They pried the hairs apart, searching for each individual letter. "Salt me and call me pickle if I know," said Gloria. "It doesn't look like a standard registration."

"Maybe he belongs to a game farm?"

"Maybe," she agreed. "Here, Martin, give me the pencil and papers."

Her son, now returned with a massive leather satchel perched against his hip, rooted through her tools and found what she requested. Gloria scribbled down the letters and read them aloud in one long line. "Opera," she paused. "Maybe he belongs to a theatre company? I'll look into it for you, Soph, and let you know what I find."

Martin handed her a curved needle with a long black tail of wiry thread. She checked the surface of my abrasion, then asked him for peroxide to sterilize the area and a topical anaesthetic to dull the pain. I turned my face away.

"Hold his head down, Soph," she said. And pulling a length of white cotton from her satchel, added, "Wrap this around his muzzle to keep him from nipping."

Sophie dragged my head onto her lap and wound the cloth around my snout, and she stroked the hair back from my eyes as Gloria poured peroxide liberally over the open flesh. My legs stiffened, I ground my teeth and a small howl of agony escaped despite all of my efforts to be tough. Sophie cooed in empathy.

But Gloria was efficient in her talents, and in only a few moments she was finished, snipping the final stitch with a pair of heavy steel clippers. She slapped her hands to her thighs. "I can't do much about the ribs, but I wager they'll heal straight as long as he rests and doesn't move around too much." She returned the bloodied needle to its black patent case and tossed it into the satchel. "And believe me, Soph, he won't go far. He'll be fighting for an easy breath for the next couple of days."

Three sets of footsteps approached the threshold. Simon entered, leading two wiry men with identical Nordic features, one blond and the other dark. Standing side by side, they appeared to be reflections in a mirror that only altered the colour of their hair. "You got that blanket, Martin?" Simon said, kicking the hay from my side. He gestured to the brothers to take opposite corners.

Martin grunted and they spread the woollen throw over the ground. If I thought Gloria's ministering was painful, the move to the blanket proved me wrong; the men spared no time to be gentle, and the barn swam as I dipped in and out of consciousness. They strained and grunted under the shared burden of my weight.

Sophie held open the door that led from the front porch to the entrance hall, and they heaved and shuffled until I was lying haphazard on the corner of the living room rug, breathing in short, shallow bursts from the throbbing in my chest. I thought I might be sick from the agony, all over the threadbare carpet.

"Thanks guys," said Simon.

They each nodded and held up a hand.

Sophie stepped towards the kitchen. "I'll make some tea. Jan, Knut, you want a cup?"

"That would be nice," said the blond in a slight Norwegian accent.

"So," said Gloria, sitting on the nearby couch and scribbling down a few notes on my condition. "What are you going to call him? I need a name for my files."

"Barfy," said Simon.

I jerked my head up in horror.

"Oh God, no," shouted Sophie from the kitchen.

"It was the name of a dog we had when I was a kid," said Simon. "He was named after the dog in Family Circus. It was a good name."

"Seriously?" said Gloria. "You had a dog named Barfy?"

The dark-haired man, who had not lost his accent to the extent his brother had, said, "What about we call him Paddington, ja? Like the bear?"

"It would be shortened to Paddy, Jan," said Simon. "No, I like Barfy."

"We are not calling him Barfy, Simon," came the reply from the kitchen.

"We had a dog called Hogarth once," said Knut.

Jan shook his head. "He was nasty, though. We don't want to name this one after a bad dog, eh?"

171

"Snowy," said Martin.

Gloria regarded her son with disdain. "He's black as pitch, Marty."

His eyes half-closed, he shrugged his indifference. "Pitchy then."

"We're not calling him Pitchy," said Gloria.

Sophie returned with six mugs on a tray, and the scent of Earl Grey filled the sitting room. She set the tray on a small side table and handed out cups as she said, "We can call him Gorlagon."

"What?" said Martin. "Gor Lo Gun?"

"Gorlagon was a wolf in an Arthurian legend," Sophie explained, and at this, Gloria snickered.

"You don't change."

But Simon wasn't amused at all and openly scoffed. "You already have a ewe called Gorlagon."

"Fine, if that's too confusing," she said, sitting down next to Gloria. "Call him Logan."

Before any arguments could begin, Gloria scribbled the name on her form. "Logan it is then."

I heard the sound in the hall before all the others.

"What's going on?"

Sophie held out her hand toward the stairwell. "Maddy, remember the wolf in the barn?" And she looked quickly at Simon. "Did you put her to bed?"

"I didn't know how long we'd be so I tucked her in before I came up with the gun," he replied. "Hey Maddy. Come to Daddy."

But the little girl shuffled closer to me, her flannel pyjama pants reaching past her feet and dragging on the carpet. She possessed the same shaggy chestnut hair as Sophie, and it hung over her sleepy blue eyes in thick tangles. I guessed her age to be no more than five, no less than three. I saw Gloria rise to pull the girl away, but I thumped my tail twice against the floor and waited without twitching another muscle.

Sophie slipped from the couch and knelt between my head and her daughter. "This is Logan. Can you say 'Hi Logan'?"

The little girl waved at me by opening and closing her hand.

"Logan is going to live with us for a little bit, and I want you to be very careful around him, okay? Promise? Don't go near him unless Daddy or I are here. Promise?"

"Okay."

"Good girl." She pressed a kiss against the tousled hair. "Now, back to bed."

"I wanna stay up."

"No, you need to sleep," said Simon, standing. "Come on, I'll take you."

The girl balked, reaching out one hand towards me. Sophie intercepted the movement and pushed herself between Maddy and me. "No, not until Logan is better. He's sick right now and I don't know if he'll snap at you."

"I wanna pat Logan."

I thumped my tail again, quite unintentionally. She was absolutely adorable.

"Tomorrow, Maddy," said Sophie, kissing her on the tiny bump of a nose.

Gloria smiled to herself as Simon lifted the little girl and took her back down the hall. Maddy's head flopped against the crook between his bull neck and his shoulder. "See that?" Gloria asked.

Looking after them, Knut said, "What?"

"He wagged his tail when Madeleine said his name." And she bent over her notes. "Hey Logan."

I looked at her, wagged the tail again. Let's face it, when it came to a new name, it was a hell of a lot better than Barfy.

6

I SLEPT.
I wanted to listen to their conversation but I was exhausted, and the fire in the wood stove made the sitting room too cosy to ward off sleep. The blanket smelt pleasantly of horse sweat; the air was filled with the swirling perfume of tea and bergamot oil. The gossip of Gilsbury Cross became a pleasant hum in the background.

I slept and I dreamt of Gwen.

Nothing in particular, no plot or story, but images of our life together that fell one upon the other in rapid succession, and each was so vibrant that I forgot it was only a dream. When the images began to slip away, I struggled to stay in her embrace, but grasping at dreams only makes them melt more quickly. The woollen blanket itched against my cheek. A gentle tugging persisted at my neck. I opened my eyes.

Madeleine, sitting cross-legged at my head, entwined her hands in my fur. Her round face and big grey eyes filled my field of vision, and the morning sun shone brightly across her wide, innocent grin. With the flat of one palm, she patted the top of my head. She still wore her flannel pyjamas, which were decorated with little rabbits carrying paintbrushes and ladders.

When she noticed the glimmer of moisture in the corner of my eyes, her smile disappeared.

"Logan crying?" she asked.

I nodded.

"Poor Logan has an ouchy," she whispered.

I nodded. Both inside and out.

"Hungry?"

I nodded.

"Mummy?" she called towards the kitchen, once more patting my forehead. "Logan says he's hungry."

"He does, does he?" Sophie shouted back. Then there was a pause, followed by quick footsteps on a creaking wooden floor. "Are you—Maddy, what did I tell you? Don't go near him!"

I thumped my tail against the floor.

"Logan's not mad a' me," she replied in a sombre tone. "S'okay."

Sophie regarded me with suspicion.

"And he says he is very hungry, an' he wants scrambled eggs with cheese," she continued. "And bacon with toast. And pancakes with raspberries an' syrup. And sausages." This last word came out as 'sawz-jez'.

I licked my lips. Yes, sawz-jez drenched in maple syrup would be divine.

"Well, he's getting kibble like the other dogs," Sophie said, arms crossed, bemused. "And there's no bacon left after your father made lunch yesterday. But the eggs and cheese I can do."

"Egncheez!"

"Up to the table, then, missy." And as Maddy scampered into the kitchen, she said to me, "I'll bring you your breakfast after I get hers."

I wagged the tail again in the hopes that sausages might still be on the menu.

But, while the smell of grease and melted cheddar and toast with butter wafted from the kitchen, Sophie laid down an aluminum mixing bowl of dried dog food close to my head, its bland sawdust flavour only made marginally appealing by the addition of salt. I whined.

"Can you reach that? Here." She moved the bowl closer to my head. "There you go, Logan. Eat up."

She went back into the kitchen to wash dishes. I prodded the bowl once with my nose, shuffling forward and taking one piece in my mouth. The flavour was utterly revolting. I'll eat rotten meat, I'll eat intestines and brain and skin, I'll even eat Hestia's cooking if there's no alternative, but these insipid nuggets of bone meal and grit were appalling. Every choking mouthful was made more vile by the comparison to what I knew was being served in the next room.

So I grunted, braced myself for pain, and slowly dragged myself up to my feet. The nature of a shifting body is that it heals quickly, but my ribs throbbed and my right leg buckled once under my weight. I hobbled forward to peer cautiously through the archway.

If heaven has a kitchen, I think it must look something like the kitchen of Sophie Rawlins. The sun poured through the wide windows, over wooden sills hidden with lines of ivy plants, potted ferns and clay jars of fresh herbs, and pooled on the aged hardwood floor. Silver pots and pans hung from a rack above the sink, reflecting the light of a clear October morning. The tile counters were immaculate, but the shelves

177

along the east wall were cluttered with papers, books and jars of pens. To a casual observer, the shelves looked like the wake of a tornado, but I suspected that this was a purposeful mess, hiding a complex system of organization of which only Sophie knew the logic. Maddy sat at the broad oak table with her back to the windows, perched on a dictionary to add height to her chair, eating her breakfast with a plastic fork and spoon. Sophie, her head down over the sink, was engrossed in scrubbing a pan.

I limped close to the table and bumped my nose against Maddy's arm.

She patted my head.

My weight stays the same in either body, but it has a tendency to displace itself when I shift, so while I'm only slightly taller than an average man when I stand on two legs, I'm much bigger than an average wolf when I take to four. Gloria had called me a brute lying down, but what would she say if she saw me standing? A wolf that's two hundred and five pounds stands only slightly less than four feet at the shoulder, and from tip of nose to base of tail, I measured six feet in length. Standing by the breakfast table, I easily laid my head on the waxed, pitted surface. I looked between the eggs and Maddy, imploring her for a bite, and with her fork gripped in her chubby hand, she scraped half her breakfast onto the place mat and pushed it towards me with an impish grin.

"There, Logan," she said.

Sophie turned to see the last of the eggs disappear as I licked the place mat clean.

"Oh!" was all she said, startled by my size and pressing her back against the counter top. I was no threat when lying on the living room floor, but now that she'd turned to find a huge carnivore in her kitchen, Sophie's face blanched. She dropped the dishrag into the sink and dried her hands on the thighs of her jeans. "Uh, sit," she said, fighting for composure. "Sit down."

I did as she asked, huffing as the pain squeezed the air from my lungs.

"Well," said Sophie in a hushed voice. "At least you know one command."

Maddy reached out and patted my nose. I licked her hand in gratitude.

"Gloria said you couldn't move."

I bumped the empty plate with my muzzle, sending it a foot or so across the table towards Sophie, and cocked my head to one side.

Staring at the bowl, she said, "If I don't give you more, I'm afraid you'll eat us."

I shook my head.

Sophie paused, unsure if I'd answered her or if my reaction was a curious coincidence. When she decided it was simply a fluke, she opened the refrigerator and took out a carton of fresh eggs. Dirt still clung to the shells. Seven went into a ceramic bowl, and this she placed on the floor at my feet, saying, "I hope you don't mind if these ones are raw."

They disappeared almost instantly. I licked the bowl clean.

"Logan finished."

179

"Thanks, Maddy. I see." Sophie stood at the side of the table, one eye continuously trained on me, and she gestured to her daughter to move away. "Why don't you go upstairs and put your clothes on, Maddy? And then you can come up the barn with me to check on the sheep."

"Okay," she shouted and she scampered into the hall, up the stairs.

Sophie regarded me with more caution than she had last night, and her eyes never left mine as she bent down to retrieve the bowl. "You seem friendly enough," she said, reaching out slowly, cautiously, to lay her hand on my head.

How do you tell someone you have no interest in harming them when your voice has been stolen away? I licked her palm. She tasted of sausages and butter, dish soap and hay.

Amused and reassured, Sophie ran her hand over my forehead. "I can't give you any more or I'll have nothing for dinner," she said. "If Simon doesn't have a poached egg for supper on Mondays, he gets really cranky."

Pausing, she studied my face for a hint of reply, and I regarded her in the same analytical way. Sophie smelt of honey and lavender, of mown grass and morning breezes. A wide scar ran above her right eye and bisected her brow while another marred the cheek below, and I noticed the bridge of her nose was crooked, once broken and poorly set sometime in her distant past. She was not stunning like Gwen. She'd been beautiful once, before domestic life had caught her and claimed her, but no man would call Sophie beautiful now. She was too timorous, too plain, as if she didn't want the world to notice her. When she tore her eyes from mine, there was a cuteness to

180

her movements much like Stella's, but the confidence to turn cuteness into beauty was gone.

I didn't mean to startle you.

I turned and hobbled back to the sitting room, and lay heavily against the side of the couch. My stomach rumbled. The eggs had done little except whet my appetite, but I didn't want to eat these people out of house and home. The dog kibble was sour in my mouth as it filled my stomach, but I forced it down in even, measured bites.

I WOKE FROM A DEAD sleep to the sound of wood scraping against wood. I lay in the middle of the living room, and when I lifted my head to look for its source, a sharp pain skittered through my chest and forced me to collapse back onto the carpet. I whined. The scraping stopped.

Sophie's head appeared from the other side of the couch, close to the hall entrance. "You okay?" she said.

I whined again.

She stood and came to my side, quickly examining the bullet wound. "No infection. But oh, you poor thing." She ran her fingers over my neck. "I didn't mean to wake you. Go back to sleep, puppy."

She vanished behind the furniture again.

Bracing myself, I rose on shaking legs and lurched forward as the scraping sound resumed; now, with my head above the height of the couch, I could see Sophie sitting before an old

181

spinning wheel in the corner of the room, a basket filled with puffy woollen clouds at her side. The wheel dragged against the axle with each revolution. Her narrow hands pulled the strands and separated the fibres, her head was down and she hummed a disjointed tune.

I sat at her side and watched, fascinated.

"You've never seen anyone spin, Logan?" she said absently, plucking more wool from the basket.

No, never.

"If I sell the wool to a manufacturer, I get next to nothing. If I spin it myself, I make a bit more selling it to tourists." She glanced up from her work. "Not quite what I had in mind for my life, I admit, but you've got to make do with what fate gives you, right?"

I'm really not the one to ask that question right now, Soph.

"Lighten up, Logan." She laughed. "You look so concerned." She paused to scratch her fingers behind my ear, and I leaned into her touch, eyes closed in the sheer pleasure of it. Her fingers departed to pluck more wool from the basket and I shook my ears straight as she continued to talk. "I adore animals and, really, they make living in this boring little town bearable, but I have to justify them to Simon somehow, and if the ewes bring in a bit of money, they get to stay." She pushed the pedal and the wheel began its clunking rhythm again.

I can't believe Gwen left me. I should have listened to Hestia. I should have paid more attention. I sighed with great bitterness. *All I saw was her face, Soph. You'd think I'd know better. I mean, me, of all people, should know that appearances are worthless.*

"I got my degree in music theory. I never for a moment thought I'd be a shepherd when I grew up," Sophie continued, deaf to my thoughts.

And now look at me. Reduced to this. I can hear Andre laughing already.

Sophie tipped her head to one side as the wheel jerked, and she snatched another bundle of wool before the one in her hand was swallowed by the spindle. "My mom was off the wall when I moved up here with Simon," she said. "I tried everything to console her, but now she can't even look at a sweater without cursing."

I shouldn't have said a word. I shouldn't have told her. But I knew this was wrong. Truthfully, Soph, I shouldn't have been so blind.

"Still, the lessons keep her from thinking my degree was a complete waste of money. But there's only a few kids in Gilsbury Cross who are interested in the violin, and even less with parents that can afford it."

You teach violin?

The spindle whirled. Sophie's fingers moved in a graceful ballet, long and slender, pinky held at a discreet angle. "But I don't mind the sheep. We used to have goats, but they were a hassle. Always getting out, running away. And the billy stank. They almost drove me crazy."

Soph, you're holding a conversation with a wolf. I'd say they succeeded.

"At least the sheep are happy to be where they are." She cast me a weak smile that held no mirth. I lay my head against her hip.

"You need to go out," she said as a matter of fact, and she slowed the wheel with the palm of her hand. "You've been sleeping for hours. Here I am, rambling on, and you need to go out."

No, I'm quite alright, don't let me interrupt you…

But she was up and walking to the door. "Come on, puppy. We'll go for a stroll around the yard." Sophie held the door open as I hobbled onto the porch, huffing and wheezing for breath, and we walked slowly along the driveway. The two dogs bounded after us, and when the russet bloodhound dared to pounce next to me, I bared my teeth and sent it racing for the garage. Its grey companion retreated just as quickly.

When we reached the end of the driveway, she held her arm aloft and waved. Across the street was Jan, the dark-haired brother, digging a trough between the gravel road and his land. He waved back and thrust his shovel into the dirt before walking towards us, greeting Sophie with a booming hello.

"He is good today, ja?" he said, nodding towards me.

"Yep. He's already walking around," she replied. "And fending off Morgan and Lancelot."

"He is sounding like he got a tractor in his chest." Jan bent forward and ran his calloused palm along my spine. "But clear eyes, ja? Crafty."

"He seems to know a command or two, and he already knows his name," she said. "And he's very patient with Maddy."

"Patient until he get hungry, maybe?"

You insult me, I thought, sitting and sighing heavily.

Sophie smiled and rested back on her heels, arms crossed, regarding me warmly. "I don't think so. He seems trustworthy enough. In fact, Jan, I think he enjoyed watching me spin."

"And Simon? He okay with Simon?"

She shrugged. "Simon was off to school by six this morning. I don't see him all that much these days."

A small current passed between them. Jan lowered his eyes and brushed a wayward pearl of sweat from his brow. "This is good?"

Sophie's smile vanished. Her eyes grew cold, sheltered. "As good as it can be."

"I wanted to say… I been wanting to say… well—" He shifted his weight from foot to foot, nervous, wringing his grimy hands. "I am sorry. Knut said that it was the best thing to do, but some things are not everyone's business."

"There's no need to apologize, Jan," she said. "I would have done the same thing if I'd heard screaming coming from your house. The police were very nice, even when I said there was no reason to press charges."

"Ja, but Simon—"

"Simon and I have our problems, it's true. But don't feel badly for acting out of the goodness of your heart, Jan. I appreciate it."

He paused as he searched for the proper words. "If you need anything, you come to our house," he said, straightening. "Our door is always open."

"Thank you." Sophie patted his forearm to show there were no hard feelings between them. "But I can handle my husband. I knew what I was getting into when I married him." She ran her fingers over my forehead. "Come on, Logan. We'll let Jan get back to work. I've got a whole basket of wool to finish before lunch."

AFTER SHE TRANSFORMED the wool into countless skeins of dimpled yarn, I followed her around the main floor of the house, watching her dust the furniture and vacuum the carpets. When she climbed the stairs to the second level, though, I couldn't follow. My ribs ached just thinking about it. Instead, I continued to wander the first floor, to satiate my curiosity and snoop through their belongings. The square layout of the main floor reminded me of my mother's home, with its turn-of-the-century wainscoting and parquet floors, but the Rawlins had neither the money nor the resources to renovate their house. The fixtures were antiquated, the floors sloped, and small cracks had formed in the plaster ceilings. The main entrance hall faced west; to the right of the door rose the stairway, which doubled as a place to stack boots, shoes, coats and sundry, and to the left was a wide arch between the foyer and the welcoming kitchen. A narrow dining room linked the kitchen to the living room, but it was filled with bookshelves and a hulking china cabinet instead of the traditional table and chairs. I rambled through the living room, past the wood stove in the south east corner, past the spinning wheel and stool, and sniffed at the layers of countless fragrances trapped in the frayed fabric of the old sofa. A second arch joined the living room to the entrance hall again and, under the stairwell, a long corridor connected the main entrance foyer with two rooms in the rear of the house; one, the laundry room, contained an old piano, while the other smelt predominantly of Simon. I assumed this was his office.

I pushed the door open with my nose and crept inside. A corner bookshelf supported a variety of instruments: a concertina, a clarinet, a trumpet, an assortment of drums, and on his desk were piles of papers covered with handwritten music. An open briefcase under the desk contained pens and a standard textbook of Beginners Musical Theory. From what I could discern, Simon was a music teacher at the local high school. A series of books on a low shelf caught my eye, and I pulled one out and flipped it open to see what sort of topics interested him. It proved to be a biography of Glenn Gould. I was turning the page with my damp nose when Sophie stuck her head through the door.

"Oh God! Get out of there," she said. "He'll have a fit if he comes home and finds his office a mess."

It already is a mess, Soph.

"Come on, come on. Out." She shut the door behind me. "Listen, you can wander around all you want, but stay out of Simon's things."

This is how you handle your husband? You avoid him? I followed her into the sitting room. She returned to cleaning the windows, a job that required great care as the panes were cracked and broken. Where the glass was patched with duct tape, the silver surface was decorated with drawings of little flowers or suns or, after careful study, what appeared to be rabbits. Did Sophie draw them, or Madeleine? I sat and studied one for a long time, finding it charming.

THE CLOCK STRUCK FOUR as the door opened and Madeleine burst in, her arms thrown wide and her boots covered in mud. She vaulted onto Sophie, who lay on the couch with a tattered paperback. "Quiet! You'll wake the wolf." She giggled as the little girl peppered her face with kisses.

I'm up, I thought, having been wrenched from a dream about Gwen and the art exhibit.

"Is he better?"

"I think so... No, Maddy, don't—"

I was roughly embraced and I yelped as her arms connected with the bruise. Maddy didn't notice and planted a kiss on my nose.

My heart melted.

The little girl scurried upstairs to grab a book, and as Sophie prepared dinner, Maddy perched on the couch and read a story aloud about a bunny and a bridge. *She's so young to be reading,* I thought, but my amazement was replaced with amusement when I looked over her shoulder and saw that the words on the page were not the same as the ones coming out of her mouth. She was making up the story as she flipped the pages; how could I not adore her?

SIMON CAME HOME LONG after Sophie and Maddy had gone to bed. I heard him shuffle through the front hall, curse when he bumped into the closed door of his office, and the light in the living room flickered on. "Hey, boy," he said to me as he sat and took off his shoes.

He smelt strangely familiar. I couldn't put a finger on it, but I sidled close and sniffed the hem of his pants. Tobacco. Steak and ketchup. Beer.

"As soon as you're better, you're out of the house and into the barn," he said as he tossed his shoes in the corner next to the spinning wheel. Without another word, Simon climbed the stairs in tired paces and batted the light switch. The room was again plunged into darkness. I lay down on the horse blanket and covered my nose with my tail.

This time, when I dreamt, my nightmares were tainted with the scent of burning clothes.

7

"I NEVER SAW IT coming," said Sullivan. He stood and moved to the window, looked down upon the grey city streets. "I should have suspected something, shouldn't I?"

"No one ever does," Caufield replied. "Believe me, buddy, I've been in divorce law for eighteen years, and no one's ever said they expected adultery. I mean, hell! If you expected it, you would've done something about it, right? Gotten a divorce before it reached the breaking point, or signed up for counselling, or—"

But Sullivan shook his head as crossed his arms over his chest and glanced towards the twilight mountains. "No, I should've known. The way Ethan was mysteriously disinterested in Gwen but happy to introduce us; that was out of character for the competitive bastard. And there was the scent on the bed sheets." He turned to the desk, baring his teeth. "That was a slap across my face, and I'd overlooked it in the naïve belief that she spoke the truth, that she really loved me, that she didn't care for anyone but me."

"You aren't the first guy to be betrayed by a girl for his money."

"No, I suppose not," he replied, looking down and away. "But realizing that doesn't make it any easier, Morris. Gwen wanted to know the location of my father's cabin because it was a secluded place to kill me and bury my corpse. She and Ethan had planned my death from the very beginning, waiting for me to reveal where I went each spring and fall. And while neither of them suspected the lycanthropy, they'd waited too long for their opportunity to let that little surprise deter them. Now they had their prize, my money, and I was reduced to eating dog food and sleeping on the floor for the rest of my life."

"But they failed," he said, gesturing at Sullivan as if making an example of him. "Somehow you got back on two feet. Your clothes were burnt, you were trapped; how'd you return?"

"Come on, Morris," Sullivan replied. "You're a lawyer. You know there's a loophole in everything."

SIMON WAS UP AT SIX and out the door by seven, his arms loaded with instruments and papers. After his departure, Sophie took Maddy to the barn to tend to the animals, and as soon as they returned, she made breakfast for the little girl, dressed her in good clothes, washed her clean of the barn's grime, and escorted her to the bus stop. Sophie returned ten minutes later, kicked off her boots at the door, and flopped across the couch to rest before attacking her own chores.

I struggled to my feet and laid my head on the arm of the couch. Her eyes were closed. My breath ruffled her hair.

"What do you want, Logan?" she said, eyes still shut.

I want to watch you spin wool again. That was fascinating, almost hypnotic.

"Hungry?"

Not at all.

She opened her eyes to judge my reaction, but when there was none, she batted my head away and smiled. "Quit staring at me, Logan."

I raised one paw to the arm of the chair in an attempt to return the gesture, but the muscles along the side of my torso didn't appreciate the movement, and I winced as they cramped.

"Poor puppy," she said, and before I knew it, she had taken my paw in her hand and crushed her nose against the pads. "Mmmm... Nothing smells better than a dog's foot."

I looked at her quizzically, and sniffed at my own paw. The aroma of earth and crushed grass lingered there.

You wouldn't be so eager to smell my feet if I'd just come home from a game of racquetball, I thought with a small chuckle.

"Was that a growl or a laugh, Logan?"

Dropping the foot to the ground, I opened my jaws, tongue lolling, in the closest canine approximation of a grin.

"You're the weirdest animal I've ever seen," she said, and parted her lips to say more, but the phone in the kitchen rang. I waited for her to return, but Sophie didn't come back to the sitting room: there was a lawn to mow and bread to bake. She sang to herself while she worked, but spinning would have to wait, and she wailed a rendition of 'Swinging from a Star' that made me want to hide my head under the cushions of the

192

couch. She could play the violin and hit perfect pitch while humming, but she sang like a goose trapped in a dishwasher.

ON THE THIRD DAY, MY bewilderment at my predicament was gone, only to be replaced by searing rage. The thought of Gwen made my fur bristle and my heart race. When Sophie invited me outside for a walk, I took out my fury on the dogs, chasing after them with teeth bared until my damaged torso threatened to explode.

"Look at you," Sophie exclaimed. "Three days and you're feeling better!"

Don't tell Simon.

"I won't tell Simon, though," she continued. "I'd rather have you around the house than tied up in the barn."

I paused, and when she finally stepped beside me, I burrowed my head under her hand to show her this impulse of joy. *Thank you, Soph. Even if you can't understand me, it's nice to pretend.*

AT TWO O'CLOCK, THE doorbell rang.

"Hey! Hi! Come on in!"

The loud, squealing, happy greeting of women filled the house. I raised my head from the blanket, torn out of my nap by their shrill chattering.

"This isn't a wolf, Sophie. It's a grizzly bear!" One of them laughed, and as my eyes focused, I saw two women strolling into the sitting room. The younger one, with smooth dark skin and vast curls of chocolate hair, was thick in the waist with child. She glowed like a streetlamp, and when she squatted beside me, I had the quick terror that she'd drop her baby right there at my feet.

"Whatcha call it?"

"Logan," Sophie replied from the kitchen. "What did you want to drink, Naomi?"

"Ach, just some milk," she said. "What's he eat, when he's not terrorizing the villagers?"

I heard Sophie giggle. "He's got a sweet temperament. Looks aren't everything."

The pregnant woman smiled towards the third woman, who was older than Sophie and Naomi, perhaps in her late thirties or early forties. A shock of grey ran through her auburn hair, the creases at the corners of her eyes deepened when she grinned. "Gloria told me he was the biggest wolf she'd ever seen, but this? Hah! You could fit your head in his mouth."

Sophie set a tray on the coffee table, carrying a plate of lemon wedges, a salt shaker and three shot glasses, as well as a tumbler of milk. Sophie handed Naomi the milk before reaching deep into a cupboard under the bookshelf and withdrawing a hidden bottle of tequila. "He follows me everywhere, even into the fields, and he's been a very well-behaved house guest. He seems to like the sheep."

"Oh, he's just sizing up which one will make the best snack," said Naomi, running her fingers over my neck. "Hey, boy. Betcha you'd love a lamb dinner."

After a week of kibble? I wouldn't complain.

"Here you go, Annie," said Sophie as she handed the older woman a shot glass and took one herself. Both of them picked up a slice of lemon. "No, I honestly think he'd eat the dogs before he touches one of the ewes." Then in my direction, she said, "You hate them, don't you? Poor old Morgan and Lancelot haven't left the garage in two days."

"Territorial?" said Annie.

"No," Sophie replied, pouring out a round of tequila. "I think he knows that the dogs aren't all that bright, and he doesn't want to associate with the great unwashed." A knock upon the door summoned Sophie from the room. When she returned, Gloria followed her and set a sack of cookies on the coffee table.

"How're you today, Mr Wolf?" she asked me, and then said to the other women, "Told ya he was mean-looking, didn't I?"

"Sophie, you're either a brave woman or a fool," said Annie as she sat in the chair farthest from me. "I wouldn't keep an animal like that in my house."

"Pah!" Sophie sat down on the couch behind me. "Until he gives me reason to worry, I'll trust him."

Annie flashed Gloria a look of bewilderment, brows arched and lips pulled down in a disapproving pout. She mouthed the word, "Fool."

"I think he's sweet," said Naomi as she hauled herself to the opposite couch. She took the glass of milk and held it up. "Well, girls? Now that Glo's arrived? To your health."

The shot glasses were emptied.

"My God, Soph, you make this shit yourself?" said Annie after biting her lemon wedge. And then, in a hushed voice, staring at the opposite wall, said, "I think I'm blind."

Laughter filled the room.

"I'd rather have that than this," said Naomi, looking down her nose at her glass of milk. "God, I miss Tequila Tuesday."

"You look great," said Sophie.

"Because she hasn't touched this rotgut crap for eight months," Gloria said, refilling her glass.

"No, really," said Sophie. "I never did the pregnancy thing very well, but Naomi, you look fantastic."

Naomi blushed but said, "I still want this little parasite outta me." She spoke to her stomach. "The free ride's almost over! Hear me? I'm sick of wearing these damn maternity dresses."

Annie hooked her legs over the arm of the chair and reclined. "I'm happy to have that part of my life over with," she said. "Tubes tied. No more worries." She drained her glass. "If he can keep it up, Steve and me are a couple of minks, and thank God for small miracles."

"Which is the small miracle, Ann? Keeping it up, or the plumbing itself?" said Naomi.

"Hey there, chickie, everyone knows that size doesn't matter."

All four of them laughed uproariously.

Do women talk to each other like this? Embarrassed but far more intrigued, I wondered with no small measure of worry that Gwen had discussed me so casually with her female friends. Had my wife been as open with our marriage secrets as these four? Naomi lumbered onto the floor next to me, caressing my ears and leaning against the couch, as she regaled in every hilarious detail how her baby had been conceived. The other three listened attentively, and encouraged her, and dissolved into fits of rollicking mirth. Maybe it was the tequila talking; they giggled and tittered and talked of such raunchy subjects that I wished I could laugh. Worse than drunken sailors, the lot of them.

As if to prove that liquor had nothing to do with it, Naomi refilled her glass of milk from the kitchen and returned to the sitting room. "But girls, I tell ya—" she said, and she waited for the other three to quiet their laughter. "I checked out Ian's hands and feet when I first met him, and believe you me, some things don't lie."

"Oh, c'mon Naomi, that's an old wives' tale," said Sophie.

"Hell! What else are we, girl?" said Ann. "What size are Simon's feet?"

Sophie pursed her lips and lowered one eyebrow. "Fourteen."

"And?" said Naomi, leaning forward.

Sophie blushed and smiled. She held out her hands as one would size a fish.

I caught a glimpse of Gloria blushing too, and wondered if the conversation was too much for the vet to bear, but she refilled her shot glass and took another wedge of lemon.

"Lucky gal," she said. Naomi clutched at her belly as she laughed, and when she'd caught her breath and wiped a small tear from the corner of her eye, she said, "You two thinking of giving Maddy a little brother or sister?"

"I don't know," said Sophie. The smile died on her lips.

"Have another glass, girl," said Annie, pouring out more tequila.

"I heard about last week," said Naomi. "Is everything okay with you two?"

"Fine. No problems," said Sophie, taking up her glass again. She gave a large sigh, but it was easy to see this was only a pause while she considered what to say. Her grey eyes flashed down to the carpet, away from the faces of the other three women. "It was one of those stupid arguments that gets out of hand, y'know? No big deal. I don't even remember what it was about."

Sophie's jasmine scent took on a musky anxious tinge, like a cornered animal. She knocked back the tequila and wiped the droplets from her frowning mouth.

After an awkward pause, Annie said, "Steve and I fight like cats and dogs. Married couples fight. It's all part of getting to know each other better."

Gwen and I never fought. I lowered my head to the ground. *She knew she'd always get her way.*

Naomi fiddled with her empty glass, embarrassed, and Sophie straightened her shoulders, just a fraction, and masked her tone with feigned happiness. "Simon's a good father. No matter how often we scrap, at least I know he loves Maddy."

She grinned. "And he's a size fourteen. How can I possibly complain?"

"Ah, priorities," laughed Gloria, and they all raised their glasses again.

THAT MIDNIGHT, LONG after all had gone to bed, I heard the first hint of howling, faint on the wind. I struggled to my feet and slunk to the front entrance hall, and when I pressed my ear to the door, I recognized a single voice amongst them. My heart hitched in my chest.

With a twist of my head, I easily flipped the dead bolt between my teeth, and rolled the knob open with one shoulder until the latch bolt clicked free. The door swung inwards on squeaking hinges, and I slipped into the cool October night like a phantom, my blood now pounding in my ears. The ache in my chest had been all but forgotten by the sound of wolves singing, by the sound of one voice raised above the others. I ran as far as the edge of the yard, struggling for breath, and closed my eyes to listen.

It was my mother. I'd stake my life on it.

She was miles away, on the other side of the mountain and close to the lake. Her song was full of concern, and I knew she'd found the charred ruins of the cabin and assumed the worst. Bracing my paws on the dewy grass, I threw back my head and answered in a long, wavering note, nothing more than a marker of my position, and prayed the wind would shift to carry my answer further. Backing up a step and lowering my head, I tried again, filling my lungs with damp autumn air until they suffered, lifting my voice to a higher pitch. Now the sound bounced from the side of the barn and carried upwards. Once more, a little louder, and she'd hear me, she'd know I was alive…

"Dammit, you'll wake up the neighbours," said Simon from behind me, as a loop of chain circled my head and pulled tight against my throat. The howl broke into a strangled cough. He gave a forceful yank and towed me after him, his pyjama bottoms dragging in the mud and his bare toes blue from the cold.

I struggled but it was useless. I had no sound left in me.

The door slammed behind us and he locked it with a deft flick of his wrist. Sophie was leaning against the wall at the base of the stairs, a bathrobe around her body. Her eyes were wide, staring at me, and I saw her hands were quivering.

"Did you leave the door open?"

"No. I'm sure I didn't," she said swiftly, shaking her head.

"How'd he get out?"

"I don't know," she replied. "Honest. I know I locked it."

Simon grumbled as he dragged me into the laundry room and tied the opposite end of the leash around the stout leg of the piano. I heard their voices rise into an argument as they ascended the stairs, and when at last their conversation was done, the pleading notes of my mother's cries were gone as well.

PART III

"Banish this loathsome animal shape, return to me the sight of my friends and family, restore Lucius to himself; or if I have offended some power that still pursues me with its savagery and will not be appeased, then last let me die if I may not live."
Apuleius, *Metamorphoses*

1

THE INTERCOM BUZZED. "I'm going home, sir," said Sandra's voice.

Caufield checked his watch and seemed startled at what it told him. "Damn! Of course… I didn't realize—"

"Helen called. I told her you were in a meeting."

"Thanks, Sandra," he said. "Look at the time."

Her dispassionate drone continued. "I'll lock the office on my way out. I left a brief for tomorrow's first client on my desk." The intercom beeped and fell silent.

"I'll come back," said Sullivan, rising to his feet. "You need to get home."

But Caufield pursed his lips and reclined. "Sit down. I don't have to be anywhere." He reached into the briefcase at the base of the desk and withdrew a silver flask. "Pass over your cup, Dan. You aren't going anywhere till you've told me the rest of your story."

"And who's blackmailing you?"

"I've seen two wars and been through one hell of a marriage. I've lived in eight cities, travelled through twenty countries and take a cruise to relax every May. Yet, for all I've seen and done," he said, pouring amber liquid into their mugs. "I've never met anyone as convincing as you."

"I've graduated from crazy to convincing now, have I?"

"So shoot me. I'm curious."

Sullivan sloshed the contents of the mug back and forth. "Poor choice of a saying, all things considered."

"I don't mean anything by it," he laughed. "You drink bourbon? That's the best in the city, right there."

"Vancouver isn't known for its bourbon."

"So it's not the best in the world. It's still good stuff."

Sullivan peered into the cup. "I'm not one for drinking." He glanced at Caufield's stony expression. "But, hell, I don't want to waste it."

"That's my boy." Caufield knocked the contents of his cup back and refreshed it from the flask. "So you were rescued by your mother."

"No, I never saw her," he replied. "And why would my mother rescue me? My union with Gwen insulted her and, on my maternal side, once you turn your back on your family, you're on your own."

"Bit harsh, isn't it?"

Sullivan shrugged. "Pack rules. In every group there's an alpha male and an alpha female, and the woman leads the family and makes the rules. You don't question them."

"Wolf packs aren't led by the male?"

Shaking his head, Sullivan said, "All the male does is make sure everyone's happy. Like the host at a party, collecting concerns and bringing them to the alpha female, acting as a mediator in debates. He doesn't make decisions or lead in any manner. In fact, if he chooses a side or questions the female's authority, he's expelled from the pack and forced to fend for himself."

"Seriously?"

"Most documentaries have it all wrong. Wolves are not a patriarchal society. The males look as though they're leading, but in truth they're only carrying out the orders of the females."

"You rebelled against Eve's opinions."

"So now I'm alone."

Caufield grunted. "That's not fair, is it? I mean, she's your mother—"

"Not in any human sense," said Sullivan. "If my father was still alive he might have stood up for me, pleaded my case with her. But Mom gave up her life on two legs. 'Fair' is a human concept, Morris. For a wolf, the hierarchy of the pack is a matter of survival and not to be disrespected. When she left us, it meant I was on my own."

"Still." Caufield shook his head, trying to understand. "She was concerned. You said so yourself."

"But I'm an adult and an outsider," Sullivan said. "Plain and simple."

"Don't you miss her? Don't you wonder if she's doing okay?"

"How many people stick their ageing parents in retirement homes and only call on Christmas?" he asked, taking a swig of bourbon. "My mother is free to do whatever she wants and go wherever she wishes. I don't worry and I don't miss her."

But Sullivan's mouth pulled down a fraction and small creases appeared at the corners of his eyes; he fidgeted in his chair as he drained the rest of the bourbon from his mug. Caufield thought of his own mother, whiling away her final years in a beachside condo in Florida, and silently resolved to give her a quick phone call as soon as he got home.

GLORIA DROPPED OFF her youngest daughter, Elsie, for violin lessons on Thursday afternoon. The scampering of young feet broke the afternoon peace, and as Elsie vanished into the music room, Gloria craned her neck over the threshold. "Do you mind if I stay? See how Logan is doing?" she said at the door.

"Are you going to charge me for a visit?" said Sophie with a wry grin.

"Naw, I'm just curious," said Gloria.

"Come on in, then. He's doing fine."

They found me lying under the kitchen table, depressed and melancholy.

"Logan," called Sophie, and I glanced sideways at her, uninterested. "Come here, Logan. Be good. You remember Glo, don't you?"

"You collared him?" Gloria said, as Sophie crouched low and wrapped one hand around the slip chain, yanking it until I slunk from under the table.

"We had to secure him last night," she replied. "He was howling at the moon in the middle of the backyard."

"Oh, Sophie… not a choke chain," said Gloria, her words low with disapproval. "You know what I think of those."

"I know they're terrible," she said helplessly. "But we tried using one of Morgan's old buckle collars, and when we weren't looking, he undid it. He even managed to get the choke chain off until Simon replaced the end ring with a larger washer."

"Really?" She was looking in my ears, feeling the way my ribs had knit back together, examining the stitches. "These can come out. I've never seen anything heal up so fast." She rocked back on her heels, hands on her knees, to look up at Sophie. "You're serious? He undoes buckles?"

"And he unlocks doors, and he turns on the faucet in the bathtub instead of drinking from the toilet like the dogs."

"Amazing."

"You're telling me," said Sophie. The first squeals of Elsie's violin pierced the still of the afternoon. "I'd heard wolves were more intelligent than dogs, but he's a freaking genius."

I grunted in disdain and embarrassment. The dogs weren't submitted to the humiliation of wearing a heavy chain around their throats. Each time I moved, the modified end banged against my sternum to remind me that I was collared. I had tried without success to wriggle it over my head, and accomplished nothing more than snaring my feet and crushing my ears. *It's not enough,* I thought indignantly as Sophie untangled me, *that my wife wants me dead and my best friend set me up. I have to be shackled too.*

As Gloria tucked her fingers under the collar to ensure there was room for me to breathe, I implored her with mournful eyes to take it off. She didn't notice.

"I'm going to start Elsie's lesson," said Sophie, wiping her hands on a rag at the end of the counter. "If you want to stay, help yourself to cookies and tea, Glo."

"Thanks, sugar pie," she said.

Sophie disappeared, and I heard her voice in the next room grow fainter as she closed the doors behind her. "Right, Elsie. Let's hear those scales from last week."

Gloria searched through her purse and brought out a pair of reading glasses, and she studied the stitches with the wire frames perched on the end of her hawkish nose. "Healing nicely, Mr Wolf," she said, dipping her fingers into her purse and withdrawing the tiny brass scissors. "Now, are you going to bite me if I pull these stitches out?"

I collapsed in a heap at her feet, positioned in such a manner that the kitchen light fell straight upon the injury.

When she was finished she held a scrap of paper towel to the wound to dab up the few spots of blood. "There you go, Logan. Done. Good boy."

The creak of the door caught my attention, and through the archway I caught scent of Simon entering the house by way of the sitting room doors. "Hello," said Gloria as he became visible through the archway, his hands piled with books and papers, an old clarinet case balanced under his left arm. He dumped the papers on the sofa in the sitting room and leaned against the passage that joined the rooms.

"What are you doing here?"

"Elsie's having her violin lesson."

"Sophie says she's doing well for twelve years old."

Gloria rocked her weight back on her heels and, as she stood, the bones of her spine clicked and popped. "She really adores it. Martin hated piano, but I'm thinking, if I'd made him play the violin, he might have kept up with music."

"He doesn't strike me as the kind of boy who enjoys the arts, no matter what instrument he's playing." Simon laughed, and he opened the fridge and drank straight from the milk jug. "How's he doing?" he said after swallowing, nodding in my direction.

"Fine," she said, thumping her hand on my rump as she pulled herself to her feet. "The stitches are out; his ribs are almost back to normal; there's still some bruising. Give him another week, and I say he'll be as good as new. I've never seen anything heal up so quick."

"Sophie told you about the buckles?"

"If anyone else was doing the telling, I'd accuse them of lying."

Simon shook his head. "The other dogs aren't half as bright. I don't know much about wolves, but sometimes I catch him listening to us, and I swear he understands every word we're saying."

"So," she said with a roguish glint in her eye. "We better watch what we say."

"Right," said Simon, grinning. "Good to see you, Glo. Glad to hear Elsie's enjoying the violin." He put the milk back in the fridge and closed the door, and sauntered back into the sitting room to collect his books.

I LAY ON THE FLOOR at the end of the couch and listened to Madeleine's nightly rendition of *Juniper Bunny*. Maddy curled up in the nest of Sophie's lap, the book laid out before her. Every few moments, the soft flip of well-worn pages interrupted Sophie's voice, and her bare foot rested on my back, lazily moving back and forth to the rhythm of the poem.

"Hop hop hop past the wild dark wood

Hop hop hop by the rickety bridge

Up through the hills and down to the field

Here comes the Hopping Brigade!"

And then, Sophie's voice, asking questions. "Where's Juniper Bunny?"

"There," said Madeleine, pointing to the book.

"Do you see the town? Which one is the church spire?"

"This one."

Their voices were nothing but a pleasing murmur to the simmering thoughts in my head.

I wanted revenge. I wanted to tear Gwen's heart out and eat it, still beating, and then I wanted to rip Ethan to pieces and piss on his corpse. I wanted to see them tremble and cower in fear. I wanted them to know how much they hurt me, but I didn't care for any apology other than the screaming and crying that would come with the knowledge that they were going to die. I licked my paws and pulled once more at the collar and imagined the taste of their pulsing blood between my teeth. The lilting tones of *Juniper Bunny* and the caress of Sophie's foot didn't soothe me. *They will pay for this,* I thought over and over again. *I don't know how, but they will pay.*

"Okay, time for bed," said Sophie, shutting the book with a puff of air. "Eight o'clock."

"I'm not tired."

"Oh, yes you are," she replied. "Look at that! Another yawn. C'mon, off we go."

I heard Madeleine slip off the couch, and I felt her arms encircle my neck before I had a chance to get to my feet. "Good night, Logan."

In reply, I bumped my cheek against hers.

Sophie ushered her down the hall and up the stairs, and before she could return, Simon appeared from his office. He collapsed on the sofa, hands folded in his lap, rolling his foot over the edge of the coffee table.

"Finished with your papers?" she said when she returned, pushing her wayward hair from her eyes.

"Almost. Maddy in bed?"

Sophie nodded and sprawled next to him. "I had three lessons today." She pressed her palm to her head. "Leslie's having some trouble with her fingering and I don't think Dawn will last another year, but Elsie's really good. I'm thinking of entering her in a competition this season."

"Glo would be thrilled."

"We have to find something new for Maddy to read. That Juniper Bunny story is driving me crazy."

"She's already got a ton of books. It's the only one she likes."

"Maybe if you read one of the others to her—"

211

Simon rubbed his palm over his face. "I just don't have time to read to her. Not until I've finished these damn reports."

"You get home so late now," she said. "I never see you anymore."

"It's the jazz choir. They're a group of little monsters. They're sucking the life out of me."

What kind of revenge could I hope to do? I was stuck here. The city was a formidable barrier for a wolf in my position, and there was no way for me to return without risking my freedom and my life. Somewhere in the urban sprawl they were spending my money and living in my house and driving my car, and for the simple fact that I walked on four legs instead of two, I couldn't come near them by fifty miles. I had the brief impulse to phone them, but that was laughable. Prank calls. Huffing and puffing on the other end of the line, threatening to blow the receiver down.

I was utterly powerless.

A distinct silence filled the room. Lying on my side with my eyes closed, trying to determine a method of exacting my revenge, I hadn't noticed the end of their conversation. A flutter of cloth touched my back. I rose to my stomach, surprised. Sophie's shirt? I looked up to see a tangle of naked limbs hanging off the edge of the couch, with various articles of clothing pushed up or abandoned.

Sex is a staple in movies and books, but I'd never seen real people ravaging each other only a few feet away, enjoying themselves without a care in the world. I sat up, entranced. They didn't care at all that I was here. Sophie, her legs astride Simon's hips, gripped the arm of the sofa and arched her body to meet his thrusts, and when she laid her breasts against his chest, he bit at her shoulders and hurtled against her.

At length, Simon looked up, and he smirked. "Hey, we have an audience."

Under all those flannel shirts and baggy pairs of jeans, Sophie had a fantastic body.

"Hey, Logan," she said, patting my head. "Go into the laundry room."

I sat.

"He's normally good with commands," she said.

"Can you blame him?" Simon laughed. "Hell, I'd want to sit through this show too."

Sophie batted him in the shoulder and laughed, and then pulled herself off of his body. "Come on, Logan," she said, grabbing the chain around my throat. "You don't get to watch if you're going to look at me like that."

Could I help it? She was radiant. Gwen may be fair of face, but she was positively anorexic compared to Sophie's curves, and at Sophie's slightest encouragement, I followed after her happily. She swayed with each step, and the scent of sex on her skin made me crave her like a landlocked sailor thirsting for the sea. I followed her into the laundry room, panting slightly, wondering who had turned up the thermostat.

"Here you go," she said, releasing her grip on the collar. I brushed against her leg and, closing my eyes, breathed in the sweet smell of her sweat. The touch of her hip against my shoulder spawned a flutter in my veins and a pulsing between my legs.

Then she was gone, closing the laundry room door.

Dammit!

I pressed my shoulder to the doorknob and twisted it with the friction of my skin against the brass, budging it a fraction, but when the latch clicked the door didn't open. There was a hook and eye on the outside of the door, and Sophie had flicked it closed as she returned to the sofa.

Who puts a lock on the outside of a room? Through the wall I could hear them coming to climax and it drove me insane, listening to her gasping his name, hearing the springs of the couch squeaking in time to their bodies. I paced back and forth with my head slung low, feeling denied what little voyeuristic joy this life afforded me.

"WAIT A MINUTE, WAIT a goddamn minute—" Caufield said, pitching forward over his desk. "Don't tell me you got a thing for Sophie Rawlins?"

"Maybe," said Sullivan with a pleased grin.

At this, Caufield tipped back his head and laughed.

BUT BY THE TIME Sophie returned, flushed and tired, I'd talked myself out of my resentment. She was married, a mother to a little girl, while I was a smelly beast that had come limping out of the wilderness, mute as a log and, as far as she was concerned, only slightly smarter than the hounds cowering in the garage. The rancour I felt mellowed into a consuming misery. When the lock clicked and the door to the hall opened, Sophie opened it to find me curled in the corner with my paws over my nose.

"Poor Logan," she said, scratching behind my ears. She was wearing Simon's sweater and nothing else, and I tried very hard to refrain from looking at the delicious naked shadows between her legs. "Do you want something to eat?"

I'd rather have a night alone in your company, but I guess, under the circumstances, that's a little too much to ask.

I rose, shook from my nose to my tail, and followed her into the kitchen.

"We have any more milk?" said Simon as he looked in the fridge, naked and glistening with perspiration.

"Bottom shelf, behind the orange juice."

"Ah, right. I see it."

He had an awful appearance, paunchy and soft in all the wrong places. Sophie had hid her curves well and, apparently, so had Simon. I regarded him with haughty contempt. A single disbelieving glance at his crotch made me want desperately to ask if he'd been ill as a child, and I cast a jealous glance at Sophie. *This pathetic bit of flesh? Come on, Soph. That can't be all you were screaming about.*

"I thought I'd make Logan and I some pancakes. You want some?"

Simon cast an amused smirk at me, but his eyes were flinty. "Oh, he gets pancakes now, does he?"

The kitchen chilled.

"He doesn't have to." There was a tremor in her voice.

"I don't care," he replied, shrugging one shoulder. "You can make whatever you want."

The phone rang as the first portions of batter sizzled in the pan. Simon looked at his watch before picking up the receiver.

"Hello?"

Sophie prepared the food and I sat at her side, watching her face. Her hair fell across her eyes and she pushed it back with one finger, lost in thought, and I caught a hint of desolation in her features. When she flipped the hot pancakes from the skillet onto a plate, her eyes focused on me.

"What?" she asked.

I pushed against her leg.

"Do you need to go out?"

I rubbed my cheek against her elbow.

"Why're you being so cute, Logan? I'm already making you something to eat."

Simon's voice rose in volume and he laid his hand over the receiver. "It's Glo."

"Kind of late for her to be phoning, isn't it?"

"She's found Logan's owner."

My ears pricked up.

"How?" said Sophie in surprise, dishing half of the pancakes into the aluminum mixing bowl and drizzling maple syrup over them.

"She posted a notice to other vet clinics in the area, looking for information on the tattoo, and his owner called her office tonight. Just a second." He went back to the phone conversation.

"Well, Logan," said Sophie, bending over to place the bowl on the floor and exposing a fraction of her beautiful cleavage. "It looks like you're going home soon."

The phone clicked back into its cradle. "You'll never believe this, Sophie. There's a reward," he said, his eyes gleaming. "Ten thousand dollars."

"You've got to be joking," she said.

Mom heard me! I thought with joy, and I took a few bites of pancakes. *We'll figure out how to get my body back. Andre will know some trick or ambiguity in this stupid curse…*

"No, not a joke. His owner was hiking up here last weekend with her fiancé and they lost him, and she's been looking for him ever since. She was relieved to hear he was still alive." Simon grabbed his pants from the side of the sofa and pulled them on. "Can you believe it?" he yelled from the living room. "Ten thousand dollars!"

I choked on my food. *Fiancé?*

"That's fantastic," she said. "When's she coming to get him?"

"Glo said she's stuck in the city with some business, but she can drive up next week to pick him up."

Sophie glanced quickly at me. "How do we know that she's his legitimate owner?"

"Glo gave me her number. You can call and talk to her yourself, if you want."

"Yes, I do," she said. "I don't want to hand him over to the first stranger that shows an interest."

"As far as I'm concerned, for ten thousand bucks, any stranger can have him."

Sophie scowled in his direction. "He got that bullet wound from someone."

"No one's going to pay money just to shoot him again," Simon replied. "Martin said the pelt was worth a small fortune—"

"Oh, don't tell me you're listening to that little bastard." A hearty laugh followed this statement.

Sophie crouched down and wrapped her arms around my neck, and gave me a crushing hug. Maybe sex was out of the question, but I couldn't help wag my tail with those fabulous breasts pressed against my side. "I just don't want to give him up to the wrong person," she said as Simon returned to the kitchen. And with a smile, she added, "Besides, don't you want me to tell her who to make the cheque out to?"

"Here." Simon pinned the scrap of paper to the board next to the phone. "Give her a call. It's only nine-fifteen—it isn't too late." He grabbed a bag of raisins from the cupboard and sauntered back into the sitting room, and I heard the television come to life.

Sophie looked at the number and yanked it from the wall.

She took the receiver and dialled. It rang, and her eyes ranged over the message board until an answer forced her to focus her attention.

"Hi, this is Sophie Rawlins of Gilsbury Cross—yes, hi. I just got the call from Dr Gloria Rutledge."

I crept closer, staring up at her.

"We found him in our barn last weekend. He's yours?" She leaned against the wall, swinging the coiled cord back and forth absently. "No, I didn't think he was wild. He's far too friendly." She leaned against the counter and crossed her bare ankles, stifling a yawn with the back of one hand.

I listened, but the noise of the television interfered with my ability to hear the other end of the conversation. I yapped, low in my throat, desperate for an identity.

"What did you say his name is?" And she chuckled. "We've been calling him Logan for the last week... Why am I phoning?" She sounded taken aback. "Well, I hope you can understand that I'd like to ask you a few questions before we hand him over to you."

I saw a look of agitation cross her features.

"No, I'm not accusing you of anything, and I'm well aware of the reward."

She listened, and her face flushed.

"If you have no time to talk now, would you mind meeting with me? I don't mind driving down to Vancouver... No, I'm not accusing you. I already said that. But I've grown fond of him, and I don't want to give him to the wrong person."

And I heard the shouting on the other end of the phone. The voice was unmistakable.

"There's no need to be rude, Ms Herve. Do you want your wolf back or not?"

A pause on the other end of the phone was quickly followed by the buzzing of her reply.

"I'll see you on Saturday, then. Yes, I can find it. I know the city well." She wrote down an address above the phone number, and when I peered more closely, I saw that both belonged to Ethan. "Yes, that sounds fine. Right. Goodnight." She slammed down the receiver.

"Well," said Sophie as she turned to face me. "It seems your owner is desperate to have you back, Daniel."

At the sound of my real name, a shiver scuttled down my spine.

"How'd it go?" shouted Simon from the next room.

"What a freak show," said Sophie. "Crikey! I'm heading down on Saturday to meet her."

"You're going to meet her?"

I followed Sophie into the living room, eager to listen.

"She's awful! I don't know if I want to give Logan... Daniel... up to her."

"But it's ten thousand dollars, Soph."

She sat next to him on the couch, plucking her clothes from the floor. "Owner or not, I wouldn't be surprised if she's the one who shot him."

"Not our business if she did."

"Simon!"

He smiled at the rise from her. "You talked to her for, what, thirty seconds? She can't have been that bad."

"I think she's mad as a hatter."

He faced the screen again. "It isn't our problem and Logan isn't ours to keep. 'Nuff said."

"Still," she said, snuggling against him. "I'm going to drive down to the city on Saturday and meet her and her fiancé for lunch, and just make sure they're legit."

Her fiancé. I growled.

"Sounds like Logan doesn't want you to go," said Simon.

"She said his name's Daniel," Sophie replied. "And he's a rare breed of wolf, an endangered pureblood Himalayan imported from Nepal; that's why he's tattooed and why he's bigger than any of the wolves around here."

"And why there's a reward."

I sat at Sophie's feet and laid my head on her knee. She scrubbed her hand over my head.

"Why'd they call him 'Daniel'?" said Simon. "Dumb name for a dog."

"I didn't ask," she replied. "I barely had enough time to get their address before she hung up on me."

Simon pulled her away from me and hugged her close. "So you're going on Saturday then? Abandoning me for the day?"

"I'll go first thing in the morning, and I'll be home by dinner."

He stared at the television screen, scowling. "I'd planned to fix the fences in the back pasture this weekend, Sophie, and I can't do that if Maddy's underfoot."

"Maybe we could get Naomi and Ian to look after Maddy while you're working," she said. And before he could argue, she added, "I'll phone them in the morning. I'm sure they won't mind. It'll give them a little bit of practice before the baby comes."

They spooned together on the couch and watched the evening news, and I paced back and forth between the kitchen and the hall, thinking. At last I vaulted up the stairs and made my way to Madeleine's darkened bedroom, where the sound of the television was faint, and crept inside. It was small and rectangular with a single window that looked towards the woods, and Maddy's bed was pushed underneath it. I drew close and heard her breathing.

"Hi Logan," she said, slurring her sleepy words together.

I wriggled my muzzle under her hand. Gwen was coming to fetch me. *Do I leave and head north?* The stitches were out but my chest pounded if I ran too far; even climbing the stairs had made me dizzy. Madeleine moved to the opposite side of her bed and she patted the mattress with her hand, so I accepted her offer and lay down on my stomach beside her, looking at the sky through the open window. *I could head back to the ruins of the cabin, try to find my mother's tracks and follow.*

But if Gwen was coming here, this might be an opportunity to exact my revenge, whatever it might be. Would Ethan come too? Surely they didn't think I'd willingly leave with them. They'd be ready to slaughter me at the first chance.

The centre of my torso ached.

She was living with him. Less than two weeks, and I was nothing but a memory. She was already referring to Ethan as her fiancé.

I looked at Madeleine, her round face a milky blue in the darkness. Her eyes were closed, and her dark lashes created

222

perfect crescents. I found I'd grown rather fond of her, and I wasn't willing to leave quite yet, especially if I could never have my other body returned.

She flopped her hand over my back, connecting with a lingering bruise and eliciting little shards of pain, but I didn't flinch. The beautiful Sophie, the tolerable Simon, the charming Madeleine. If I could never be a man again, I supposed there were worse fates than this.

Listen to me. I'm giving up.

I looked again at Madeleine, her expression one of complete tranquillity.

But I don't know what else to do.

I closed my eyes and replayed the awful moments of watching my clothes burn, and Maddy could feel my body tremble under her arm with quiet sobbing. She curled closer, half asleep, unaware of the comfort she gave me with such a small gesture.

2

"I DON'T WANT YOU taking him out without a leash, Soph," said Simon at the breakfast table. "He's worth way too much to risk him bolting into the hills."

"What good is a leash going to do?" she said, cutting up a sausage into bite-sized chunks for Madeleine. "If he wanted, he could probably drag me from here to Maple Lake and back."

"Then leave him inside and clean up whatever mess he makes. I don't want to risk losing him."

Losing ten thousand dollars, you mean. I growled low and deep in my chest.

"But he opens doors, Simon. Locked ones. I can't keep him in if he doesn't want to stay in."

"Have you actually seen him open a door? Of course not, Soph, because he can't. That's stupid." Simon finished the last of his breakfast and pushed his plate away. "You haven't been closing and locking them properly, that's all."

I sat alongside Maddy and waited for her to drop a bit of sausage off of her plate. This was a game we'd devised, she and I. As soon as Sophie's back was turned, that morsel would be mine, but until then, we did nothing to merit punishment. We were angels. Sophie watched us with suspicion, tempered with humour.

"I know he can," she replied, taking the empty juice vessel and walking to the sink. "I've locked the door, double-checked it, and the next thing I know, he's in the front yard."

Her back was turned. The sausage flicked onto the place mat. Gulp! Gone.

Simon, who caught a flicker of movement out of the corner of his eye, narrowed his gaze. "Maddy, don't feed him from the table."

"I just thought you could take him with you when you fix the fencing on Saturday, that's all," Sophie said as she returned to the table with the container refilled. "Glo said his ribs are almost healed, but he's still out of breath when he climbs the stairs. I thought a bit of fresh air would be good for him."

"I cracked a rib once when I was rock climbing and it took weeks to heal," said Simon. "He's probably not as good as Gloria thinks. He's probably putting on a brave face, but he's in pain and he can't tell us."

"Look at that face," she said, gesturing towards me. "That's not pain."

I licked the grease from my lips.

"Maddy, I told you, no feeding from the table," said Simon.

The little girl nodded, the flipped ends of her brown hair bouncing up and down.

"Do what your father says," said Sophie. "And I don't want to find him in your bed again tomorrow. No animals in the bedrooms." She waggled her finger.

"He just came in on his own," said Maddy.

"Alright then," Sophie replied, and jabbed the finger in my direction. "No sleeping on the bed. Understand?"

225

"Stick a leash on him and take him to the barn and back," said Simon. "And if he's not too winded, maybe I'll take him with me tomorrow. But it depends on him. If I'm mending fences, I don't want to be distracted." He straightened his tie. "Can Ian and Naomi take Maddy tomorrow?"

"Only for a bit of the day," she said. "They'll drop her off back here at two."

He shrugged. "That's okay. It'll allow me to get most of the work done in the morning, at least."

"I thought I'd leave around seven and be back by five."

"Sounds good."

She stood, cleared the plates and cleaned the kitchen. Simon bundled his papers and instruments into his old sedan and tore out of the driveway in a roar of gravel. I watched him leave from the windows that flanked the front door, and suppressed a shudder when Sophie clipped a frayed leash to the end of the choke chain. "Come on, Logan. Up to the barn."

I sat heavily in the foyer of the house.

Sophie tugged again. "Come on."

But I continued to sit. I was a veritable horse compared to her. She could tug all she wanted and never budge me by strength alone.

"Fine, then," she said, clasping both sides of my head and staring into my eyes with an adorable snarl. "You don't go."

As soon as she unhitched the metal clasp, I stood expectantly at the side of the door.

Sophie rolled her eyes, motioned towards me with the end of the leash, and I sat again.

"So, what? You won't go if you wear the leash?"

Nope.

"Don't be difficult, Logan. Daniel. Whichever name you prefer."

I leapt up, put my front paws against the front door and flipped the dead bolt with my teeth, and with my shoulder against the knob, rolled past until it sprang open. I nudged the door open with my nose. As I stood on the threshold, I watched her and waited.

"Jesus! Sometimes you actually scare me, you know that?" she said, pulling on her boots and shrugging a shapeless denim jacket over arms, dropping the leash in a heap by the rest of the shoes. "No wonder that horrible woman wants you back. You can probably crack safes and decipher government codes too."

I never went farther than ten paces from her side. Madeleine scampered around the base of an apple tree in the backyard and finally crawled into the rope swing hanging from a low branch, but Sophie and I continued past the chicken coop, past the bowers of raspberry canes, to the gate of the paddock. Sophie took one look back to ensure Maddy was safe before she stepped into the cool, dim interior of the barn. Fissures of sunlight seeped through the wooden panels and the cement foundation was patterned with eggshell cracks, but the structural posts that held up the roof and hayloft seemed safe and secure. The building smelt thickly of manure and alfalfa.

"Good morning, ladies," she said, pushing two of the sheep aside as she poured a pail of grain into the trough. "Galahad, let Lamerocke have a bite of oats. Out you go, get on." She threw wide the back doors to the pasture and stood back as the ewes meandered into the field. "Hurry on, Parsifal, Gorlagon." She swatted the last on its rump to hurry its pace.

I watched the sheep stumble from the rear of the barn. *Those are all medieval characters,* I thought, and glanced up at Sophie. *I have three books at home that you'd love. One's a collection of French folktales from 1817, with these amazing illustrations…*

My thoughts trailed away. Gwen had probably sold them by now. Even she'd recognize their worth.

I grumbled under my breath as I followed her out to the water trough on the opposite end of the pasture. *I'd love to sit and talk with you, Sophie. I want to know what books you read and what artists you like. I want to know how you found your way here, to this little town, and why you married Simon.* I pressed my forehead against her palm. She patted it absently as she surveyed the fencing. *You have no idea how much I want to talk, Soph.*

"That was quite the sigh, puppy," she said over her shoulder. "Is the state of the world getting you down?"

I doubt you need me to talk, Soph. You seem to have a talent for holding a one-sided conversation.

The trough had once been a gleaming claw foot bathtub but now boasted just three legs and a crack down one side. The garden hose, with its constant trickle of water, had fallen from the stained tub during the night, and Sophie replaced it and lodged it on the bottom with a rock. The sheep trailed us in a close pack as we walked the boundary of the pasture, keeping a constant distance, stopping here and there to nibble on tufts of grass. They knew this woman equalled food, but she circled the field every morning to ensure the fences were secure before

228

leaving them here for the day, and she paid them little attention now that they had been turned out to pasture.

Our route brought us to the riverside where I had dragged myself from the water. I paused for a moment and listened, hoping in desperation to hear my mother's voice again, but there was nothing except the rushing of the current.

"Come on, Logan," she said then, seeing my interest, looked towards the bend in the river. "What is it?"

I miss Gwen, Sophie. I hate her and miss her at the same time. I gave her my heart and she smashed it into a thousand pieces.

Her hand rested on the crown of my head. "It's the bear, isn't it? Knut saw it on the edge of their pasture last week." She shuddered. "Some of the guys are organizing a hunt; it's getting too close for comfort."

The bear hasn't returned. The scent is too old.

"I don't want to stay out here a minute more. It's too dangerous."

I'd protect you, I thought with a small hint of glee, and the longing for Gwen dissipated, if only for a moment.

Did Sophie hear my thoughts? She cast me a knowing smile. "But you'd scare him off, wouldn't you?"

I bared my teeth and bristled, bracing my feet and lowering my head playfully, and this made her laugh.

"Yeah, exactly," she said. "Come on, puppy. I'll make us lunch." As we returned across the shorn autumn fields, she chattered about bears and sheep. She told me they'd lost a lamb to coyotes last year, and she'd hoped they'd have more in the coming spring. She spoke easily, sweetly, never once faltering

229

into an awkward pause. I listened and walked close beside her, delighting in her undivided company.

The sound of a car in the drive interrupted her stories. The hounds had slunk into the garage when I left the house, but now they bounded towards the rusted Pinto, throwing their heads back and baying.

"Hi Ian," Sophie shouted, and the sheep scattered. She waved her hand over her head.

The driver waved back. He threw the vehicle into park, slammed the car door closed, and jogged towards the pasture.

"Hey, Sophie! I thought I'd drop by on my way into town," he yelled as he neared us. His round, boyish face and scruffy brown hair made him look much younger than Sophie, and even though he had dressed in a t-shirt and jeans, he didn't seem to notice the cold snap in the air. He slowed down when he saw me. His scent, which reminded me of wood chips and raked leaves, took a faint turn towards fear. "Holy crow, Soph… this is what Naomi's told me about? The wolf that you found in your barn?"

"Yep," said Sophie. She tousled my ears. "I'm heading to meet his owner tomorrow."

He stared through the wire fence with wide, unblinking eyes. I wouldn't have been surprised if he'd picked up a stick to poke me through the bars. "Look at them fangs," said Ian.

He still smelt scared, so I kept Sophie between us. Maybe with her as a barrier, he'd relax a little.

"And he's modest too," Sophie said, mistaking my reticence for shyness. "You don't have to hide behind me, Logan. Ian won't do anything to you."

230

Ian glanced towards the apple tree where Maddy swung in a wide arc on the rope swing. She had flung her head back, watching the sky, as her feet scuffed in the dirt. "You aren't scared with him around Madeleine?" he asked.

"He hasn't done anything to warrant it," said Sophie. "Look, thanks a bunch for taking Maddy for a few hours tomorrow, Ian. I know Simon's been wanting to replace this old fencing for weeks, and he'll be happy to have some time to himself."

"We'd love to have her, Sophie, but that's what I dropped by about. It seems Naomi has an appointment with her obstetrician and she wants me to drive her home afterwards, but they needed to reschedule, so we can only look after Maddy until twelve. Is that going to be a big hassle?"

"I don't think so," said Sophie, leaning against the fence post. "Simon will be here all day. I'll leave the door open and you can drop her off."

"Thanks a million," said Ian. "Soph, you're a doll."

"You're doing us a favour. I'm almost done with the sheep. Would you like to stay for tea?"

"No, can't. Got to run," he said. "When Naomi wants pickled onions, she wants them *now*."

"I'll tell Simon about tomorrow."

Ian waved back as he raced back to his car, his long legs carrying him in jouncing steps.

231

BUT, BY DINNER, SHE'D dismissed the message from her mind. They put Maddy to bed and locked me in the laundry room again, but let me out and retired to their bedroom an hour later, and I thought no more of it.

I watched Sophie climb into her rusted Dodge and leave at seven. Not long afterwards, Maddy jumped down the front steps and into Ian's car with a merry wave to her father. The house seemed unnaturally quiet and still with the two of them gone.

He ate with his head bent low over his plate, watching me devour my own breakfast of eggs and kibble. Unlike Sophie, Simon said nothing to me, and kept all of his thoughts to himself.

I didn't mind. I licked the bowl clean and waited for him to finish his own eggs and toast. The day would pass quickly enough. We'd have a bite to eat, fix the fences, and I'd keep a wary ear open for Maddy's early return. No problem.

When he was done, Simon dumped his plate in the sink of water and beckoned. "Come on. Up to the barn."

Already? Man, you're organized. It took Sophie an hour to visit the sheep yesterday. She did the dishes, called her mother, spent fifteen minutes looking for a useless leash. I followed after with tail held high. *Don't get me wrong, Simon. I like Sophie, but she's got a mind like a sieve and easily distracted. Did you know she talks to her sheep?*

He had a brisk pace and purposeful stride, but I loped alongside him and kept my nose to the air, detecting the joyful scent of pine sap on the morning breeze. Snow dusted the higher elevations and last night had boasted a heavy frost, but the morning sun was unseasonably warm and the ground had already melted, releasing its heady perfumes of decay and dew. By the time we reached the barn, his pant cuffs were soaked up to the calf. The wide gate slammed against the wall as he threw it open. Without a word he scooted the ewes out the back door to the field, slapping them unkindly on their rumps to hurry them up, and closed the doors behind them without checking the water or fences. I paused. No oats for them?

Sophie would have a fit if she knew you treated them so casually.

I took a step towards the back doors.

A rough hand grabbed the collar and hauled me backwards as my breath was interrupted. A sharp click.

"Stay," he said, and turned to leave.

What…?

A heavy chain led from the iron ring of my collar to a loop around the post supporting the hay loft, and before I had time to think, he slammed the barn door behind him. My first frantic instinct was to pull, but that only tightened the manacle around my neck, and I clawed at the fetter with my front paws to release the pressure on my throat. The chain was as thick as Maddy's wrist and rusted from seasons out of doors. If I kept my head low to the ground, I could breathe, but if I stood, the weight of the increased length pulled the collar uncomfortably tight, so I was forced to lie at the side of the pen and fume. He wanted me out of the way for a day. I heard the dogs in the yard baying in joy now that I was imprisoned.

Simon, you fucking bastard, how dare you restrain me?

I raised my head again, coughed and sputtered.

If I had fingers, I'd shove this slip collar so far up your pudgy ass, you'd be spitting rust for weeks. I could hear the sheep returning to the other side of the back doors, one after another, to listen to me struggle against the metal restraint. All to no avail. I paced my breaths to keep the pain in my chest from rising.

And then, I heard the roar of an engine.

Where's he going?

But when the engine died, a car door slammed, and the front door of the house shut. Simon had gone nowhere, but someone had arrived.

I lay in the pen, my head to the ground, wondering what he was doing. Who had come? Why would he bind me here? I'd done nothing to deserve this, and if he was frightened that I'd leave before he could collect his reward, he could have simply locked me in the music room. There was no need for the preparations that he'd taken, selecting a length that would keep me down, securing it around the post with a heavy lock before bringing me here. Twice I tried to worry the opposite end of the chain from the fixed support but Simon had secured it well around the widest beam, and I could no more gnaw the post apart than chew the links open. He certainly wasn't mending any fences. I'd heard no movement in the yard other than the moronic hounds.

A crack in the ceiling showed the progress of the sun, and as the line of light it cast on the floor moved in a steady pace across the barn, I tried again to free myself.

I heard a second engine coming down the drive. I recognized it from yesterday; it was the Pinto.

Maddy was home.

I howled as loud as I could. I tugged again at the chain until I could barely breathe. The light shone straight through the hole above, marking noon, and I heard a single door slam, followed immediately by Maddy's heavy steps ascending the front porch and her high voice chirping a cheery goodbye. The tires skidded on the gravel as Ian's Pinto roared away.

I held my ear to the wall, holding my breath.

Help me, Maddy! Come to the barn and let me out!

I was about to make a noise, a howl to call her or a bark to let her know I was here, when a throaty, animalistic scream rose from the house. It was sharp and high, the sound of a terrified child, and my skin turned to ice with shock of hearing it. For a moment I was frozen, and then every muscle in my body filled with fire, and I stood and pounded my front paws against the wall. It held firm. The chain dragged me down as it tightened around my throat.

I backed up a step and lowered my head, and I didn't think of the consequences. I launched myself against the post, hitting it with the full force of my shoulder, and the entire structure shifted.

Again, another scream.

And again, I threw myself at the support beam. Showers of dust fell from the hay loft. A bale came crashing down, almost striking me, but the post now stuck out at an awkward angle. I tensed my legs and sprang.

The wood splintered. I seized the loop of chain in my teeth and pulled, and as the hay loft buckled, I yanked the chain clear of the broken column. I sprinted to the door as the loft collapsed with a bang under its burden of hay bundles, sending clouds of fodder and shards of wood in all directions. By the

235

time I'd vaulted the gate into the paddock, the weather-worn barn was caving in from all sides like a house of cards.

I held the loop of chain in my mouth to keep from strangling myself. The dogs, seeing me sprint from the crumpling structure, dashed for the safety of the garage, and I hurtled through the front door of the house with the force of a locomotive. The door cracked and tore away from its hinges. The long windows that flanked the door shattered in spider web formations.

Maddy cowered in the middle of the hall.

I broke through in time to see Simon, naked and flushed with rage, raise his hand and strike the girl full across the head with an open palm, sending her flying towards the kitchen. He looked up and saw me, blocking the remains of the front door.

I'd never seen a man hit a child; it stole my breath. She'd landed the length of her body from the point of impact, and her ashen face had crinkled with terror. Maddy inched forward, wailing with panic, and a trickle of blood issued from the right corner of her swelling lip. A patch of urine darkened her trousers and puddled on the floor.

The hall filled with the stench of their fear, a thin ammonia smell from Maddy and a heavy primal musk from Simon. I lowered my head, bared my fangs and slunk forward, to stand over the fallen girl as he stepped back, fists raised. I'd never before attacked anyone, never had a call for it, but in that moment all I desired was to bury my jaws in his ribcage and tear out his heart. With adrenaline clarity I knew, too, that this was not the product of a monstrous background, not the culmination of my ancestors' blood that I'd repressed all my life, but the instinctual reaction to protect someone I loved. It didn't matter if I was a man or a beast, I would have killed him then, all the same.

Simon didn't flinch and he made no effort to run, but in a steady voice he said to a shadowed figure in the hall, "Get my rifle. Under the bed."

Maddy whimpered at my feet. She clutched at my ankles, breaking my focus.

I seized the hood of her jacket in my jaws and dragged her after me. Simon found his courage as I retreated, and I heard footsteps in the hall coming from the stairway.

3

"SO HE *DID* HIT HER," Caufield said under his voice, scratching notes over the legal pad.

"But that's not anything you can use in court," Sullivan said. "As far as the law is concerned, I wasn't there."

"Yeah, but—"

"Morris, you can't use my testimony. God knows I'd love to see Simon thrown in prison for hitting a child, but I can't be a witness. They'll think you're as crazy as me if you try and admit my story as evidence."

Caufield glared at the man in the client's chair for a moment before scratching out the sentence with sharp, violent jerks of the pen. "Right now it's Simon's word against Sophie's, and the little girl is too afraid to speak to social services."

"I know, Morris, I know," said Sullivan, slouching. "But I can't get involved. At least, not yet."

"And the person in the hallway?"

"They know what happened," said Sullivan, his eyes ablaze. "They saw everything."

MADDY WEIGHED ALMOST nothing, but the chain around my neck dragged through the grass and caught on every protrusion. We raced down the driveway and across the road to the farm on the opposite side and, as I leapt a culvert, the sharp snap of Simon's gun echoed across the fields and startled ravens from the trees.

Fucking idiot. He's shooting at his own child.

The notion must have occurred to him as well, because no other shot was fired, and I carried Maddy through the neighbours' yard and towards the trees that bounded their property. My breath was ragged, my feet faltered. When we reached the woods, the chain finally caught on a tree root and I was yanked backward in midstride. Maddy fell hard against the loam.

I whined, pulled, and tried in vain to untangle it from the bracken.

A small hand found its way to my throat. "I help you," she whispered. The fragility of her tone terrified me.

Maddy knew how to unhook a dog's leash, and she sprang the clip with only a small amount of difficulty. I studied her face, swollen on the right side, and licked the blood from her chin.

We heard voices of men from the fields. I recognized Jan, Knut and Simon, but there were others that I didn't know, and I estimated seven or eight followed us. I grasped her jacket in my mouth again and we resumed our flight through the trees. I tried desperately to ignore the fire in my chest and the aching of my ribs. We forded a shallow stream and followed a ridge through a stand of elms. I took great care to avoid open land,

239

clinging to the edges of fields. The countryside immediately around Gilsbury Cross was fairly flat but rose sharply towards the north, and as the ground inclined I picked my way with less care, now speeding towards the mountain forests at a full run. Maddy was a dead weight in my grip, her boots leaving furrows in the soft earth, and as the adrenaline began to wear away, my neck cried for a rest.

Twilight turned the branches into black veins against a rich violet sky. I looked back at our trail through the forest, listening and hearing nothing, so I dropped her in a hollow filled with fallen leaves.

She cried, afraid. The darkness came with incredible speed and no moon, turning the naked pines into malformed trolls, turning the landscape into twisted monstrosities. Every noise was magnified, from the mouse scurrying in the leaves to the swish of an owl's wings to the creaking of the boughs in the wind. I curled my body around her and wiped the tears from her cheeks with my own, wishing I could say anything to comfort her, but at long last, her sobbing ceased, and she laid her dirt-stained head against my shoulder.

The only thing I could think to do was hum the cadence of *Juniper Bunny and the Hopping Brigade.*

And Maddy, her eyes closed, recognized it and filled in the words.

"hop hop hop past the wild dark wood
hop hop hop by the rickety bridge
up through the hills and down to the field
here comes the hopping brigade"

240

She said the words mechanically. I licked her face and flicked my tail over her legs.

"I hurt, Logan. I'm hungry."

I know, Maddy, I know.

"And he was hurting a lady and she was crying and I wanted him to stop and then he hurt me too."

I thought of Simon being startled in his bed by a wailing little girl who didn't understand what she'd discovered. *It's okay, Maddy.* I ached to say it. *He won't hurt you again.*

Her tiny body shook as she started to sob. The sound of her cries bounced through the silent woods, breaking my heart. I had no arms to hug her, but I pressed her closer to my shoulder with my muzzle, and she snuggled her hands into the mane of fur around my neck. Eventually, her crying subsided. Madeleine, too tired to care about the dark or her rumbling stomach, fell fast asleep.

I MOVED HER TWICE during the night, once when the barking of dogs drifted through the trees from a mile to the south of our location, and once when the scent of a nearby black bear caught my nose. Maddy didn't care. She wrapped her arms around my neck and clung to my fur, weeping piteously from fear, before settling again for a shallow nap at the next spot of my choosing. I reclined at her side to keep her warm and remained vigilant. For the first time in many days, my own plight had vanished from my mind.

241

As the eastern sky turned from black to gold, I rose and stretched, and looked down on the elfin form that still slept in the depression my body had made. I walked a short distance away to urinate, and when I came back, she was stiffening her limbs against the autumn temperature and blinking slowly like a cat. She yawned, and so did I. I nudged her awake with a cold, wet nose.

"Uh oh! I did a no-no," she said, looking at her pants with horror. The stain over her lap had dried and reeked of apple juice.

I don't care, Maddy. There's worse things than peeing your pants. I sniffed her face, checked her limbs, made sure she'd suffered nothing worse than bruising. The definite outline of fingers and a palm was visible on her cheek, crossing over her right eye and turning a violent indigo, and her lip had split in two places, but she didn't seem to have broken any bones or sprained any muscles. She walked with her legs spread, hopped from foot to foot like Juniper Bunny, and skipped in a little circle.

"I'm hungry, Logan."

I bumped her in a single direction, but she had difficulty navigating the terrain. The crusty fabric of her soiled pants caused her obvious discomfort. At last I stopped her by seizing her coat sleeve in my teeth, and I bent my head low to the ground and grunted.

"I don't know what you mean."

I guided her towards my back with my nose.

"Up?"

Yes, yes. I nodded my head.

242

She climbed between my shoulders, grabbing handfuls of fur and clinging with her knees. *She's had a riding lesson or two,* I guessed as my damaged ribs sang under the pressure of her grip, but I swallowed hard and started south at a brisk trot. Madeleine's peals of laughter were reward enough. Her voice echoed through the ridges and ravines, and it seemed the ride distracted her from the memory of last night's distress. I was tempted to trace yesterday's route but thought better of it, for as we descended from the hills, I heard the high pitch of motors, of ATVs and dirt bikes, and knew without a doubt that they were following my original direction. I had no desire to backtrack only to meet hunters and hounds face-to-face. We kept to the deer paths, winding our way between thick braces of blackberry brambles and down steep, rocky ravines. When we reached a shallow creek, I waded through the icy water for more than a mile, heading east and then south.

The stream grew deeper as it narrowed and the banks rose from sloping sandbars to shale escarpments, garlanded with ferns. Instead of clean, alpine breezes, the air held the thick, sour stench of automobile exhaust, wood smoke, and sheep manure; there were roads above and a farm or two. When we followed a bend in the waterway and saw a wooden bridge spanning the small valley, I hauled us out of the gulch and onto the verge of a main road.

I knew this place more from scent than sight. The Rawlinses' farm lay on the other side of those fields, over the swell in the land. This stream to our backs must feed the river which had swept me down from the cabin. I loped across the fallow fields with my head held high, Maddy clinging to my back with her bony knees and unrelenting grip.

We approached the farm from the northeast, parallel but hidden from the road by the rise in the land, and Maddy shrieked with joy as she bounced against my spine. She bumped her boots against my torso in a bid to make me go faster.

I ignored her appeals and kept my pace constant, steady and wary.

The barn had slumped drunkenly to one side and the sheep remained in the pasture, huddled under an orange tarpaulin that had been hastily erected. They mewled and moaned in agitation, ignored this morning by their mistress, as hungry and cold as the little girl on my back.

I prowled closer, sniffing the drafts that came from the south. A rusted Dodge was parked in the driveway, and I recognized it to be Sophie's; its engine smelt cold. The front door had been covered with a sheet of plywood.

"I want Mummy," said Maddy. "Lemme down, Logan."

Simon could still be here. I smelt his feet on the gravel and the lawn, crossing back and forth, but every path was relatively fresh. No barking came from the garage. He'd taken the dogs. I crept a little closer, gingerly.

I heard the click of metal on metal.

"Put her down."

Sophie, to my right, crouched in the shade of the chicken coop with the rifle raised to her shoulder. I shifted slowly so that Maddy wouldn't lose her balance.

My first instinct was to bolt but I stood my ground.

"Put her down, Logan," she said, eyes narrowed. "I know you understand me. Put. Her. Down."

I lowered myself to my stomach and Maddy slipped off, wrapping her arms around my neck and kissing my cheek before toddling towards her mother. She threw her arms around Sophie's legs, but still the woman kept me in her sights. "Madeleine? Are you okay?"

"I slept in the woods!"

"I know. I was so worried. I came home, and I didn't know where you'd gone."

I remained as still as possible. Sophie stared at me, the gun aimed at my head. She was so tense and reactive that the slightest twitch of my tail was liable to make her pull the trigger. I was made of marble and she was made of springs.

"When I got home," Sophie said, "your father said that Logan had attacked you, and he thought you might be dead."

I heard Sophie's voice crack under her emotion, and noticed that her eyes were swollen and crimson, her hair tangled, her skin as pale as a corpse.

"Logan read me *Juniper Bunny and the Hopping Brigade*," said Maddy. "And he slept next to me, but we weren't in a bed so it was okay. I know he isn't s'posed to sleep on beds."

"Did he bite you, Mads?" she said, and for the first time, she looked down at her daughter's face. A gasp caught behind her clenched teeth. "Oh, dear God!"

She lowered the gun, but I remained close to the ground, motionless.

It was a handprint on Maddy's swollen face, there was no denying it. Sophie laid aside the rifle and gathered her daughter into her arms, and studied her face with rapid, erratic movements. "Who did this to you? Who hit you?"

The sound of fear in her mother's voice made Maddy's chin quiver, and tears rolled down her cheeks and dripped onto her torn jacket.

"Tell me, Madeleine. Who hit you?"

Words poured out of the little mouth. "He was making her yell and I wanted him to stop so I yelled and then he hurt me and I fell down and I did a no-no and I'm sorry."

Sophie pressed the little body close to her breasts and, as the girl sobbed, she watched me over Maddy's shoulder. "Well? Is it who I think it is? Is this Simon's handiwork?"

I drew myself to my feet and lowered my head, understanding her betrayal.

"And who's the woman?"

I saw the hollowness in her eyes and felt my own wounds break open afresh, but even if I'd known, even if I'd had the capacity to speak a name, Madeleine answered before I realized I'd been asked.

"It was the lady who fixes the animals," she said innocently. "It was Elsie's mummy, Gloria."

4

THE FIRST THING Sophie did when she went inside the house was give Maddy a bowl of cereal and a glass of juice. "You must be hungry," she said, frigid, as if her heart was dead.

Maddy, with food before her, didn't notice the distance in Sophie's gestures, and tucked into her breakfast without hesitation.

I followed Sophie upstairs into the master bedroom, and I sat at the end of the bed as she tossed Simon's clothes into a pile on the floor. She muttered under her breath, and her words dripped with venom. "Fucking bastard," she spat. "I'll fucking kill him." Sophie strode into the adjoining bathroom. I heard the slam of a cupboard door and she returned with a garbage bag in each hand. "I told him, right after we were married, if he ever raised a hand again, I was fucking leaving." Her fingers drifted to the scars on her face. For a moment, she looked as though she might burst into tears, then her eyes hardened again as her task became clear. She flung open the closet doors, ripped the suits and shirts and sweaters from the hangers and shelves, and jammed his clothes into the plastic bags. Her rage tainted every movement. I lingered in the doorway, a little afraid of what she might do to anything that barred her way, but at last she slowed and bowed her head, her shoulders trembling.

"I suspected there was someone else, but I kept telling myself I was wrong. Do you know how goddamn stupid I feel? I'm an idiot."

I really want to tell you that I understand, Soph. You are no more an idiot than me.

Sophie took a deep breath to fortify herself, then dragged the two bags of clothes to the bedroom window. It looked over the driveway, providing a wide view beyond of misty fields and woods. Sophie shouldered it open with the creak of wooden panes, then unceremoniously hurled the sacks out.

She slammed the window shut. "And they're out there looking for you, and here I was, positive you'd come back, and ready to blow your fucking brains out." She strode across the room and grabbed my head in her fierce hands and hugged it to her chest. "Thank you. Thank you for saving my baby." Her anger at Simon was so overwhelming that her appreciation sounded more like an accusation than gratitude. She bared her small square teeth. "I can't believe the bastard would pin Maddy's injuries on you."

She released me and swept out of the room like a tempest, down the stairs to the main floor. I followed in her wake as she burst into his office and tore the sheet music from his desk. It became confetti in her strong hands.

Maddy sidled next to me in the hallway. She said quietly, "Mummy?"

"Yes?" Red-faced, with beads of sweat appearing on her brow, Sophie turned to Madeleine.

248

Where the bruises hadn't discoloured her skin, the little girl's face was pale. She pointed towards the front door.

"Daddy's here."

Sophie pressed her lips together and raced to the remains of the front door. She shoved the plywood to the side in one fluid motion.

In the middle of the driveway, Simon stood between the two bags of clothes. One had burst open on impact and scattered his underwear across the lawn. The hounds had already grabbed a pair of y-fronts and were tugging it apart between their jaws, tails wagging.

He looked stunned, surrounded by his rumpled clothes. "Soph? What's going—"

"You," she said, pinning him with one sharp finger. "Can get the hell off my property."

"What?"

"You heard me."

I pushed alongside her and saw him drop his hands to his sides. His expression shifted from confusion to anger—a restrained, paternal anger that warned of punishment, should she continue. "Honey," he said, and even though the tone was placid, I heard the threat veiled between the words. "Sweetheart, I don't know what you're talking about."

"I do," she said. "That bruise on Maddy's face wasn't made by any animal except you. I remember your temper, Simon. I remember the broken beer bottle, the blood, the pain. Eighteen stitches to close the lacerations—yeah, I know exactly what I'm talking about, Simon, and I have the scars to prove it."

"Honey, we should talk about this."

"No more talking," she said. "I have the rifle, Simon, and I'm not afraid to use it."

He slouched his back, retreated a step.

"Can I at least collect my papers?"

"Here."

She tossed the strips of paper into the wind. They fluttered over the banister of the veranda and settled in the barren rose bushes. As she pushed the plywood back into place, I caught a glimpse of him collecting the remains and holding them like a bouquet in one hand.

SOPHIE GAVE MADDY A warm bath and put her to bed. After a night spent outdoors, the girl was asleep as soon as her head touched the pillow.

Then Sophie grabbed a hammer and nails from the closet in the hallway, secured the plywood over the front door with twelve spikes the length of her finger, and nearly drove the head of the tool through the wall in her rage. When she tossed it aside, the hammer skittered across the hardwood floor, leaving a visible dent at its point of impact.

Sophie said nothing but moved like an Amazon, her hair now loose from its braid. She tore every instrument out of Simon's office, hauled them to the backyard, and set them on fire in an old iron barrel between the barn and the chicken coop. The smell of his belongings burning made me pace back and forth with agitation.

She flew back inside, up the stairs, and threw herself over her bed, sobbing. I waited at the door, unsure if I should leave her to her misery.

At last, I crept near. She lay on her stomach with her head in her arms, her nose buried in the quilt, and when my breath fluttered on the skin of her elbow, she looked over the rise of her upper arm at me. "What?"

I whined, and rubbed my muzzle against the back of her hand.

"You feel bad for me, do you?"

How could he do this to you? He was the luckiest man alive, and he tossed you aside for a beat-up hag of a farm doctor. James Herriot's got more sex appeal than Gloria.

She reached out one hand and touched my forehead. "I should have known this would happen eventually. I just wish Maddy hadn't been the one in danger." She rolled to her side, looking towards the window. "I should have left from the first. I shouldn't have bothered to give him a second chance. The nurse in the emergency ward warned me that if I went back he'd eventually just snap again, and I tried so hard to make sure he was happy, but I should have packed my bags and gone." She took a deep, shuddering breath. "But, if I'd left, we wouldn't have had Maddy, and she's my entire world, and I can't bear to think what my life would be like without her." The words dissolved into a trembling chin and a river of tears spilling over her hands.

I circled the bed and leapt up behind her, and I lay down along her back, wrapped my arms around her body, and enfolded her as best I could with my awkward limbs. She settled into the embrace, crying, and we lay together as the shadows grew long and the bonfire crackled in the backyard.

When twilight fell, Sophie was breathing steadily again.

"You're not leaving," she said. "When that dreadful woman gets here on Thursday, I'm telling her you're staying with me."

My tail thumped twice against the mattress.

"And if she dares to complain, I'll shoot her."

When my tail wagged again, she looked over her shoulder at me.

"That makes you happy?"

God, how I wished I could tell her it did.

SIMON RETURNED THE next morning. The police were called. Fearful of charges that would jeopardize his teaching career, Simon got into the passenger seat of Gloria's truck and left without any arguments. On Monday evening, Jan and Knut dropped by with sentiments of remorse and gifts of food, and told Sophie that Simon wanted a few of his belongings. Toiletries. His father's watch. The clarinet and the bassoon.

"You can take his toothbrush and the watch," Sophie said. "And I'll give you a paper bag for the instruments. You'll find their remains in the iron barrel out back."

"I am sorry for dis," said Jan, his meaty hands fidgeting.

"It's okay, Jan," she replied. "It's for the best."

"And Maddy?" said Knut.

Sophie looked back inside the house, towards the kitchen. "She's drawing right now. She doesn't quite know what's going on, but—" Her voice faded, and she shrugged.

"Ja, well," said Jan, uncomfortable with her sorrow. "We grab de stuff and go. Give you your privacy."

The lawyer, a certain Mr Caufield from the city, came to the house on Tuesday afternoon to draft the papers for the divorce. He was an odd fellow who seemed a bit out of place in the backwoods town of Gilsbury Cross, but he said kind things to Sophie and consoled her when she began to sob. I was much impressed by his humanity.

Maddy wailed when Sophie told her that her father wasn't coming back, but I pressed my nose to her bruise to remind her as delicately as I could that the contusion had come from his hand. While Sophie and Mr Caufield talked in sombre words in the kitchen, I shepherded Maddy into the sitting room and urged her to wait on the couch. When I returned from her bedroom with *Juniper Bunny and the Hopping Brigade* clasped in my mouth, she clapped her hands and moved to one side of the sofa, brushing the last moisture from her face with delicate fingers. I curled along its length, she sat cross-legged with her back against my belly, and she read her fanciful version of the story as I looked at its illustrations.

On Wednesday, a wrinkled, gangly man from Gilsbury Cross delivered a new door and stayed most of the day to install it. The frame had to be rebuilt and, as the door was a few inches shorter, the lintel had to be lowered. When the construction was done, he pushed his sweaty cap back from his high forehead, rubbed his wrist along his brow to wipe away the perspiration. "This here's all busted in like," he said, pointing to the fractured pieces that now lay on the hall floor. "You have someone rob ya?"

Sophie handed him a cup of tea. "Logan wanted in."

I wagged my tail.

"Most dogs is tryin' to git out," he replied, sipping.

"What will the bill be?"

He hummed and ground his teeth together, regarding the door that waited on the front porch to be joined to its hinges. "What with labour and all, I'm thinking sixty bucks. Plus the price of the door itself, now."

"And that is?"

"124.99 plus tax. But it's a good door, solid construction. Real secure, with a dead bolt like you asked."

Sophie sighed. "I'll give you fifty now. Can I pay the rest on Friday?"

He puffed up his chest. "A hun'ed now."

"Alright," she said. "But I'll have to go next door to borrow the extra fifty from Knut."

"S'alright, then," he replied, returning the cup. "I'll just finish up here, and be on my ways when you gets back."

When he was gone, she sat on the steps of the porch, her head in her hands.

"Logan," she said when I sat at her feet. "I don't know how I can afford to keep you. We don't have enough money to last the week, and I can't feed Maddy kibble."

The thought of Madeleine starving was appalling.

I'll hunt for you, Sophie. I'll bring back deer and rabbits. I'd never let you or Maddy go hungry.

But she couldn't hear my thoughts any more than I could speak them, and her mind was a million miles away. Softly, she said, "That ten thousand dollars is starting to look damn appealing."

I laid my head on her lap, and she leaned over me to run her hands down my back. I felt her sweater against my ears and the rise of her breasts against my face, and when she sat up, she planted a kiss on the spot between my eyes. Her hair brushed over my nose.

"Will you forgive me if I give you back?"

I stepped back a few paces and looked towards the hills.

"You'll bolt before you go back to them," said Sophie, dark shadows under her eyes, defeated. "I understand. If I could run for the freedom of the woods, I'd do it too."

THURSDAY DAWNED cloudy with a hint of moisture in the air and the first real chill of winter. The morning frost left ghostly patterns on the windows. Sophie built a roaring fire in the woodstove and made Maddy stand in front of it to chase the cold from her bones, and I remained close by, staring out of the living room windows towards the fields and the wild mountains beyond. I had lain awake at Sophie's side for the entire night, contemplating the idea of flight, but it was accompanied by a sharp sense of guilt, for I'd be denying her the reward money that she so desperately needed. If I wanted to pay her back for everything she'd done, I'd wait until Gwen arrived and accept my fate. If I wanted to be selfish, I'd flee. I watched her sleep and decided that I couldn't live my life knowing I'd denied Sophie anything, even if that meant that my life was cut short by a bullet to the head from Ethan's gun.

She fell asleep with the full expectation that I'd leave in the night. When she woke and found me dozing on Simon's side of the bed, a flicker of happiness crossed her face, only to be replaced by one of woe.

At eight-thirty, there came a knock on the door.

I smelt Gwen's cloying perfume on the landing, and I pressed closer to Maddy, afraid.

"Hi, come in."

Two sets of footsteps entered. One set was heavy and masculine, while the other was the sharp taps of a woman's heels.

"You've got some beautiful countryside up here." My stomach clenched at the sound of Ethan's voice.

"Can I get you something to eat? Breakfast?" said Sophie. "You must have been on the road early to get up here so quickly."

"We spent last night in a bed and breakfast outside of Rosedell," said Gwen.

"That sounds lovely."

"It was far too expensive for what it was," she answered. "But I suppose people out here have to make their living somehow, and it's easiest to try to screw the wealthy when they can."

"Sorry you feel that way," Sophie said. "I left the city because I suspected it was the other way around."

Ethan coughed to defuse a growing argument. "So," he asked with feigned friendliness. "Is the old boy here somewhere?"

"He's in the next room."

I lowered my head, glaring. Ethan stopped at the entrance between the hall and the sitting room. When he saw me, his face became pallid, but he covered his trepidation with a merry grin and held out his hand. "Ah, Daniel, that's a good boy. We've come to take you home."

Gwen appeared behind him. Her hair was pulled on top of her head, her white leather coat buckled around her slender waist. "Hello, Daniel."

I bristled but didn't move.

Sophie brushed past them and towards me. "He'd been shot when we found him. But see? Like I told you when we met, the wound's already closed up."

"Shot?" said Gwen, never taking her eyes from mine, her voice a steely monotone. "How awful."

"But he hasn't been any trouble?" said Ethan, still loitering at the edge of the room.

Gwen, with a hint of a sneer, said, "Chewing up slippers? Messing on the carpets?"

"No, not at all," Sophie said, running her hands over the thick ruff of my neck. "I've never seen any animal so intelligent."

Maddy took Gwen's hand. "He took me when I did a no-no and he read me *Juniper Bunny*."

"I have no idea what you mean," Gwen said with a grimace, wiggling her fingers out of the little girl's grasp. Seeing that

Ethan wasn't advancing any farther, Gwen pushed him aside and drew an envelope from her pocket. "Here's the reward. Ten thousand dollars, all in small bills." She handed it to Sophie, and when the woman took it with desperate eagerness, Gwen smirked. She wrapped her fingers around the dangling end of the choke chain. "I hope it covers all his expenses."

"Yes, it was no trouble—do you have to go so soon?"

Gwen slipped a stout cord through the slip chain and yanked the collar as I braced my feet.

"I don't want Logan to go!" said Maddy as she scrambled forward, suddenly realizing what was happening. She threw her arms around my neck. "Don't take Logan. I won't let him on the bed again, I promise!"

"I'm sorry," said Sophie to Gwen, prying Maddy from me. "My husband left us last weekend. Maddy is really upset."

"This is mine," said Gwen to the girl. "Get your mother to buy you your own dog." And she yanked again, hard enough to dig the chain into my flesh and grind against my tendons.

"We can take care of him," said Maddy, struggling against Sophie's grip.

"No," snapped Gwen, her eyes narrow. "And if you don't shut the fuck up, I'm going to give you a matching bruise on the other side of your face."

Sophie reeled and slapped her, hard enough to send the clip that held Gwen's hair flying.

"Don't you dare come into my house and threaten my child!" Sophie roared. Her teeth flashed like a lioness's, her heartbeat skyrocketed. The scent of rage filled the close air, and she lunged forward with one fist raised while the other hand

258

pressed Maddy close. "Take your damn money, leave him, and get out!"

But Ethan jerked forward and grabbed the braided cord. He was closer to my weight, and he dragged me with gritted teeth out the front door and towards the driveway, where they'd parked my Bronco—of course they wouldn't want fur and dirt on the upholstery of their own vehicle. I thrashed against him, and wondered with hackles raised how Gwen could stand it, to be seen in such a dilapidated, lowly form of transportation.

She unlocked the back and they hauled me in. I grappled against their efforts but I was struggling to breathe against the constrictions of the choke chain. At last the hatch slammed shut, and as they each took a seat in the front of the car, I pressed my shoulder against the window to force it open. It refused to budge. The back of the vehicle had been segregated from the front with a metal grate, screwed in place and immovable. When I glanced out the window, Sophie, holding a frantic Madeleine, stood on the front porch with a look of seething fury contorting her features.

"Can you believe it?" Gwen said. "She hit me! That white trash bitch hit me." She rubbed her cheek with one hand, examining herself in the rear view mirror. "That's why there should be mandatory sterilization. I can't believe they let people like that breed."

I threw myself against the gate with teeth bared, frenzied.

"Calm down, Daniel. You should be thanking me," said Gwen, turning in her seat as she fixed her hair. "Did you want to spend the rest of your days lying on the front porch, snapping at flies and scratching fleas, while Grammy darns socks and Ellie-May minds the moonshine? We're doing you a goddamn favour."

Ethan threw the car into reverse and slammed the accelerator to the floor. "I thought the little girl was sweet."

"I thought she was a troll. And the bitch *hit* me." She grimaced again. "And you didn't defend me, Ethan."

We raced away from the Rawlinses' house leaving clouds of dust in our wake, and the vehicle jounced over potholes and fishtailed on the gravel curves. Ethan maneuvered the Bronco like a stagecoach, and each time he took a sharp corner, I was thrown against the spare can of gas or the luggage.

"Did you remember the hacksaw?" said Gwen.

"Damn. I knew there was something," he said, and as he threw it into third gear, the engine bucked and almost stalled. "This thing's a tank. Daniel, I'll never figure out why you didn't get a newer car."

"Maybe there's a hardware store in town," she said, looking back over the valley. "But it probably doesn't open until ten."

"I'm not waiting an hour and a half to buy an overpriced hacksaw," said Ethan. "We have to be back home by two; I've got a meeting with Roy at four."

Gwen glanced back at me. "I'm not just dumping the body. What if he changes back after death?"

"You said he couldn't."

"Maybe he didn't tell us everything. God knows he took his own sweet time breaking *this* news to me."

I glared at her, baring my teeth.

"Look, it's easy enough," said Ethan. "We take him into the woods, shoot him, and use the petrol to burn the body. Simple. No one will ever find out."

I thought of all the nights when we were housemates, watching crime dramas on television while we ate dinner—I never thought he'd use any of their tips to hide my murder. Ethan's betrayal stung as much as Gwen's, and now he was openly planning to destroy all trace of me. I let out a piteous whine.

Gwen turned in her seat. "Don't be so glum," she said. "Surely you knew what we planned. I can't have you running free in the hills, especially once your family finds out you're missing. Do they know about this little secret of yours?" She reached down to a purse between her legs and, withdrawing a small revolver, checked the number of bullets in the chamber. "Ah yes, you said your sister does."

"Dammit, I forgot about Hestia," said Ethan. The Bronco bounced and jostled over a bump in the road.

"We'll be sunbathing in Guyana before she figures it out."

"She's bloody persistent," he replied. "You don't know her like I do. She doesn't lie back and take lame excuses."

"She'll need a body to claim a murder, Ethan."

He glanced towards the back of the Bronco. "Hestia won't stay still until she knows what happened."

Gwen had reached the limit of her patience with his morality. "So we'll send her the pelt with an apology. 'Sorry, Hessie, but I didn't recognize him without his human face on.'"

At the idea of Hestia receiving my hide in the mail, I leaned my head against the grating and whined.

261

"One quick shot, Daniel, and it's all over," said Gwen. "There's worse ways to go."

"Don't the bullets have to be silver?"

She scowled. "If they did, he wouldn't have run so damned fast the first time."

I paced back and forth, watching the farms give way to woods, my heart beating faster, my ribs aching. The leather suitcase at my feet hopped with each bump, and I thrust my head towards it, tearing it to pieces and burying my nose into the soft clothing inside in search for anything I could use. Lingerie, an overnight bag of perfumes and make-up, a hairdryer. Nothing heavy enough to break the window. The sound of fabric tearing attracted Gwen's attention, and when she gave a strangled cry, I looked at her with the remains of her lavender silk nightgown clenched in my teeth.

"Stop it," she yelled.

I shook it like a terrier shakes a rat, simply because I knew it would send her into a tantrum.

Ethan was unaffected. "We'll buy you another." He eased the vehicle to the verge and turned off the engine, and farther down the road I saw the red convertible I'd bought Gwen after our wedding.

"I'll kill him, right now, in the car," she said, raising the gun level to my head. "Get out. It's going to make a terrible noise."

"Jesus Christ, Gwen," Ethan shouted, pulling the gun down. "There's a can of gasoline back there! That'll go up in a fireball if you hit it with a hot slug, and it'll take us with it." She lowered the weapon, looking dour, but Ethan continued in the same calm, calculating voice as before. He adjusted his shirt, rolling up the cuffs. "Don't be so reactionary, Gwen. He'll get blood everywhere. No, we'll do this like we planned. Give me the gloves."

She pulled a pair of heavy cowhide sleeves from the bag on the floor, the kind used by dogcatchers to protect their hands from bites, and Ethan slipped them over his arms as he jumped out of the car. I watched him circle to the back hatch. Gwen mirrored him, and met him on her side of the car with the gun in one hand and a roll of duct tape in the other.

I pressed myself against the partition but I was too large to move away from the door. He looked at her.

"Ready?"

She set the gun on the top of the car and nodded, holding a strip of tape between her hands.

He threw open the door and seized my head, dragging me forward with a vicelike grip. I braced my legs against him, but as hard as I closed my jaws, my teeth couldn't pierce the hide. Suddenly I felt a crunch, and he shouted, high pitched—I released him as I felt his flesh compress into jelly under the glove. Gwen dipped forward and encircled my muzzle with the tape. Once secured, Ethan dragged me out with my head under his arm, and even with my body writhing and my paws clawing at his shirt, he held firm. Still, I could feel his strength flagging. I felt hands on my front feet, forcing my wrists together, and more tape binding them.

As soon as this was done, he dropped me, and I crashed to the gravel road.

"Back feet, we have to secure his back feet," said Gwen as Ethan stomped away, his face violet.

263

"He…" Ethan peeled off the right cuff, exposing a hand that was purple and distended. "… crushed my… wrist…" He tried to take off the left glove, but his right hand wasn't working. "… hospital…"

"We have to finish—"

But he shook his head, beads of sweat rolling from his face like pearls, his breath coming in clipped, strained pants. "… now… now… hospital…"

Gwen glared at him. "You can wait ten seconds," she said, grabbing the handgun from the roof of the car. I cowered in the shadow of the vehicle as she pressed the cold circlet of the muzzle to the centre of my brow.

When the explosion came, she didn't even bat an eye.

5

GWEN PAUSED, HER vision clouding and her eyes unblinking. At first, I was certain that I must be dead, but then I watched her topple to the side, and after a full five heartbeats of lying in front of me, she parted her lips and shrieked like a stabbed pig. Her howls were so piercing that I flattened my ears and tried to escape from the shrill arrows of her voice. Her lips formed a perfect circle. Her teeth were square and unnaturally blue-white against the black cavern of her throat.

Beyond her, two hundred feet down the road, Sophie stood to the side of her car and lowered the rifle.

She hadn't killed Gwen as she'd promised, but she'd taken out her knee, and the gaping wound in the left leg below Gwen's thigh was a mass of exposed tissue and bone. I dragged myself to the side of the vehicle, shocked, and saw that Ethan had the same expression on his face as me.

The woods were perfectly still as Sophie approached. The birds had ceased to chirp and the breeze had fallen quiet, as if the world was hesitant to make a sound in case the smallest noise incurred her wrath. She kept her eyes on Gwen, not once diverting her attention to Ethan's shivering form.

"I told you to leave him with me," she said, driving the toe of her boot into Gwen's wounds.

Gwen answered with a piercing yowl.

Sophie shifted her eyes to Ethan, and before she could raise her gun, he buckled to his knees. His voice was a rasping caw from the agony in his arm. "If you kill me, make it quick. I was going to give Dan the same consideration."

Sophie looked at me, gagged and bound, and her mouth was pulled down in a scowl. "If you wanted to show him any consideration, you wouldn't kill him at all." She took a knife from her belt and slit the tape around my feet, but it stuck to my fur and wouldn't pull away. Sophie gave a sympathetic moan and said, "We'll get this off when we get home."

I nudged her face, ecstatic.

"Get in my car, I'll take you to the clinic," she said to Ethan, and as blood was oozing from Gwen's leg, Sophie took the roll of duct tape and bound the wound shut. She hooked one arm under Gwen's and dragged her to the car, and I hobbled after her with my front legs stuck together. The last thing she did was grab the keys from the Bronco and lock the doors, intending to come back later to claim it for herself. Anyone raised in the country can tell you, the best entertainment at an autumn bush party is the abandoned car set ablaze, and Sophie was too practical to let a perfectly good vehicle be burnt to a crisp.

THE CLINIC IN Gilsbury Cross was small and efficient. It sat back from the main street behind a lawn and rose garden, in a tiny white house that, through the years, had been the mayor's house, a Depression-era bordello and an accountant's office. It boasted three rooms with five beds and equipment to save you from anything but the most dire of accidents. For that, there was a helicopter pad behind the parking lot.

Before she unlocked the child-safe doors, Sophie turned in her seat and fixed Ethan with a fierce stare. "Tell me why it's so important to kill him."

He shrugged.

"You pay me ten thousand dollars, only to butcher him on a logging road?"

No answer came except for Gwen's laboured breathing.

Sophie looked between me, perched in the passenger seat, and Ethan, who slumped in the back with Gwen lying across his lap. "I'm not letting you out until you tell me, and that arm sure as hell can't feel good."

Gwen's skin was the colour of oyster shells and she glared at Sophie with livid abhorrence. "Keep him," she spat, her voice cracking with agony but still spiteful. "He's been nothing but trouble. I got my investment out of him and he's all yours." Little specks of foam collected at the corners of her grey lips. "You'll be… hearing… from my… lawyer."

"Get out of my car," Sophie said, and she unlocked the doors with the flick of a switch. Ethan helped Gwen hobble into the parking lot, and as they limped up the walk to the little white door, Sophie rolled down her window. "If I see you anywhere near my property, I aim for the head. Understand?"

He nodded.

I watched them disappear inside.

When I looked back to Sophie, her eyes were wide and bright, staring into the centre of the steering wheel. "Holy shit. I shot someone."

You did a good job of it, Soph.

"I think—" She fumbled at her door latch. "I think I'm going to be sick." Sophie threw open the driver's side door and vomited a thin gruel onto the street, and when she sat upright, she looked calm, composed, and oddly pleased with herself. "I end up with you and the money," she whispered. Then, in a louder voice, more assured and concerned, "She's going to sue. She's going to sic her lawyers on me like the hounds of hell."

Payton isn't a hound, Soph, and I'm sure he'll understand. He never had much of a fondness for Gwen.

She put the Bronco's keys on the seat and drew a penknife from her pocket. With deft movements she sliced the hair under the remains of the tape and freed my legs, and when she did the same with the restraints on my face, I stretched and yawned. "I have no idea why anyone would want to get rid of you, Logan, but I'm happy to have you back. Maddy will be thrilled to see you again."

She pulled the Dodge into the sparse traffic.

I laid my head on the seat and listened to her humming, but I wasn't sure how I felt. The closest description I could think of was unfinished, unresolved. I blinked slowly and sighed. Sophie talked about Simon, said that the divorce would be as amicable as possible under the circumstances, but that she feared there'd be a quarrel regarding custody and visitation rights. She fretted over Gwen's threat, then waxed again with wonder at the idea of shooting another human being. I laid my head down, wondering myself if Gwen deserved that title, and felt my old depression lingering in my bones. My old key chain bounced in time to the swaying of the car, and wished I had hands and feet to drive again.

I was stuck, and as much as I'd wanted to see both Ethan and Gwen pay for their actions with blood, nothing had changed. My loyalty to Sophie would keep me with her, but it was going to be heartbreaking to watch her live her life, meet new people, fall in love with another man, while every morning I'd wake to this body. There would be no conversations with her, no chance of telling her how I felt about her, no hope of thanking her for all her generosity. Gwen and Ethan would return to the city and live off my inheritance. My situation remained as hopeless as the moment Gwen burnt my clothes and sentenced me to this form.

Sophie continued to talk. I didn't listen, and she was too engrossed in venting concerns to the dumb animal at her side to notice my dismay. The key chain jumped from the seat as the car hit a bump in the road.

A shard of light hit the keys and glinted more brightly than aluminum or steel.

I raised my head, focusing.

They shifted and jingled against the seat, and I extended one paw to flatten them, to hold them still.

There, slipped onto the coil for safekeeping, was my wedding ring.

Clothing!

Well, sort of clothing.

I'd never experimented with what I needed to remind my body of the change. My mother had been explicit in her instructions and your form wasn't the sort of thing to gamble. I'd heard that Andre had once used only his hat to change, but it was one of those stories told over family dinners that no one actually believed. A ring, however, is a most human accessory, like a necktie or a sock, and if my hands could recall the action of slipping it on, why couldn't the rest of my form follow suit?

I picked up the key ring between my teeth and shook it at Sophie, whining and pawing at the seat. My sudden action startled her. She pulled to the side of the road under the shade of a willow denuded of its leaves, and as she let the car idle, she shrank back to keep the dangling metal in my mouth from hitting her in the nose.

"What?"

I shook it at her again, making a merry sound.

She took it from my grasp and examined it, and made a little gasp. "Look at this, it's a gold band."

I whined, stretched forward as best as I could in the enclosed space.

With quivering fingers she released it from the key ring and examined it in the sunlight. "Who'd keep such a nice band with their car keys? It's all scratched from the other metal," she said, and noticing I was shifting my weight from foot to foot, she raised one eyebrow. "Do you want this?"

I whined, nodded.

Unquestioningly, she held it out.

"Here you go."

The morning sunlight sparkled over its surface, and I took it delicately in my mouth, trying to refrain from swallowing it in my excitement. Placing it on the middle of the seat, I took a deep breath.

The cells of my skin began to tingle, resonating, remembering.

The paw was a hand even as I reached out to grab it, and as I motioned to put it on my finger, I felt the hairs receding up my arms, my bones lengthening and shortening according to their altered form. There was an audible pop as my spine curved and my shoulders were forced back, my legs lengthened and my bare feet touched the floor. I coughed as my larynx settled into place and my canines ebbed into my gums until only square teeth remained. I turned my head away, ashamed, for I'd always been careful to change in private, but the discovery of the ring had chased any modesty from me.

When it was done, a minute or two later, I turned to her and smiled.

Her back was pressed against the car door and her hands gripped the seat. Sophie's face had turned a peculiar shade of white, but her mouth had not fallen open, and while her eyes stared in astonishment, she held no scent of fear.

"Hi." This was my first word to Sophie, ever, and I cringed when it sounded bashful and shy.

"I have a naked man in my car," she replied, more as a matter of cataloguing her situation than warning me of my nudity. She shuffled a fraction closer, and the corner of her mouth turned up in a shade of a smirk. "A naked man with a chain around his neck."

Now with deft hands and opposable thumbs, I slipped it over my head and dropped it to the floor. "Do you know how awful that thing's been?"

"I didn't… I mean, it was—" And she took a deep breath and shook her head, just a little, to clear her thoughts. "Oh… my… God."

"Do you want me to drive? You look like you might be in shock, Soph."

"I think I'm going to pass out."

I held her hand, soft and supple in my own. I'd spent so many days looking up at her, looking at the underside of her chin, that I found myself amazed by her smallness. "Don't worry. If you faint, I'll drive you home."

She held her other hand over her mouth and giggled. "No, no, I'm okay. This just isn't something you see every day, y'know?" And, reaching forward with one cautious hand, she ran her fingers over my tangled, uncombed hair. "How did you… the ring… is it magic?"

"Nope. Only a ring."

"And you?"

"Just a guy."

"Who turns into a wolf."

I shrugged. "Everyone has to have a hobby."

Her colour was returning, and she glanced back towards the clinic.

"And those two?"

"Gwen and Ethan?" I looked towards the distant clinic with venom. "My wife and her lover."

Her face soured. "You were married to that?"

272

"I could say the same thing about Simon."

She blushed.

"They destroyed my clothes to keep me as a wolf but—" I turned the ring on my finger. "They forgot one piece."

She tipped her head to one side, regarding my body with open curiosity. "Nice tattoo."

I looked at the words, now wholly visible without fur to cover them. "Thank you."

"What is it?"

"A medieval talisman to ward away bad fortune."

"It looks like it worked."

We exchanged amused glances.

"So it's Daniel, right?" she said, her composure returning.

"Dan Sullivan." I shook her hand formally.

"So what—" She gave a little shrug. "So what do you do?"

I couldn't help but laugh out loud, and the sound of my own familiar voice, a sound I thought I'd never hear again, made me laugh once more. "Take a deep breath, Soph. You still don't look all that well." I smiled warmly at her. "If I've learnt anything in my life, small talk just worsens a stressful situation."

She relaxed back into her seat and crossed her hands in her lap. "I think I'm feeling a bit better."

"I really didn't mean to startle you."

"I should've guessed, shouldn't I? The faucet. That should have tipped me off."

"Don't be hard on yourself," I replied. "No one believes in werewolves anymore. We like to keep it that way."

She laid one hand on the small of her throat. "You have my word, Mr Sullivan, that your secret's safe with me."

"I don't doubt that at all," I said, crossing my arms and shivering slightly. "And please, no 'mister'. You've seen me naked; we can skip right to first names."

She giggled, then paused, a blush rising furiously from her throat. "And what you've seen—"

I cast her a mischievous wink and she laughed in return, covering her mouth with both hands. Her grey pallor was completely gone, replaced by a charming shade of pink.

"Simon would be so embarrassed."

"And so he should be. Size fourteen, my ass. Do you mind if I turn the heater on?"

Sophie covered her whole face with her hands, laughing. "This is ridiculous. You must think I'm awful, listening in on my conversations, watching me burn all of Simon's possessions—"

"I don't think you're awful," I said, and I pried her hands away from her eyes. "Thank you. Thank you for saving my life."

We sat for a moment and I let her study my face, bewildered and amazed.

"What will you do now?" she said at last. "What are your plans? Where do you go from here?"

"Clothes might be a good first step."

"And then?"

"I'm in no hurry to go home. I'm sure Gwen left it in shambles." I chewed my lower lip in thought. "It never felt like home, anyway. But I liked being in your company, Soph. If I chose to stay a little longer, would you have me?"

"Let's find some clothes for you first, chat a bit, have a bite to eat for lunch," she said, throwing the car into drive and casting me a smile as bright as the sun. "Then we'll see."

THE NEXT MORNING I made a point of visiting Gwen.

She was sleeping, her head thrown to one side with her bandaged leg poking like an immense white worm from under the thin blue covers. I laid the bouquet of pink larkspur and coltsfoot on the bedside table as I sat on the plastic chair, and I rested my elbows on my knees, watching her chest rise and fall with each breath. The remains of Simon's clothes had proven a good fit, although a little tight across the shoulders, and I felt the fabric strain as I slumped in the chair.

A nurse offered me a drink of water, but I refused with a simple wave of my hand and he placed it beside the flowers before continuing on his rounds. After an hour, Gwen stirred, and smacked her lips.

"Are you thirsty?"

Her eyes flashed open. She said nothing, but her mouth formed my name.

"Hi Gwen."

The afternoon sun warmed the room, and we sat in silence for a few moments as she found her voice.

"How did you… I thought—?"

"Our marriage was a huge mistake, Gwen."

"A mistake? That's all you can say?" she said, and gave a sharp laugh, but it held a faint quiver. "I tried to kill you. You don't seem very angry."

I shook my head. "I'm not. I mean, I was before, but I realized I didn't really know who you were when we met, and so how can I be sad to lose you?" The thought of her and Ethan, scheming to meet me at the Adua Gallery and play their sinister parts in the theatre of our marriage, bubbled into my mind, but it was accompanied by a forlorn regret rather than betrayal or rage. I shrugged. "I never had you to begin with. You hid your true face better than I hid mine."

She sat upright, unwilling to take her eyes from me, and winced as she dragged her bottom closer to the headboard. I helped her arrange the pillows at the small of her back.

"You're taking this very well."

I shrugged. "If it wasn't for you, I wouldn't have met Sophie."

Her eyes narrowed. "You've got to be kidding."

"Don't like the fact that you've been dropped for… what was it you called her again? Grammy?" I said as I sat down. "Sophie's only in her thirties, Gwen, and she's got fewer grey hairs than you do."

"You? And her?"

"We're only friends for now. She's dealing with her own separation, and neither one of us wants a relationship. Yet."

Gwen, speechless with suppressed rage, chewed her cracked lips and fought for composure. I knew what she wanted to ask, but she didn't know how to phrase it without screaming.

I took the initiative. "I can't press any charges against you, but I also told them I don't know a thing about your injuries," I said. "Some sort of hunting accident, wasn't it?"

The edges of her lips were rimmed with white.

"Whatever story you told them about your gunshot wound, I'll support it, and I'll pay for your medical care as long as you keep your mouth shut."

"You want me to keep quiet about you?"

I shook my head. "I'm not worried about me. About Sophie."

She wrinkled her nose, disgusted but well aware that she was in my debt. The knee injury was a glancing blow due to Sophie's merciful aim; she could have easily destroyed the joint and left Gwen without a leg. As it stood, she'd live with a limp, and I could see in her feral eyes that she knew she was lucky. "And—" She was panting. Little beads of sweat peppered her brow. "And us?"

"I'm filing for divorce. I'll see Payton tomorrow."

"You can't divorce me. On what grounds?" she said, and I saw that my friendship with Sophie was a better revenge than any physical wound. This cut her to the quick, damaged her pride, and made her sarcastic with envy. "Because I stole your clothes and forced you to live as an animal? Because I burned your cabin?"

"Because you're a cheating, manipulative shrew, Gwen," I replied.

"They won't believe a word—"

"I can't charge you with attempted murder, but destruction of property, theft of funds and adultery are all valid reasons too," I said.

Her face flushed with rage.

"You can't leave me."

"I already have," I said, standing. "I hope you and Ethan are happy with each other. I'd drop by his room myself, but I don't feel much like visiting him, and I don't care if I ever see either one of you again."

She said nothing as I left, but her gaze was a rain of daggers in my back. I thanked the attendant at the desk as I passed, and suggested a sedative for Ms Herve, who was not in very good spirits. "She's a little off balance," I said.

He guffawed. "You're telling me? You should have heard the stories she was spinning last night," he said. "Are you her husband?"

"Nope," I said. "Not anymore."

"So you came to me."

"That I did, Morris," Sullivan said. "And it's getting late. You probably need to go home to your wife, and I have a long drive back to Gilsbury Cross."

"Back to Gilsbury Cross?" A crafty grin spread over Caufield's face. "Why, what could be there to keep your attention, Mr Sullivan?"

Sullivan shook his head. "It's not what you think, Morris." He set his cup on the desk and leaned forward, resting his elbows on his knees. "I do like Sophie, very much, but it's not the right time for either of us. I'm tempted to jump right into a relationship with her, I admit it, but there's more important things to do first. Sounds like a cliché, but I need to find my independence, and so does she. Once the divorce is settled, I'm putting my money into a few well-chosen, stable investments. Then I'm parking the Bronco in Sophie's driveway, I'm changing my skin, and I'm going for a holiday." He grinned. "A long, long holiday. And when I get back, maybe after a month but more likely a year, I'll ask Sophie if she wants another man in her life."

"And what does Sophie have to say about that plan?"

Sullivan tipped his head to one side. "True to form, Sophie had a lot to say. She doesn't want me to go, but she agreed it's best for both of us to sort out our separations on our own."

"Probably wise," Caufield said.

"And if you can persuade Gloria to testify, you'll have no problem securing a decent settlement for Sophie and Madeleine, true?"

"I wasn't sure how to get the little girl to admit that her father hit her," said Caufield, scratching at his thin hair above his ear. "If Gloria Rutledge is willing to testify, it'll help Sophie's case."

"Just don't tell Gloria who knew she was there."

279

"Please, Dan," he replied with disdain. "Give me a little credit. You tell me who's blackmailing me, and I'll never say a word."

Sullivan grinned.

"Ah, yes," he said quietly. "The blackmail."

"I'll take on Gwen as a client, that won't be a problem. I'll listen to her claims and gloss over them in my report… I'll even chalk them up to stress brought on by her hunting accident, how about that? Wouldn't be difficult. And when I draft up the papers with Payton, I'll make sure to tell him I don't believe a word of it. Because I don't. I still think you're a loony." He smirked. "But tell me, Dan. Who's got the photos?"

6

ON THE TUESDAY THAT Mr Caufield visited Sophie, to draw up her divorce and comfort her as the magnitude of her situation sank in, a snow as fine as ash began to fall over the mountains. I reclined on the rug next to the dining room windows, looking into the overcast sky, listening to Maddy play with her plastic horses behind me. I did not yet know that I would walk again on two legs; instead I thought of other options, of running in the hills during the first stirring of spring, and finding my mother to beg her forgiveness. This would be a dangerous plan, depending on the strength of the pack that had welcomed her, but the fact that I considered such an idea only measures how desperate for sympathetic company I had become.

Maddy whinnied and snorted. I felt the pin prickling of plastic legs galloping over the landscape of my back.

The contusions were fading. Half of her face was pattered with gold and lavender, and in the sanctuary of her imagination she'd forgotten the uncertainly of her surroundings. I studied her, lost in play, and wondered how I could leave when she needed something, anything, in her life that wouldn't vanish. What else could I do but offer my companionship to this little girl who'd lost so much so quickly?

Don't look at me like that, Morris. Werewolves are a loyal bunch; some, like Hestia, would claim it's our worst trait. Werewolves follow blindly those we love, for little reason.

As the doorbell rang and Sophie ushered her lawyer into the kitchen, Maddy roused herself from her pretending and gave me a sweet smile.

"Maddy?" said Sophie. "Say hello to Mr Caufield."

Both Maddy and I looked towards the arch between living room and entrance hall to see a stout middle-aged man in a tweed coat, half-moon glasses perched on his nose, removing his fedora from his balding head. He set his briefcase on the ground and hung his coat from a peg on the wall.

"Hello Madeleine," he said. His manners, though coarse, were worldly and well-educated, casual and confident. From his professional charm to his polished shoes I saw he was not from Gilsbury Cross. I wanted to ask Sophie how she'd come by his name, but it wasn't until after my return to the world of men that she explained. Morris Caufield had presided over her uncle's estate, two years before, and was an old family friend.

Maddy, hand shy, gripped my coat and curled closer.

"And that's Logan," said Sophie.

"Good dog," said Mr Caufield, reaching down to tousle the fur between my ears. They retired to the kitchen table where he proceeded to open his briefcase.

Dog. I supposed with absent helplessness that I'd have to get used to that.

For more than an hour they convened over cups of tea and slices of banana bread. Maddy slipped in to steal us both a morsel or two while the adults discussed assets and mortgages, visitation rights and police reports. I gathered Maddy's book in my jaws and she read to me as we sat on the couch, and I heard Sophie crying as Mr Caufield embraced her like a father. I admit, envy roared in my blood.

His coat pocket began to ring.

"I'll be back in a moment," he said as he came into the hall to find his cell phone, and he pressed it to his ear as I lay on the sofa, studying him through the archway. His eyes glazed and he watched me as he spoke.

"Caufield here."

The house was peaceful and I could hear both sides of the conversation. I expected to hear a secretary or client, but instead the voice was harsh and mechanical, neither male nor female.

"Drop instructions."

"Dammit, not now," he hissed. "I'm with a client and—"

But it was a recording, not a living creature capable of mercy. It continued, unabated. "Place payment in sealed garbage bag... You will find ticket to this evening's performance of *La Bohème* in jacket pocket... Place sealed bag with payment in trash receptacle on stage right of dress circle after performance... You will be followed... No tricks this time."

A beep and a click.

Mr Caufield, his face twisting into a scarlet expression of frustration, replaced his phone and jabbed his hand into the other pocket, only to withdraw a plain white envelope. He tore this open, and a single opera ticket fell out.

"Damn," he said.

"Is everything alright?" said Sophie from the kitchen.

"Fine, fine," he said, grabbing the precious ticket and placing it in his wallet, smoothing back his thin hair to regain his composure. "Just Helen asking me to pick up a few things on the way home. I'm afraid I'll have to cut the visit a bit short tonight, Sophie, but remind me now, where were we?"

SULLIVAN TOOK A folded white envelope from his pocket, torn and rumpled from Caufield's frantic fingers. Caufield stared at it, brow creased and lips clamped tightly closed.

"So I picked this up."

"You listened? I thought—" And Caufield gave a short, strangled cough. "Fifty thousand dollars at each drop. It's draining my accounts. You know why they want it?"

"In all honesty, Morris, I don't. I have no idea why they want your money, but I know now who they are, even though I didn't know before I came to visit you today."

"Huh?" It was an undignified sound from such an educated man.

"Your blackmailer is a nervous sort, Morris, and their sweaty palms left their scent all over this envelope. I picked it up because I felt badly for you, after you were so kind to Sophie and took her case gratis, but, honestly, I don't know why they're squeezing you."

284

Caufield leaned back in his chair. He took a deep breath. "You know how you want to help Sophie and Maddy, give them a little support? I was stationed in Cambodia for four and a half years and, during that time, I hired a prostitute and found out she had a little boy, some soldier's kid, but bright as button. She could barely feed him, and I couldn't just leave them, so I've been sending money to them over the years. Not much, but enough to help. My wife doesn't know. Hell, she'll think the boy is mine, and I don't want my life turned upside down because I tried to make someone else's existence a bit easier.

"Last year the boy flew out here and wanted to meet me, so I arranged a visit and… well—" Caufield dabbed at his eyes with a cotton handkerchief. "Nhean's a fine boy. Real fine. Makes me prouder than hell."

"But someone found out?"

"They took pictures. They have copies of my bank records too, the bastards. If they show my wife how much I've been skimming off our accounts, she'll have my head. And if they show her the pictures, she'll have my balls as well."

Sullivan glanced at the envelope in his hand, weighing Caufield's story.

"Tell me who it is, Dan. I want to fly Nhean out here and set him up, send him to a good college, but I don't want to lose Helen. I'll pay anything you want to stop these fuckers."

"I don't want your money, Morris."

He waved his hands. "I know, I know, you want me to represent Gwen. But what if she's hired an attorney already? You won't get what you want. I'm shit out of luck."

"She's currently confined to bed in the Gilsbury Clinic, heavily sedated and hobbled with knee surgery. She hasn't found anyone to represent her, Morris, I'd stake my life on it." He laid the envelope on the desk. "When you visit Sophie on Friday, drop by to see Gwen and tell her Payton sent you. Easy as that. Gwen was always quick to take the easy route if it ensured her a bit of money, and you can offer her the world at a very cheap price." When Caufield opened his mouth to protest, Sullivan said, "You'll have your blackmailer off your payroll. You can afford it."

Caufield stared at the envelope. "If she's my client, Dan, I'll try and take you for all you're worth."

"Good luck."

"You have a hell of a lot of faith in Payton's ability."

"If he's half as vicious in litigation as he is on the hunt, I'm secure," Sullivan replied, and when he smiled his teeth seemed sharper, gleaming like stars.

Caufield flinched in his chair. "So—" He pulled at his collar, his heart beginning to pound and his blood racing. His skin was clammy with perspiration. "Who is it? Who does your overzealous nose detect on that little scrap of paper?"

Sullivan's grin faded. He leaned forward to rest his broad hands on the edge of the desk. "I'll tell you, but can I make a suggestion?"

"What?"

"If I'd been honest with Gwen right from the beginning, scared her off with the truth of my nature, you and I wouldn't be sitting here, Morris, and I wouldn't be paying the deposit on Payton's new yacht. Maybe you'd better tell Helen before she hears it from someone else? She'll be angry, sure, but I wager she'll be less angry to hear it from you."

Caufield narrowed his eyes. "Point taken. Now who is it?"

Sullivan picked up the empty tray. He raised it to his nose and, closing his eyes, smelt along the edge for a trace of a scent. With a faint smile, he said, "I didn't know until I walked into your office, but I'm positive. The scent on the envelope is the same as in your waiting room, on your papers, and here on this tray. Morris my friend, your secretary thinks her wage isn't high enough."

EPILOGUE

"When a man steals your wife, there's no better revenge than to
let him keep her."
Sacha Guitry

ALMOST A YEAR PASSED, far too quickly for Caufield's comfort. It seemed the closer he got to retirement, the faster the years peeled away, and looking back over his life was like watching a speeding train vanishing in the distance. Ten months had flown by in the blink of an eye.

Sandra had not questioned her speedy dismissal. She had not questioned her lack of a severance package, nor her replacement by a younger, more buxom redhead with a cheery smile and a quick step. Instead, she went straight to Helen Caufield with the photos and the bank statements.

Helen was more enraged that Sandra would blackmail Caufield out of their savings than she was about Chey Nhean and Chey Chanda-ji. Caufield, ruefully taking the advice of a lunatic, had told Helen all about them before firing his secretary, and Sandra found herself with no surprises to use in her defence.

As nervous as a schoolboy, Caufield introduced Helen to the frail Chanda-ji and her lanky son in the airport lobby, two weeks to the day after Sandra was found guilty of extortion. As Caufield took Chanda-ji's luggage, both women graciously exchanged pleasantries and, in faultless English, Nhean gave many thanks for Helen's generosity, softening the tension in the air. Helen's anger would fade. Caufield had a great deal of gifts to buy and back rubs to give, but he took relief in the knowledge that his wife would eventually forgive him and he wouldn't be in the doghouse forever.

One Saturday in late September, he and Nhean drove to Gilsbury Cross to visit Sophie, but when he asked after Sullivan, she just smiled mischievously. Madeleine played Parcheesi with a lean older woman in the living room, and the little girl's shrieks of joy pierced the still house. Nhean sipped his tea and grinned whenever she squealed in triumph.

"He comes to visit, now and then," said Sophie. Then, louder, "Maddy! Play fair."

"She's beating me again," the babysitter said.

Sophie chuckled and signed the last of the papers dissolving her marriage. "There you go, Morris. Done."

"Thanks, love." He bundled them into his briefcase. "Tell him… tell him I say hello."

"I will," she replied.

"Tell him I'm sorry about the last few months."

"Sorry?" she said, and laughed. "What are you talking about?"

"I warned Dan, with Gwen as my client, I'd take him for everything he was worth, but I—" Caufield gave a shrug. "I feel bad about it. I played down her claims, as he requested, but I still secured her a good chunk of his father's money. He obviously isn't all there." Caufield tapped his finger to his temple. "And it seemed wrong to win."

"A lawyer with a heart?" said the older woman, who had left Maddy in the living room and now loitered in the doorway of the kitchen. "I'm the first to admit that Danny's a little slow

292

when it comes to social graces, Morris, but he's not as daft when it comes to saving his own assets."

Caufield studied the woman, and recognizing the shape of her eyes and the quirky curl of her lips, he said, "Eve. Eve Sullivan."

"It's been many years since we met, Morris," she replied. "You look well."

"I… I didn't mean—"

"You didn't mean to what?" she said, strolling in and sitting next to him. Her eyes were bright and merry, her voice jocund. "Insinuate that my oldest son is crazy as a loon? Oh, Morris." She clapped her hand on his knee. "He's a bright boy with a vibrant imagination, and far from insane. I'm pleased to say he's also getting better at judging a person's character."

"Well, don't tell anyone you've discovered a lawyer with a conscience," Caufield said. "I'll have all the basket cases clamouring for my attention. Between your crazy son—" He nodded his chin towards Sophie. "And your nonexistent bill, I'll be working for double my fee to meet my obligations. I can't have the whole world knowing I've gone soft."

"Your secret's safe with me," Eve said, and cast Nhean a wink. She lowered her voice and leaned towards Caufield. "And I shouldn't be telling you this, in case Gwen's lawyer is around, but only a fraction of Jack's money was ever in Danny's name. The tip of the iceberg, Morris, is all Gwen got." At this, she cast him a wink too. "An ice cube, nothing more."

Caufield took the last sip of his tea and smiled behind the rim of his cup. Eve engaged Nhean in polite conversation, asking about school and classes and culture shock. At last

Caufield said, "Will you tell Dan to call me when he comes back to civilization? I hoped to introduce him to Chey Nhean."

Eve turned to face him. "Why not go for a hike? He's in the area. If he hears you coming, he'll find you."

"And Nhean, why not stay here and help me with dinner?" said Sophie, pulling a pot from the cupboard. "Maybe Morris can drag Dan back here to join us, should he find him."

"I would like this very much," said Nhean, and he stood to help clear the cups.

Caufield found himself walking through the wilderness behind the farm, and he complained under his breath as his shoes slipped on the packed earth of the trail, his pressed slacks captured burrs and nettles, and his bleached shirt collected smears of dirt and pitch. The woods conspired against him. They rallied against anything that was clean and orderly, and Caufield was not in the same shape he'd been in as a younger man. He huffed like a tugboat and loosened his tie.

When he reached the pebbled edge of a creek, he squatted at its bank to scoop a handful of water to his mouth. "Damn woods," he spat, swatting at a mosquito that feasted on the side of his neck.

"Out of breath, Morris?" came a familiar voice from the opposite shore. Startled, Caufield stood to see Dan Sullivan sitting on a fallen log, naked and covered in mud from his hands to his elbows and his feet to his knees.

Caufield laughed and the sound echoed up and down the gully. "I didn't know if I'd find you," he said. "You're a hard fellow to get a hold of."

"No phone, never mind voicemail," Sullivan said. "You're looking well, Morris, even if you're a bit out of shape."

"At least I've got my modesty," he said.

Sullivan looked to the cloudless sky. "It's too nice of a day to bother with clothes." He stood and splashed through the stream, and Caufield suddenly felt awkward with his feet enclosed in fancy, yet cumbersome, Italian leather. Sullivan strode onto the shore without a hint of pain from the stones under his feet. "You're here to finish Sophie's divorce?"

"Yep. And I met your mother again." He grinned. "I apologized for taking so much of your assets, but she assured me my concern was completely unfounded."

Sullivan tipped his head to hint at that statement's truth. "She's been staying at the farm, watching Maddy while Sophie works in town," he said. And then, after a pause, he added, "We've worked out our disagreements. It wasn't so difficult, once I admitted she was completely right." He shrugged and Caufield chuckled.

"Sophie tells me you've been out here for a while."

"Five months, give or take a week. I've lost track, to be honest," Sullivan replied. "It's been nice, but I'm starting to miss the little things, like television and french fries." He scratched behind his ear. "And an absence of fleas."

"How long until you return to the real world, then?" said Caufield. "You're always welcome at my poker night, buddy, if you need something to entice you back."

"Oh no… Payton's told me stories about your poker nights, Morris," he said. "I'd be a lamb to the slaughter."

295

"Ach, we'd be kind," Caufield said. "But, no kidding, I want to introduce you to Nhean. When are you coming home?"

"I don't know," Sullivan said distantly, crossing his arms over his mud-spattered chest. "I'm mustering the courage to ask Sophie to marry me."

Caufield's eyebrows arched into his forehead. "Really?"

"Don't look so shocked." Sullivan chuckled. "It's just taking me a little longer than I thought."

"Once bitten, twice shy."

Sullivan nodded. "But Sophie isn't Gwen, not by a long shot, and I'd rather be Maddy's stepfather than an eccentric who stumbles out of the woods once in a blue moon to join them for dinner."

"If it means anything," said Caufield. "I'd be a poorer man without that boy in my life. If I ever questioned all the money I gave them or all the stress of the blackmail, he proves it was worth it."

"You'll come to the wedding?"

Caufield laughed, sharply, and the sound bounced through the pines. "If you're a fortunate man and she says yes," he replied. "But take it from me, you don't look like much of a prize right now, Danny boy. Covered in mud with sticks in your hair, stinking to high heaven, bare-assed as a bullfrog. If she takes you in, don't you forget how lucky you are."

"I count my blessings, Morris, every time I see her."

"She and your mother are teaching Nhean how to cook spaghetti," Caufield said as they meandered along the banks and tossed flat stones into the water. "I should be getting back. God only knows what they're telling the boy about me."

Sullivan weighed a rock in the palm of his hand before pitching it far across the stream and into the bushes on the other side. He listened to the rustling of leaves, and breathing deeply, he closed his eyes for a heartbeat. "Winter's coming. There'll be snow before the end of October." When he looked again at the woods, there was a peace in his expression that Caufield couldn't immediately place, but when Sullivan smiled, Caufield recognized it as the relief of a man reaching the end of a journey, of a weary traveller arriving home.

"You coming back with me?" he said with a crooked grin.

"Sure," Sullivan replied.

"Sophie's going to be happy. Maddy too."

And as they broached the bank and climbed onto the sweeping pastures, he heard Sullivan say, "You know what, Morris? So will I."

ACKNOWLEDGEMENTS

THE FIRST DRAFT OF *The Tattooed Wolf* was written as part of a three-day novel writing contest, when I sealed myself in a room with a laptop, ignored any urge to sleep, and immersed myself in a world of werewolves, shepherds, love and loss. I had no idea then how far the manuscript would go.

Since those three crazy days, the book has grown and evolved, so I wish to acknowledge the help and support of my family, who provided encouragement and assistance during this project: Ron and Cindy Bannerman, Mike and Trisha Bannerman, John Bannerman, Rob and Laura Pigott, Craig Pigott and Kate Blood, Rhonda Pigott and Tom Thorndale, Kailli Pigott and Jen Thorndale. Thank you, too, to Jennye Stark, Tracy Ford and Laurie Farkas, who have read my work and provided invaluable feedback for literally decades. I'd also like to thank Mark Gilliland, Will Sengotta, Tamara Sengotta, Alice Munro, John Belshaw, Sophie Yendole, Sarah Redmond, Sarah Bynoe, Deron Douglas, Dinah Roseberry, Conan McPhee, Alex Khan, Claire Guiot, Andrew Thomas and Kim Manky for their help, whether it came in the form of writing advice, suggested edits and/or revisions. I'd also like to thank Adele Wearing of Fox Spirit for her encouragement; Evo Terra, Mike Menninga and Joe Murphy of Dragon's Page Radio Talk Show for their kind reviews of an earlier edition of the book; and of course, the two most special wolf-pups in my life, Zoe and Linus.

Thank you to Hannah Kate and Rob Shedwick of Hic Dragones for publishing *The Tattooed Wolf*. To Hannah, thank you for your skillful edits; your suggestions enriched the story in countless ways. To Rob, thank you for a cover that beautifully represents the world within these pages.

Finally, thank you to Shawn Pigott. You encourage me to write when I'd rather watch TV, you listen to my scattershot ideas with patience, you temper my flights of fancy with good sense, and you notice when the real world needs a bit of my attention. You simultaneously keep me grounded and help me soar. For that, thank you.

ABOUT THE AUTHOR

K IM BANNERMAN LIVES in a tiny house surrounded by forests on Vancouver Island, Canada, where she writes short stories, novels and plays. Her stories have appeared in journals like *Room of One's Own* and *Parabola Magazine*, and in anthologies like the ground-breaking *Paraspheres* (2006), *100 Stories for Queensland* (2011), *She's Shameless* (2009), and *The Girl at the End of the World* (2014). Her short story 'A Woman of Wolves Born' appeared in the 2012 Hic Dragones anthology, *Wolf-Girls: Dark Tales of Teeth, Claws and Lycogyny*. Kim is the author of four novels, including the historical murder mystery *Bucket of Blood*. Together with her partner-in-crime, Shawn Pigott, they run Fox&Bee Studio, where they have written, produced and directed over 100 short films.

For more information, visit www.kbannerman.com.

Dark Tales of Teeth, Claws and Lycogyny

edited by Hannah Kate

Feral, vicious, fierce and lost... the she-wolf is a strange creature of the night. Attractive to some; repulsive to others, she stalks the fringes of our world as though it were her prey. Seventeen new tales of dark, snarling lycogyny by Rosie Garland, J.K. Coi, Kim Bannerman and Beth Daley, amongst others.

ISBN 978-0-9570292-1-7 ~ £8.99 ~ eBook available

www.hic-dragones.co.uk

The stunning debut novel by Toby Stone. When her mother's cruelty is too much, Amy holds her teddy bear's paw and travels to the Other Place—a world where teddies become real bears, where children attend the Night School to escape whatever it is they face at home. A dazzling, heart-wrenching and brutal descent into the world of the imagination.

ISBN 978-0-9570292-5-5 ~ £8.99 ~ eBook available

www.hic-dragones.co.uk

Don't trust what you see. Don't trust what you hear. Don't trust what you remember. It isn't what you think. A new collection of twenty-one dark, unsettling and weird short stories that explore the spaces at the edge of possibility, including stories by Ramsey Campbell, Simon Bestwick, Keris McDonald and Douglas Thompson, amongst others.

ISBN 978-0-9570292-8-6 ~ £8.99 ~ eBook available

www.hic-dragones.co.uk

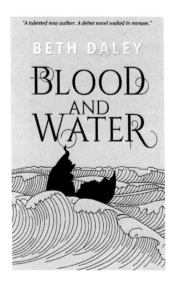

"A talented new author. A debut novel soaked in menace."

BETH DALEY

BLOOD AND WATER

Dora lives by the sea. Dora has always lived by the sea. But she won't go into the water. The last time Dora swam in the sea was the day of her mother's funeral, the day she saw the mermaid. And the sea keeps calling her, reminding her of what she saw beneath the waves all those years ago... of what will be waiting for her if she dives in again.

ISBN 978-0-9576790-1-6 ~ £8.99 ~ eBook available

www.hic-dragones.co.uk